THE EDGE OF TEMPTATION

J. SAMAN

Cover Design: Danielle Leigh

Editing: Gina J. - re-edited

Chapter One

Halle

"NO," I reply emphatically, hoping my tone is stronger than my disposition. "I'm not doing it. Absolutely not. Just no." I point my finger for emphasis, but I don't think the gesture is getting me anywhere.

Rina just stares at me, the tip of her finger gliding along the lip of her martini glass, her expression saying she's got me right where she wants me. "You're smiling. If you don't want to do this, then why are you smiling?"

I sigh. She's right. I am smiling.

But only because it's so ridiculous.

In all the years she's known me, I've never hit on a total stranger. I don't think I'd have any idea how to even do that. And honestly, I'm just not in the right frame of mind to put in the effort.

"It's funny, that's all." I shrug indifferently, playing it off. It's really not funny. The word terrifying comes closer. "But my answer is still no."

"It's been, what?" Margot chimes in, her gaze flicking between

Rina, Aria, and me like she's actually trying to figure out the mathematics behind it. She's not. I know where she's going with this and it's fucking rhetorical. "A month?"

See? I told you.

"You broke up with Matt a month ago," she continues. "And you can't play it off like you're all upset over it, because we know you're not."

"Who says I'm not upset?" I furrow my eyebrows, feigning incredulous, but I can't quite meet their eyes. "I was with him for two years."

But she's right.

I'm not upset about Matt.

I just don't have the desire to hit on some random dude at some random bar in the South End of Boston.

"Two *useless* years," Rina persists with a roll of her green eyes before taking a sip of her appletini. She sets her glass down, leaning her small frame back in her chair as she crosses her arms over her chest and purses her lips like she's pissed off on my behalf. "The guy was a freaking asshole."

"And a criminal," Aria adds, tipping back her fancy glass and polishing off the last of her dirty martini, complete with olive. She chews on it slowly, quirking a pointed eyebrow at me. "The cocksucker repeatedly ignored you so he could defraud people."

"All true," I agree. "Matt was the absolute worst sort of human."

I can't even deny it. My ex was a black-hat hacker. And while that might sound all hot and sexy in a mysterious, dangerous way, it isn't. The piece of shit stole credit card numbers, and not only used them for himself but sold them on the dark web. He was also one of those hacktivists who got his rocks off by working with other degenerate assholes to try and bring down various companies and websites.

In my defense, I didn't know what he was up to until the FBI came into my place of work, hauled me downtown, and interviewed me for hours. I was so embarrassed, I could hardly show my face at work again. Not only that, but everyone was talking about me.

Either with pity or suspicion in their eyes, like I was a criminal right along with him.

Matt had a regular job as a red-team specialist—legit hackers who are paid by companies to go in and try to penetrate their systems. I assumed all that time he spent on his computer at night was him working hard to get ahead.

At least that was his perpetual excuse when challenged.

Nothing makes you feel more naïve than discovering the man you had been engaged to is actually a criminal who was stealing from people. And committing said thefts while living with you.

I looked up one of the people the FBI had mentioned in relation to Matt's criminal activities. The woman had a weird name that stuck out to me for some reason, and when I found her, I learned she was a widow with three grandchildren, a son in the military, and was a recently retired nurse. It made me sick to my stomach. Still does when I think about it.

I told the FBI everything I knew, which was nothing. I explained that I had ended things with Matt three days prior to them arresting him. Pure coincidence. I was fed up with the monotony of our relationship. Of being engaged and never discussing or planning our wedding. Of living with someone I never saw because he was always locked away in his office, too preoccupied with his computer to pay me even an ounce of attention.

But really, deep down, I knew I wasn't in love with him anymore. I didn't even shed a tear over our breakup. In fact, I was more relieved than anything.

And then the FBI showed up.

"I ended it with him. *Before* I knew he was a total and complete loser," I tack on, feeling more defensive about the situation than I care to admit. Shifting my weight on my uncomfortable wooden chair, I cross my legs at the knee and stare sightlessly out into the bar, still feeling ridiculous in ways I wish I never will again.

"And we applaud you for that," Rina says, nudging Margot and then Aria in the shoulders, forcing them to concur. "It was the absolute right thing to do. But you've been miserable and mopey and very . . ."

"Anti-men," Margot finishes for her, tossing back her lemon drop shot with disturbing exuberance. I think that's number three for her already, which means it could be a long night. Margot has yet to learn the art of moderation.

"Right." Aria nods exaggeratedly at Margot like she just hit the nail on the head, tossing her messy dark curls over her shoulders before twisting them up into something that resembles a bun. "Anti-men. I'm not saying you need to date anyone here. You don't even have to go home with them. Just let them buy you a drink. Have a normal conversation with a normal guy."

I scoff. "And you think I'll find one of those in here?" I splay my arms out wide, waving them around. All these men look like players. They're in groups with other men, smacking at each other and pointing at the various women who walk in. They're clearly rating them. And if a woman just so happens to pass by, they blatantly turn and stare at her ass.

This is a hookup bar.

All dark mood lighting, annoying, trendy house music in the background, and uncomfortable seating. The kind designed to have you standing all night before you take someone home. And now I understand why my very attentive friends brought me here.

It's not our usual go-to place.

"It's like a high school or frat house party in here. And definitely not in a good way. I bet all these *bros* bathed in Axe body spray, gelled up their hair, and left their mother's basement to come here and find a 'chick to bang.'" I put air quotes around those words. "I have zero interest in being part of that scheme. Boring conversations with half-witted men who wouldn't know a female orgasm if it came in their face."

"Well . . ." Rina's voice drifts off, scanning the room desperately. "I know I can find you someone worthy."

"Don't waste your brain function. I'm still not interested." I roll my eyes dramatically and finish off my drink, slamming the glass down on the table with a bit more gusto than I intend.

Oops.

Whatever. I'm extremely satisfied with my anti-men status.

Because that's exactly what I am—anti-men—and I'm discovering I'm suddenly unrepentant about it. In fact, I think it's a fantastic way to be when you rack up one loser after another the way I have.

Like a form of self-preservation.

I've never had a good track record. Even before Matt, I had a knack for picking the wrong guys.

My high school boyfriend ended up being gay. I handed him my V-card shortly before he dropped that bomb on me, though he swore I didn't turn him gay. He promised he was like that prior to the sex.

In college, I dated two guys somewhat seriously. The first one cheated on me for months before I found out, and the second one was way more into his video games than he was me. I think he also had a secret cocaine problem because he'd stay up all night gaming like a fiend. I had given up on men for a while—are you seeing a trend here?—and then in my final year of graduate school, Matt came along.

Need I say more?

So as far as I'm concerned, men can all go screw themselves sideways. Because they sure as hell aren't gonna screw me!

"You can stop searching now, Rina," I suggest. This is getting pathetic. "I have a vibrator. What else does a girl need this day and age?"

All three pause their search to examine me and I realize I said that out loud. I blush at that, but it's true, so I just shrug a shoulder and fold my arms defiantly across my chest.

"I don't need a sextervention," I continue. "If anything, I need to avoid the male species like the plague they are."

They dismiss me immediately, their cause to find me a "normal" male to talk to outweighing my antagonism. And really, if it's taking this long to find someone then the pickings must really be slim here.

I move to flag down the waitress to order another round when Margot points to the far corner. "There." The tenacious little bug is gleaming like she just struck oil in her backyard. "That guy. He's freaking hot as holy sin and he's alone. He even looks sad, which means he needs a friend."

"Or he wants to be left alone to his drinking," I mumble, wishing I had another drink in my hand so I could focus on something other than my friends obsessively staring at some random creep. *Where the hell is that waitress?*

"Maybe," Aria muses thoughtfully as she observes the man across the bar, tapping her bottom lip with her finger. Her hands are covered in splotches of multicolored paint. As is her black shirt, now that I look closer. "Or maybe he's just had a crappy day. He looks so sad, Halle." She nods like it's all coming together for her as she makes frowny puppy dog eyes at me. "So very sad. Go over and see if he wants company. Cheer him up."

"You'd be doing a public service," Rina agrees. "Men that good-looking should never be sad."

I roll my eyes at that. "You think a blowjob would do it, or should I offer him crazy, kinky sex to cheer him up? I still have that domination-for-beginners playset I picked up at Angela's bachelorette party. Hasn't even been cracked open."

Aria tilts her head like she's actually considering this. "That level of kink might scare him off for the first time. And I wouldn't give him head unless he goes down on you first."

Jesus, I'm not drunk enough for this.

"Or he's a total asshole who just fucked his girlfriend's best friend," I protest, my voice rising an octave with my objection, my hands flailing outward like a chicken who has lost her way. I sit up straight, desperate to make my point clear. "Or he's about to go to prison because he hacks women into tiny bits with a machete before he eats them. Either way, I'm. Not. Interested."

"God," Margot snorts, twirling her chestnut hair as she leans back in her chair and levels me with an unimpressed gaze. "Dramatic much? He wouldn't be out on bail if that were the case. But seriously, that's like crazy psycho shit, and that guy does not say crazy psycho. He says crave-worthy and yummy and 'I hand out orgasms like king-sized candy on Halloween.'"

"Methinks the lady doth protest too much," Aria says with a knowing smile and a wink.

She swivels her head to check him out again and licks her lips reflexively. I haven't bothered to peek yet because my back is to him and I hate that I'm curious. All three ladies are eyeing him with unfettered appreciation and obvious lust. Their tastes in men differ tremendously, which indicates this guy probably is hot.

I shouldn't be tempted.

I really shouldn't be.

I'm asking for a world of trouble or hurt or legal fees. So why am I finding the idea of a one-nighter with a total stranger growing on me?

I've never been that girl before. But maybe they're right? Maybe a one-nighter with a random guy is just the ticket to wipe out my past of bad choices in men and make a fresh start? I don't even know if that makes sense since a one-nighter is the antithesis of a smart choice. But my libido is taking over for my brain and now I'm starting to rationalize, possibly even encourage. I need to stop this now.

"He's gay. Hot men are always gay. Or assholes. Or criminals. Or cheaters. Or just generally suck at life."

"You've had some bad luck, is all. Look at Oliver. He's good-looking, sweet, loving, and not an asshole. Or a criminal. And he likes you. You could date him."

Reaching over, I steal Rina's cocktail. She doesn't stop me or even seem to register the action. I stare at her with narrowed eyes over the rim of her glass as I slurp down about half of it in one gulp. "I'm not dating your brother, Rina. Any of your brothers for that matter. That's weird and begging for drama. You and I are best friends."

She sighs and then I sigh because I'm being a bitch and I don't mean to be. I like her brother. I like all of her brothers, but Oliver and I are tight. He is all of those things she just mentioned, minus the liking me part. But if things went bad between us, which they inherently would, it would cost me one of my most important friendships. And that's not a risk I'm willing to take.

Plus, unbeknownst—or maybe just ignored—by Rina, Oliver is one of the biggest players in the greater Boston area.

"I'm just saying not all men are bad," Rina continues, and I shake my head, unwilling to budge on this. "We'll buy your drinks for a month if you go talk to this guy," she offers hastily, trying to close the deal.

Margot glances over at her with furrowed eyebrows, a bit surprised by that declaration, but she quickly comes around with an indifferent shrug.

Aria smiles, liking that idea. Then again, money is not Aria's problem. "Most definitely," she agrees. "Go. Let a stranger touch your lady parts. You're waxed and shaved and looking hot. Let someone take advantage of that. And by take advantage I mean I mean take advantage. You need sex, Halle. It's been a hundred years since your orgasms weren't self-produced."

"And if he shoots me down?"

"You don't have to sleep with him," Rina reminds me, cutting a glare at Aria who clearly doesn't agree. "Or even give him your real name. In fact, tell him nothing real about yourself. It could be like a sexual experiment."

I shake my head in exasperation.

"We won't bother you about it again," she promises solemnly. "But he won't shoot you down. You look movie star hot tonight."

While I appreciate the sentiment from my loving and supportive friends, being shot down by a total stranger when I'm already feeling emotionally strung out might just do me in. Even if I have no interest in him. But free drinks . . .

Twisting around in my chair, I stare across the crowded bar, probing for a few seconds until I spot the man in the corner. Holy Christmas in Florida, he *is* hot. There is no mistaking that. His hair is light blond, short along the sides and just a bit longer on top. Just long enough that you could grab it and hold on tight while he kisses you.

His profile speaks to his straight nose and strong, chiseled, cleanly shaven jaw. I must admit, I do enjoy a bit of stubble on my men, but he makes the lack of beard look so enticing that I don't miss the roughness. He's wearing a suit. A dark suit. More than likely expensive judging by the way it contours to his broad shoulders and the flash of gold on his wrist that I catch in the form of cufflinks.

But the thing that's giving me pause is his anguish. It's radiating off him. His beautiful face is downcast, staring sightlessly into his full glass of something amber. Maybe scotch. Maybe bourbon. It doesn't matter. That expression has purpose. Those eyes have meaning behind them and I doubt he's seeking any sort of company.

In fact, I'm positive he'd have no trouble finding any if he were so inclined.

That thought alone makes me stand up without further comment. He's the perfect man to get my friends off my back with. He's going to shoot me down in an instant and I won't even take it personally. Well, not too much.

I can feel the girls exchanging gleeful smiles, but I figure I'll be back with them in under five minutes, so their misguided enthusiasm is inconsequential. I watch him the entire way across the bar. He doesn't sip at his drink. He just stares blankly into it. That sort of heartbreak makes my stomach churn. This miserable stranger isn't just your typical Saturday night bar dweller looking for a quick hookup.

He's drowning his sorrows.

Miserable Stranger doesn't notice my approach. He doesn't even notice me as I wedge myself in between him and the person seated beside him. And he definitely doesn't notice me as I order myself a dirty martini.

I'm close enough to smell him. And damn, it's so freaking good I catch myself wanting to close my eyes and breathe in deeper. Sandalwood? Citrus? Freaking godly man? Who knows.

I have no idea what to say to him. In fact, I'm half-tempted to grab my drink and scurry off, but I catch Rina, Margot, and Aria watching vigilantly from across the bar with excited, encouraging smiles. There's no way I can get out of this without at least saying hello. Especially if I want them to buy me drinks for the next month.

But damn, I'm so stupidly nervous. "Hello," I start, but my voice is weak and shaky, and I have to clear it to get rid of the nervous lilt. Shit. My hands are trembling. Pathetic.

He doesn't look up. Awesome start.

I play it off, staring around the dimly lit bar and taking in all the people enjoying their Saturday night cocktails. It's busy here. Filled with the heat of the city in the summer and lust-infused air. I open my mouth to speak again, when the person seated next to my Miserable Stranger and directly behind me, gets up, shoving their chair inadvertently into my back and launching me forward.

Straight into him.

I fly without restraint, practically knocking him over. Not enough to fully push him off his chair—he's too big and strong for that—but it's enough to catch his attention. I see him blink like he's coming back from some distant place. His head tilts up to mine as I right myself, just as my attention is diverted by the man who hit me with his chair.

"I'm so sorry," the man says with a note of panic in his voice, reaching out and grasping my upper arm as if to steady me. "I didn't see you there. Are you okay?"

"Yes, I'm fine." I'm beet red, I know it.

"Did I hurt you?"

Just my pride. "No. Really. I'm good. It was my fault for wedging myself in like this." The stranger who bumped me smiles warmly, before turning back to his girlfriend and leaving the scene of the crime as quickly as possible.

Adjusting my dress and schooling my features, I turn back to my Miserable Stranger, clearing my throat once more as my eyes meet his. "I'm sorry I banged into you . . ." My freaking breath catches in my lungs, making my voice trail off at the end.

Goddamn.

If I thought his profile was something, it's nothing compared to the rest of him. He blinks at me, his eyes widening fractionally as he sits back, crossing his arms over his suit-clad chest and taking me in from head to toe. He hasn't even removed his dark jacket, which seems odd. It's more than warm in here and summer outside.

He sucks in a deep breath as his eyes reach mine again. They're green. But not just any green. Full-on megawatt green. Like thick summer grass green. I can tell that even in the dim lighting of the bar, that's how vivid they are. They're without a doubt the most beautiful eyes I've ever seen.

"That's all right," he says and his thick baritone, with a hint of some sort of accent, is just as impressive as the rest of him. It wraps its way around me like a warm blanket on a cold night. Jesus, has a voice ever affected me like this? Maybe I do need to get out more if I'm reacting to a total stranger like this. "I love it when beautiful women fall all over me."

I like him instantly. Cheesy line and all.

"That happen to you a lot?"

He smirks. "Not really. Are you okay? That was quite the tumble."

I nod. I don't want to talk about my less than graceful entrance anymore. "Would you mind if I sit down?" And he thinks about it. Actually freaking hesitates. Just perfect. This is not helping my already frail ego.

I stare at him for a beat, and just as I'm about to raise the white flag and retreat with my dignity in my feet, he swallows hard and shakes his head slowly. Is he saying no I shouldn't sit, or no he doesn't mind? Crap, I can't tell, because his expression is . . . a mess. Like a bizarre concoction of indecision and curiosity and temptation and disgust.

He must note my confusion because in a slow measured tone he clarifies with, "I guess you should probably sit so you don't fall on me again." He blinks, something catching his attention. Glancing past me for the briefest of moments, that smirk returning to his full lips. "I think your friends love the idea."

"Huh?" I sputter before my head whips over my shoulder and I catch Rina, Aria, and Margot standing, watching us with equally exuberant smiles. Margot even freaking waves. Well, that's embarrassing. Now what do I say? "Yeah . . . um." Words fail me, and I sink back into myself. "I'm sorry. I just . . . well, I recently broke up with someone, and my friends won't let me return to the table until

I've re-entered the human female race and had a real conversation with a man."

God, this sounds so stupidly pathetic. Even to my own ears. And why did I just admit all of that to him? My face is easily the shade of the dress I'm wearing—and it's bright motherfucking red. He's smirking at me again, which only proves my point. I hate feeling like this. Insecure and inadequate. At least it's better than stupid and clueless. Yeah, that's what I had going on with Matt and this is not who I am. I'm typically far more self-assured.

"I'll just grab my drink and return to my friends."

I pull some cash out of my purse and drop it on the wooden bar. I pause, and he doesn't stop me. My fingers slip around the smooth, long stem of my glass. I'm desperate to get the hell out of here, but before I can slide my drink safely toward me and make my hasty, not so glamorous escape, he covers my hand with his and whispers, "No. Stay."

Chapter Two

Halle

STAY, he said. But I couldn't tell if he actually meant it or just said it because he felt bad for me and was trying to be friendly. If this was his way of making the embarrassed girl feel better.

I waver, my eyes drifting from the large warm hand covering mine back up to his. I can't figure out which I'd rather look at, his hand on mine or those green eyes.

"Sorry," he mumbles, hastily removing his hand. I miss the contact instantly, which has me frowning inwardly. "But I don't see how you can go back to your friends like this."

"Like what?"

He lifts his glass to his lips, taking a small sip as his eyes remain focused on mine. Then he sets it down, takes a deep breath like he needs it for courage or to steady his nerves, and pivots in his chair to face me better. "I don't consider falling on me and apologizing for it a real conversation." He tilts his head slightly with a touch of a grin pulling up the corners of his lips, and I hate how easily I sink into that.

Matt had a great smile. It's what initially drew me to him. What made me say yes when he asked me out. I remember thinking: no man with a smile like that could be bad.

Sucker.

I glance back over at Rina, Aria, and Margot. They're actually high fiving. I can't stop my groan.

"Your friends seem pretty pleased about it."

I laugh. It's the only thing to do. I turn back to him. "Yes. Like I said, they wanted me to get back out there."

"Get back out there," he echoes, almost to himself like something I'm clearly missing is coming together for him. I have no idea what, but something in his disposition most definitely shifts. When his eyes meet mine again, they're sparkling in a way they weren't before. "Then I think the only right thing to do is to sit down and let me buy you a drink. I couldn't stand it if I were the reason they wouldn't let you return to your table."

I sit down. But only because he's finally flirting with me and I can't come up with anything witty to say in response. It's those eyes. They're disarming. And hypnotizing. And unfortunately, I like the way they're gazing at me like I'm something rare and beautiful. Like I'm the best thing he's seen in a while and he doesn't want to waste the evening looking at anything else.

I've become a poster child. A cautionary tale. When smart women go stupid.

But really, I'm the one in control here, right? It's a conversation. Possibly a drink. Maybe more if I feel like it. And then I walk away. No strings. Zero expectations. No one gets hurt.

"Much better," he praises with an impish grin and a flirtatious gleam. "You're very tall when you're standing. So, why do you need help getting back out there?" He wraps his hand around his glass without raising it to his lips. "Bad breakup? That's what you said, right? I find it hard to believe men aren't throwing themselves at you constantly."

"Something like that, minus the men throwing themselves at me. That never happens."

"You're taking the piss with me now, right? That's a savage lie."

I shake my head, feeling like he just spoke to me in tongues.

"I get it," he goes on thoughtfully, ignoring my confusion as his demeanor shifts once again. More of that original uneasiness returning. I still can't place his accent. It's American with something else added to it. British, most likely. Australian, possibly. I honestly can't decide. "Things don't always end the way you anticipate."

I stare blankly, at a loss for words. I wonder if I'll ever get over the feeling of being duped by Matt. When I'm alone and allow myself to reflect on it, it drives me insane. I'm not a stupid woman, but Matt, and the asshole before him, and the asshole before him, make it difficult to believe I'm anything but. At least where men are concerned.

We both fall silent, lost in our own contemplation. This might be the worst, most bumbling start ever.

"I'm Jonah," he introduces, extending his hand out to shake mine. He's much better at this than I am. It relaxes me. Makes me feel less awkward. A sexual experiment. That's what Rina called this. I don't even have to tell him my real name, she suggested.

I hesitate. "Jade," I let spill quickly and cringe instantly. Because really? Fucking Jade? If his eyes had been brown, would I have called myself dirt? I try to brush it off, taking his proffered hand. It's large and strong and smooth with just the perfect hint of callouses on the tips of his fingers. Like he knows exactly what a hard day's work is all about but doesn't do it that often. And his voice. He must do voiceovers on commercials or audio books or something.

It's panty-melting sexy. He could read the dictionary to me and I'd get off on it. It would be my porn.

I might swoon. I know I'm smiling.

"Jade?" He laughs. Loudly. Clearly, my lie didn't pass muster. "I can't call you that knowing it's not your real name. I won't have you remembering me simply because I called you by a fake name. And I'd very much like you to remember me . . ." He waits me out, but I'm a bit stuck on the way he says he'd like me to remember him.

I stare down at my hands. "Halle."

"Halle." He says my name with something extra in his voice. A low rumbling purr that heats my blood. "Much better. Glad you fell into me, Halle."

I laugh awkwardly, taking a sip of my drink. This is my second of the night, but I am not about to stop now. I need this liquid courage more than I care to admit and the alcohol flowing through my bloodstream is making me feel warm and tingly.

"Same here."

"Do you always give men you meet in bars a fake name?"

"First time. But so is coming up to a complete stranger in a bar, so I'm going to go with learning curve over being a bitch."

He chuckles lightly, his eyes drifting methodically over each of my features before dipping down to my breasts, waist, and legs. He gets stuck on my legs for a beat, and when he finds me again, the color in his eyes has darkened into something that has me squirming in my seat.

"What are we drinking to?"

"Hmmm. Good question." We continue our private stare-down and then he snaps his fingers in an ah-ha way. "To nights we'll never remember with people we'll never forget."

I shake my head. "That's rather poetic in a weird alcoholic way."

"It's not mine. I wish I could take credit for that pearl, but it's what my mate always says." British. Definitely British to his American. It's sexy as hell.

"Then we'll go with it. Cheers." We clink glasses before simultaneously taking a sip of our respective drinks, his eyes locked on mine the entire time, making my stomach do a funny swooshy thing.

"Where are you from?" he asks as he sets his glass down. "I know it's not Boston."

I snicker. God, the alcohol must be starting to get to me if he noticed my accent so quickly. I typically have to have a solid three drinks before that bad boy comes out. "South Carolina."

He grins smugly, shifting his body toward me until we're facing each other. But our chairs are too close, and we end up with one of his knees between mine and one of mine between his. They're not touching. But they're right there and this is a surprisingly intimate position to be in with a complete stranger.

"I knew it was southern. It's lovely. Why do you try to hide it?"

I raise an eyebrow. "What makes you think I try to hide it?"

"Because when you first spoke to me you were over-enunciating your vowels and shortening your words. It was flat. Now that you're a bit more relaxed, your words are slower and more elongated, and your vowels are drawn out. Not quite a twang, more of a sweet southern lilt."

"You're way too observant, Jonah." He doesn't seem to care as he waits me out. I puff out a breath. "It's mostly habit now. I don't even realize I do it. I've been living in Boston since I came here for college, and because I'm a southern lady, I won't tell you how long ago that was. Northerners tend to believe people who speak with a southern accent are as slow as our speech."

"So you hide it." It's not a question, but I nod and shrug all the same.

"Not really. I mean, it's not intentional at this point. It started in college as a joke. A friend of mine teased that I couldn't do a northern accent for an entire day. So, I did and found not only did my professors treat me differently but so did the students."

"Wow," he muses, leaning back in his seat and rubbing his hand absently across his smooth jawline.

Propping his elbow up on the edge of the bar, he does that once-over thing again. Usually that would feel like a total check-out move —like he was trying to figure out his level of interest in fucking me. But there is something about the way his eyes rove over me. Something in the way they twinkle as they take me in. Instead of creeping me out or making me uncomfortable, I enjoy it. I like the way he looks at me.

"So, you've been a closet southerner ever since. Such a waste of something so beautiful. Will you do me a favor?"

"That depends."

His brows furrow and I sink my teeth into my bottom lip to try and hide my smile.

"I barely know you, Jonah. You could be about to ask me to help you cover up a murder."

"That's where your brain goes?"

"I might read a few too many mysteries."

"I can see that. Well, I promise not to ask you to help me cover up a murder. And for that matter, I promise I won't rape or savagely kill you tonight. You can rest easy, Nancy Drew."

"*Savagely?*"

He smiles widely, and I realize for the first time that when he does, he has twin dimples in his cheeks.

"Too far?"

I nod with a smile of my own as I swallow that thought down.

"Okay, I promise I won't murder you at all. Or hurt you in any way. That work for you?"

"It does actually. Even though that seems like a total murderer thing to say. You know, the get-your-victim-to-feel-more-comfortable sort of thing."

He laughs, shaking his head. "We're digressing here. All I wanted was for you to promise me you'd use your regular accent with me."

"You've got a deal. But what about yours?"

He gives me a mischievous grin, but just as he's about to answer, the bartender comes over to check on us. "You good here?" he asks, and Jonah pivots to me.

"How anxious are you to return to your friends?"

I glance over my shoulder and discover they're talking to a few guys they seem extremely interested in, considering Margot is practically on one of their laps.

I turn back to Jonah. "Not very."

"Good, because I'm going to be honest with you. I had a real rubbish day and you and your southern accent and gorgeous baby blue eyes are the only things that have made me feel better. Do you trust me?"

I laugh, shaking my head and trying really hard not to bite my lip. This guy has me nervous. In the best possible way. "Not even a little."

"Brilliant. How do you feel about shots?"

"Shots?" I parrot. The bartender clears his throat and shifts his weight to let us know that we aren't his only customers.

"That's what I said." Jonah doesn't seem intimidated by the bartender's looming, pissed off presence. In fact, he's patiently waiting on me, his eyes bouncing back and forth between mine while I deliberate his offer.

"I'm in."

What the hell, right?

His smile is so dazzling, I can't help but return it. "We'll have two shots of chilled Patron, please."

Shit. Tequila. "You're trying to get me drunk," I exclaim with alarm when the bartender leaves us to pour the shots.

"We'll only do the one, Carolina. I swear. Remember, I already promised not to hurt you." He did. Why is that reassuring when I feel like it shouldn't be? "Besides, you already paid for your drink and I told you I was going to buy you one."

The way his green eyes sparkle at me when he says that, I might agree to almost anything. And the way he said Carolina as a nickname has my heart tripping over itself, trying to jump out of my chest. His hand reaches out, brushing some of my wild, copper locks out of my face before tucking them behind my ear.

My breath hitches at the contact. What the hell is happening? I don't think I've ever been this attracted to someone this quickly before.

I swallow. Hard. Then I clear my throat and ask, "Why was it such a bad day for you?"

His expression instantly grows dark. Transitioning back to that hidden pain he was wearing when I first fell into him. "I'd rather not discuss it if that's all right with you. Nothing personal. You've brightened my mood considerably and I'd hate to ruin that."

I nod. I get it. I don't even need to be asked twice.

I know nothing about this man other than his first name and the fact I'm way too attracted to him for sanity's sake. He doesn't owe me explanations. I certainly don't want him delving into my past.

Recent or otherwise.

Leaning forward, I go for my most seductive pose. Yes, I'm flirting. And I do not care. In fact, I'm suddenly all-in for whatever this is or isn't.

My friends are right.

I need to rejoin the female race.

But more importantly, this feels so fucking good. I want to flirt with this man. I want more of his touches and smiles and his smooth, sexy voice. Definitely more of those long, devouring gazes. I might even want to check out the deal under his suit and see if my previous assumptions of his body are, in fact, correct.

"How's this then?" I start, "We don't ask each other anything serious. Tonight is all about fun."

The resulting smile he treats me to makes him easily the most gorgeous man I've ever seen.

"Sounds perfect, actually. All fun. Nothing serious. That I think I can definitely do."

Chapter Three

Jonah

I HAVE no idea what I'm doing right now. Why I'm talking to her. Why I didn't let her go when she tried to leave. Why I'm smiling and laughing and ordering shots. *Shots!*

I should not be doing any of these things. The majority of me doesn't even *want* to be doing these things, but it's as if I'm on autopilot and can't stop myself.

I. Can't. Stop. Myself.

It was that moment when I looked up into her eyes. I felt that . . . thing. That inexplicable warmth spreading over me. I've only felt that sensation with one woman in the history of my life.

Until now.

When I woke up this morning, I knew today was going to be one of the hardest days of my life. Same as it was last year. And the year before it. Something tells me that won't improve as the years go by. It's always going to be brutal.

Like a gunshot to the gut.

Two years of fighting and she's gone. It just goes to show you, life is essentially unfair. That it couldn't give a toss about anything other than its own agenda.

Our relationship didn't end the way fairy tales do. I spent the last year and a half of her life being her other half, her support system while she fought for her life. And the last six months of it, I was by her side, helpless, while she wasted away before my eyes.

And two years ago today, I buried her.

I had hoped that instead of utter despair, I'd feel relief. Grieving should have a self-imposed time limit. An "enough" button you can press. But it doesn't. It's a never-ending cycle.

A vicious twist.

I should feel relief because my sweet girl is no longer in pain. Relief because she's at peace.

It's been two years, and by this point, I should be living my life again.

But after I walked away from the cemetery today and went back to her mother's house for the requisite mourner's feast, all I felt was empty. I didn't want people to shake my hand or hug me while they reminded me how special Madeline was. While they reminded me of all the comfort I brought her.

Especially when they know nothing of the truth.

From the moment she was diagnosed, I wished a million times over I could switch fates with hers. I'm not suicidal; it's just that Madeline was the best person I've ever known. And if I had to listen to another person tell me it's okay she's gone because she's with God as one of His angels up in heaven, I would have either punched them or broken something.

So, I left.

I don't even think I said goodbye to anyone.

I drove into the city and then drove around it until afternoon turned into night. Then I parked my car and walked into the first pub I came upon.

This pub.

I had every intention of drinking myself into oblivion. Of getting so pissed and numb that the crushing pain could no longer register. Then a tall woman with the longest legs and the silkiest red hair and the lightest blue eyes and the fullest red lips—a few shades darker than her hair—I've ever seen bumped into me.

And even though I set out to do nothing but drown my sorrows, alone, I suddenly have company. Company I was not particularly adept at shooing away. It was her explanation for things. How her friends prodded her to get back out there, and she's brave enough to give it a go. Something about that resonates with me in a way I never expected. And that warmth I felt when I initially gazed into her crystalline eyes, spreads. Like the universe is challenging me to grow some balls and get back out there.

Even if I don't want to.

The bartender slides our shots, along with a salt shaker and a small glass of limes, across the bar. Halle glances over at me, and then, with trepidation, back to the shots we're about to take. She sinks her teeth into her full bottom lip, eyeing them warily for a minute longer before blowing out a slow even breath.

I can't stop staring at her. Dear God, she's stunning.

"Fuck it," she mutters, and once again, I'm smiling. Because this sweet, southern belle does not strike me as the type to use the word fuck. But she just did, and it has me . . . well, interested, I suppose. It also has me curious as to what sort of man would ever let her get away. Not one with any brains, that's for sure. She's captivating, even if she's nothing more than a drink and a moment of distraction. A bad breakup, she said. His loss is most certainly my gain tonight.

"All right, Jonah. You talked me into this, so you better pick up that glass and do it with me. I'm being brave here. Shots are not my thing."

"Not your thing? Then what is?"

"Martinis?"

"And those are different from shots? Hardly. They're loaded with alcohol."

"Shots are stronger. Or they at least feel that way."

"Do you like tequila then?"

"Tequila is uncharted waters for me.

My eyebrows hit my hairline and I lean into her, propping my elbow on the edge of the bar and angling my body full on in her direction. "Honestly? You've never taken a tequila shot?"

Her blue eyes shift to mine. They are as pale as a winter sky. She shakes her head slowly, turning a lovely shade of pink as that copper-penny hair tumbles over her shoulders in thick waves. She has tiny, pinpoint freckles along the bridge of her nose. They add an innocence to her otherwise sexy siren features.

"Pathetic, right?" Her nose scrunches up. "I'm almost embarrassed to call myself an American. Or a former college student for that matter. But it's true. I have never done a tequila shot. In fact, I've only done shots once. Needless to say, it didn't end well, and since that night," she shrugs an apologetic shoulder, "I just couldn't stomach the thought. Literally."

I grin, oddly enjoying her nervous rant.

One drink and then I'll leave.

One drink and then I'll tell her I'm the wrong man to aid her in her quest to reenter the world of male/female social interactions and dating.

One drink and then I'll go home to my empty, lifeless flat. My empty, lifeless life.

One drink . . .

I can't remember the last time I had a drink with a woman. I can't remember the last time I flirted with a woman. I can't remember the last time I had sex with a woman.

But more importantly, I can't remember the last time I smiled or laughed.

At least not genuinely.

Not since Madeline died. Well before that, if I'm being honest. I tried to give them to her, but I just never felt them. I was too angry and bitter and resentful for that. Too fucking heartbroken. But this woman seems to coax both of those out of me with her adorable awkwardness and sweet southern accent.

So unexpectedly wonderful.

And then it hits me. Like a sledgehammer to my overworked brain.

I don't have to be the right man for her. I just have to be the right man for her *tonight*.

She's beautiful. She's interested. She's here. And I'm fucking miserable. Been like this for so long. So long that I can't remember what it feels like not to hurt. Why can't I enjoy this moment, this time with her, and take it for what it is?

It's not like it's going to lead anywhere beyond tonight.

Leaning into her, I allow the knee that's between her enticing legs to touch hers. I like this position. It's strangely erotic, but I think I'd enjoy it more if her legs were spread and her knees were on either side of mine. Red dress. Red hair. I think red just became my new favorite color.

I glance down at her legs as I move and wonder if they feel as smooth and silky as they appear. What would they look like wrapped around my waist as I sink inside of her?

Focus, Jonah.

Right. Bollocks.

I force my gaze back up to hers. "What did you drink that night?"

"Kamikazes."

"Did you vomit your guts out?"

"Yes!" she vociferates, slapping her thighs with her hands like I get it. "I had about four or five of those puppies and I was sick that whole freaking night."

"I promise, that won't happen tonight. Those are sweet and manufactured to make you ill."

I smile. Again. Reaching out, I lay my hand on her shoulder. Why am I touching her shoulder? How on earth did that happen? I squeeze like I'm reassuring her, praying I don't come across as an asshole or a creep. She doesn't pull away, instead flashing me another of her enticing smiles. And now my heart is starting to pick up a beat or two.

"And tequila isn't?" She cocks an eyebrow at me, her cheeks flushing again as I rub my thumb along the skin of her shoulder.

She's not stopping me.

She might even be enjoying my touch.

In fact, if the fire in her eyes is any indication, I'd bet she is.

My hand drops to her knee and I leave it there. Waiting. Watching. She smiles wider, showing off her perfect white teeth, and I mentally high five myself for still having some game left. For accurately being able to read when a woman wants me.

My gut twists before it sinks so low, I can feel it in my feet.

One drink, I said. But in truth, this is too good to stop. Or maybe it's just this woman. Halle. This sexy, alluring creature and her playful, easygoing disposition. There is something about her. Something that is so very different. Something that makes me *feel* so very different.

"Okay," I concede with a small chuckle. "Maybe it is. But not good tequila, which is what this is. And one shot will not make you sick. Come on then," I cajole, running my fingers along the inside of her knee. I don't go far, but I'm making this contact with her and I can't seem to stop it.

Her eyes focus in on my fingers and the corner of her lips quirk up. And that blush. Christ, it's making my cock spring to life like it's waking up after being in a coma.

"Okay," she whispers. "I'm in." Her eyes meet mine. "I already said fuck it and I never go back on something once I agree to it. But you gotta walk me through the procedure. I mean, I've seen it in movies, but . . ." She trails off and I want to kiss her. I have no clue where the inclination comes from, but it's there.

Then again, I haven't kissed a woman in so long it's almost pathetic to admit. Except it's not, because I was taking care of Madeline and I'd sacrifice all the kisses I missed for her to still be alive.

I sit up straight and Halle imitates my position immediately. "Lick the back of your hand."

Her nose scrunches up, but when she watches me do it, her eyes darken and I'm thinking she's starting to realize how sexy taking a tequila shot with a member of the opposite sex can be.

Her pink tongue swoops out of her mouth, and as it glides along the skin of her hand, I can't look anywhere else.

"Now sprinkle some salt onto it." I shake some salt onto my

moistened skin and she does the same once I pass her the shaker. "Now, you need to be ready. Because once we lick the salt, we have to down the shot in one swallow." Her eyes widen at this. "You can do it. It's chilled, and like I said, it's good tequila."

"Let's do it then. What's with all the build-up?"

I laugh, lifting my salted hand to my mouth. She does the same, curiously watching as I lick my hand for the second time. She follows my lead, her nose wrinkling up at the taste of the salt, and then we take our shot. She swallows it all down, her face pinching before she rushes for a lime wedge, shoving it in her mouth and sucking on it for dear life.

I grab my own, popping it in my mouth, but I'm in no hurry. Mostly because I can't stop watching her.

Where did this woman come from?

"Whooo." She smacks her lips together before she shakes her head back and forth, her eyes cinched shut. Once she's gotten rid of the nonexistent burn, she opens them and smiles so big, I can see all of her pearly white teeth as they gleam against the paltry bar light. "I liked it. But I also didn't. Does that make any sense?" She tilts her head, her hair cascading down across her perfect breasts. "It was fun, but I'm not so sure about the taste. I don't think I'm a salt girl."

"The salt is more for the other person you're doing it with."

"Explain." She wiggles her shoulders, setting her posture back as she takes her martini glass with her, swallowing a small sip of it to wash down the tequila.

"You lick your hand. It's sexy. Erotic. I couldn't take my eyes off you while you did it," I admit, because why not? Chances are this isn't going past this drink and this conversation, and then I'll never see her again. "The salt is really secondary to that."

"Hmmm. I see your point. But we're done with shots now, right? I may be tall, but I don't drink all that much."

"No more shots."

"Good. Because this one is already making me feel warm, I'd hate to think what two shots could do to my body."

My jaw drops slightly at that. I want to lean into her. I want to

27

whisper in her ear, *warm where*. Or better yet, *I can make you even warmer*.

I need to slow down. Get a grip on myself.

"What do you do for work, Halle?"

"Fashion model," she declares, and I suck in a rush of air. "Ha, gotcha." She laughs, reaching out and shoving my shoulder lightly.

I return my hand to her knee, my thumb brushing back and forth against her skin. She is warm. Warm and delicious

"What? Don't laugh like that. You could be."

She rolls her eyes, propping her elbow on the bar next to her drink so she can face me better. "You most definitely have the charming part down. No, I'm not a model. I'm something else altogether. but I don't want to talk about work. I'm starting a new job soon and I'm nervous about it. Besides, we said nothing serious tonight, right?"

"Right. Nothing serious. So no discussing our jobs, or recent breakups, or my bad day." I lean in, invading her personal space, tasting the cloying essence of alcohol on her breath and inhaling the vanilla of her fragrance. "What do you want to talk about then, Halle?" I ask, my voice dropping an octave.

"You," she whispers, her pupils dilating. She swallows. Hard. Her cheeks turn that lovely shade of pink again.

"What about me, love? Do you want to know if I want to kiss you? Because the answer is yes. Do you want to know if I'm dying to take you home and spend the night inside your gorgeous body? Because that answer is also yes."

Her pretty blue eyes bounce back and forth between mine like she's trying to wade through the storm of desire to find what's hidden beneath.

"Too forward for you?" I pause, realizing I might have just killed this. My heart kicks up to a nervous pounding and I suddenly wish I hadn't let the tequila and my dick do all the thinking. I like talking to her and I don't want that to stop, so if there is a retreat button, I might consider hitting it.

"I don't know," she admits restlessly, though I don't think those nerves are directed at me. I think she's as new to this game as I am.

She hasn't pulled back. Her breaths are coming out in shallow quick bursts. She licks her lips and an image of those lips wrapped around my cock springs unbidden into my brain.

"I've never had this sort of conversation with someone."

"Do you want some honesty?" I ask.

She nods vigorously.

I stare at the beauty before me. Fuck it. I'm done fighting it. I need this. Wrong or right, I need this.

"Neither have I. In fact, I haven't been with a woman in a very long time. And I've never, ever said these things to someone I didn't know beforehand. But there is something about you, Halle. Something I cannot help but want. Even if just for tonight."

"Wow," she whispers and then pauses as she thinks all of this through. "Okay, this is too much. I need information, Jonah. Something more personal than the fact that you haven't screwed a woman in a very long time and you've never told a stranger that you want to spend the night inside her body."

"Fair enough." I smirk, willing to give her just about anything if it means she's actually considering my proposition. "I'm thirty-one. Grew up in London with my parents until my father died when I was fourteen and my American mother decided she preferred Boston over Blighty. I went to Harvard. I like running, science, and the ocean. I'm ruthlessly honest, and right now, hopelessly attracted to you. I don't even care if that comes across as a line, because it's absolutely true."

She blinks. Sucks in a breath. Blushes. "I'm twenty-seven. You already know I'm from South Carolina. I went to Boston College. I don't like running, but I do like science, and the ocean, and mozzarella cheese sticks. I have a knack for dating assholes and losers. And . . ." She trails off, biting into that lip again.

"And?" I prompt with a tilt of my head because that pink is turning into a deep rose.

"And I think I might suck in bed."

An incredulous chuckle bursts out of me before I'm able to rein it in. There is no way that's even remotely possible.

"No. I'm serious. The first guy I slept with turned out to be gay.

29

Since then, I've been cheated on, and one guy even passed out on me during the act. My last boyfriend was more interested in his computer than he was in me."

I shake my head, wondering again how there are men out there like that. How could anyone possibly cheat on her, pass out, or prefer a computer over her? I glide my fingers up and down her knee, and she shudders. Goose bumps erupt over her skin, showing me just how responsive she is. No way this woman is anything other than incredible in bed.

Unable to stop myself, I lean in and press my lips to the crook of her neck, right where her pretty red dress meets her skin. I close my eyes and breathe in her scent as my lips caress her skin.

When the expected wave of guilt doesn't hit me, I pull back and meet her steady gaze. "You just haven't been with the right men, Halle."

"Oh? Are you saying you'r the right man?"

I shake my head, because no, I'm the farthest thing from the right man.

"I can't promise you anything. I'm not looking to start dating anyone or for a relationship. I buried a piece of my soul two years ago today and that's why I've been drinking myself away in this bar tonight. But I want you. I truly do. If you're interested, I'd like to spend the night showing you just how extraordinary I know you can be in bed."

I draw back and wait, taking another sip of my drink just to give myself something to do. I have no idea what's come over me. I never do this. But I don't want this night with her to end. Even if it means I don't get into her pants.

Just as I open my mouth to tell her that, she comes back with, "Yes. I want to go home with you."

Those words reverberate through my skull, turning me on and making me just a bit mad with lust. "You sure?"

"Yes," she asserts. "Without a doubt. I have a terrible history with men and am absolutely not looking for anything after my last breakup. You buried a piece of your soul and don't want anything more than tonight. I think you're perfect for me in that respect. And you're really hot. And very sexy and I cannot tell you the last time a man gave me an orgasm that didn't require a map, a compass, and a flashlight to get me there."

Christ. She has no idea the things I could do to her. The things I *will* do to her.

"Do you need to let your friends know? You can give them my name or phone number if that helps to make you more comfortable."

She rolls her head over her shoulder, finding her friends—one is making out with a guy and the other talking to the same guy she's been with the entire time. The third one that was with them is gone.

Halle stands up, waves her hand in the air to catch her friend's attention. When she does, she points at me and gives a thumbs-up. A fucking thumbs-up.

I laugh so bloody hard.

She's sweet and shy and yet she's the antithesis of that. There is a fire hidden beneath and I cannot wait to draw it out. Her friend nods with an approving smile, giving her a thumbs-up in return and then holds up her cell phone. Halle nods and blows her a kiss, then she turns back to me, ending her non-verbal conversation.

"I'm good."

I grin, because holy hell, this girl, this night . . . "Then let's go."

Chapter Four

Jonah

WE BARELY MAKE it outside before I'm attacking her. The warm Boston summer air hits us with its stale, end of the day scent. We're in the South End and the sun has been baking the city streets all day long. It's not all that appetizing in truth.

But Halle is.

I have her pressed up against the wall of a neighboring building, my lips crashing against hers. She moans into my mouth, kissing me back with equal ardor. Her lips are soft and warm, pliant. Perfect.

Interlocking our fingers, I raise her arms to just above her head. She grins into my mouth, rocking on the balls of her feet.

"Will this kill our sexy buzz if I tell you that this kiss is already better than any sex I've had in years?"

I chuckle, dropping my mouth down to her exposed neck and running the tip of my nose up the column of her skin back toward her ear. "No," I whisper, my voice husky and filled with a want I had no clue I possessed anymore. "And if we weren't on a busy street in the middle of the city, I'd hike one of your long legs up around my waist and show you just how hard you make me."

She sighs, sinking into me. "I live three blocks from here."

"I live twelve."

"I'm closer."

"Your place it is."

"Okay." She giggles, but the sound is quickly muffled as my lips take over hers once more, my tongue gliding along the seam of her lips, demanding entrance. "I don't have any condoms," she rushes out. When I pull back, she scrunches her eyes shut like she's afraid to look at me. "God, I keep killing this." She rests her head back against the rough bricks, her chin rising up toward the sky before she opens her eyes. "But it's true. I really don't."

"I don't, either. As I said, I haven't done this in a very long time."

"There's a convenience store around the corner from my building."

"Lead on, love."

Stepping back, I release one of her hands but hold on tightly to the other. Her eye catches mine as we make our way down the mostly deserted street. It's late now, and as silence descends upon us, a stroke of guilt does, too. Madeline. I haven't kissed a woman since her. And now, two years after I buried her, I'm going home with the first woman I find any interest in.

"Did you like living in London?" she asks, drawing me away from my dark thoughts.

"Yes. It was different than here in some ways. Similar in others. Mostly your food and expressions on things. How long have you been living in Boston?"

"Nine years. I came here for college."

I nod and smile at that. "I've lived here since we moved from London. Do you miss South Carolina?"

"Sometimes. I'm from outside Charleston. It's beautiful there, mostly warm and southernly sweet. No one gets that unless they're from there or have visited it enough to appreciate the old beauty of it. But even though I miss it, I don't want to go back."

I bring her hand up, kissing her knuckles, and that sexy smile of hers curves her lips.

"How come?"

She turns away, but before she does, I swear I catch a flash of pain in her eyes. "Because I like Boston," she says simply, but that doesn't feel like the whole truth. "I have friends here, and my work is valued here more than it is there."

"And we're still not talking about that? Work, I mean."

She shakes her head, giving me a sideways glance. "Definitely not. My work is so very serious. And at the moment, stressful. Skydiving or bungee jumping?"

"What?" I laugh the word as we wait at the crosswalk for the light to change.

She laughs, too, spinning around with her back to the street so she can face me, her hand still in mine. I like holding her hand, I realize. It's never really been my thing. It always felt like a task. Awkward even. I was always too tall compared to the women I was with. We never lined up well.

But tonight, everything feels different.

"So, when you bungee jump, you're harnessed up and tethered to a long rope, right? Something to catch you. When you skydive, you freefall with only the parachute to help you land safely."

"Ah." I twist her hand over her head, twirling her around because now the light has changed and it's our turn to cross. "I think I understand. But before I give you my answer, have you ever done either?"

She smiles and shakes her head. "I'm a total heights wimp. It's why I asked *you* the question. I haven't done either, but I think I'd like to one day. You know, face my fears and whatnot. Have you?"

"Yes. I've done both."

"Seriously?" Her eyebrows hit her hairline.

"Seriously. I had someone who made me systematically go through her bucket list with her."

"Wow," she muses. "Is this the piece of your soul you buried?"

I look away, the ground dropping out from beneath my feet.

"Shit," she hisses. "I'm sorry. That was so out of line. Don't

34

answer that, okay?" She leans into me a little, begging for me to turn back to her. I do. I don't think I can look away from her for long. "I like that you've done both. I think it's pretty amazing actually. I bet I'd just pee my pants and run the other way."

"You came up to me at the pub tonight," I tell her. "You approached a total stranger, which means you're braver than you give yourself credit for."

She tilts her head as she thinks on this before her teeth sink into her lip. "Would it sour our whole night if I told you my friends bet me free drinks for a month in exchange for approaching you?"

"Nah," I say, leaning in to kiss her. "Incentives are what drive people to do things they don't typically feel comfortable doing. In any event, I'm glad you did."

"Me too," she sighs on a heavy breath like that admission surprises her. "Here." She lifts our joined hands, sticking a finger out to point to the glowing chain store sign overhead.

I open the door for her and she waltzes in, winking at me as she passes. The lights are bright in here. Compared to the darkness of the street, it's a bit disorienting. The aisles are filled with late-night shoppers and all I can focus on is getting this woman home.

"Condoms, condoms, where could you be? Family planning is my bet, though feminine products could be a winner, too."

I laugh at her cheekiness, wrapping her up in my arms and kissing her again, right here in the middle of the store. "Family planning, love," I whisper into her mouth. "Lead the way."

"They really need a better name for this section. Anyone shopping over here is *not* planning a family."

I look at her. She looks at me. We both turn back to the varietal buffet of condoms and lubricants. There's even a purple vibrator as well, which has me inwardly grinning.

"Wow," she muses, tapping her finger on her lower lip. "Clearly, I need to get out more. Who knew there were this many choices? It's a bit overwhelming to tell the truth."

"What are you thinking?" I glance over at her and enjoy the way those cheeks pink up.

"That this is sucking all the heat and fun and romance out of this. I may be a virgin at this sort of game but buying condoms before you do the deed feels a bit anticlimactic."

Oh shit. I turn and take her hand, pulling her into me until she's wrapped in my arms. And it feels . . . natural. Which is bizarre as I've only known her a little more than an hour. She's technically a complete stranger, but I didn't hesitate to hug her, and she doesn't pull away or get turned off by it.

"It sort of is," I agree, pressing her into me. "I'm sorry. I should have been more prepared. But even shopping for condoms with you is fun. A bit awkward, sure, but fun." I stare intently into her eyes. "Are you still into this? If not, you can tell me."

"So, you're saying you want to make this fun?"

"We're buying condoms with the intent of using them. I think this could most definitely be fun."

She grins up at me, running her hand up the fabric of my jacket and through my hair. I love when women do that—run their fingers through the back of my hair. It's my weakness or an aphrodisiac or whatever the hell you want to call it. It just gets me. My cock responds accordingly, and I know she feels it.

"Hmmm. Are you a magnum man, Jonah? Trojans? Ribbed for my pleasure?"

I grin. "Lady's choice."

"Oh," she exclaims, her eyes widening. "I like that."

Lowering my mouth to the shell of her ear, I whisper, "I'm going to make sure of it. Now let's pick out some condoms so I can take you back to your place, strip you out of this pretty red frock, and make you come."

Her breath hitches as I press my lips into the soft tissue beneath her ear before releasing her. Her light blue eyes darken as she wordlessly grabs two boxes of condoms. One is, in fact, Magnums; the other is ribbed for her pleasure.

"Wishful thinking," she says as she tosses both boxes at me. "And just to keep your mind in the game, my panties and bra match my dress."

She blushes when she says that and even though we're buying condoms, which isn't the sexiest of activities as she said, I'm still dying for this woman. Because condoms might not be sexy, but she sure as hell is.

"My mind is still very much in the game. But since you're all about incentives tonight, Magnums are typically my brand."

Her gaze drops down to my pants. My cock twitches, anxious for what is yet to come and loving the way she's staring like she's starving for me. "We might have to sample one of each kind. You know," she hedges with an impish grin, "to see which feels better."

"Most definitely."

We walk up to the register, hand in hand, each of us clutching a box of condoms. When we drop them on the counter, the middle-aged clerk eyes us both like we're a couple of deviants. "I'm taking him home with me," Halle says out of nowhere and I can't stop my burst of laughter. Halle giggles, too, glancing in my direction with a playful grin before she turns back to the clerk. "Aren't I a lucky lady?"

The clerk doesn't even react, she just peers in my direction and then shrugs. "If you say so."

"Ouch," I gasp, clutching my chest like she wounded me.

"What can I say, you're not really my type."

Fucking Bostonians. It's why I love this city.

Halle and I both laugh. I tug her into my side and plant a kiss on her cheek. "Lucky for me, I'm hers." I wink at the lady, grab our condoms, and yank Halle along after me.

I have no idea who I am tonight. No idea if this is how Halle typically is, either. This wild, flirtatious, confident, take-no-prisoners woman. It didn't seem like it in the pub, but maybe those were just her nerves getting the better of her, and now that she's relaxed with me, she's showing me her true self.

If I'm being honest, I like both.

I like the demure, sweet, innocent girl who blushes at everything I say. But I also like the sexy vixen who seems to know what she wants and how to get it. All I can make sense of is that I'm enjoying everything I'm seeing so far, and I cannot wait for more. More kisses. More touches. More giggles and smiles.

Maybe I should be home, crying myself into a bottle of scotch.

But I don't want to. I've been doing that for two sodding years. I won't be doing that tonight. And it's not because I didn't love Madeline. I absolutely did. Still do. Always will. Not a moment will pass that I won't miss her. I still hate life and wish it wasn't such a greedy bastard for taking her.

But I don't want to think about Madeline right now.

It just hurts too much. Tonight, I want to be selfish. Tonight, I want it to be about me and about Halle.

I don't even care if that makes me a first-rate git.

So, this one night with Halle, well, I'm not about to squander an opportunity.

Halle and I step back out into the night, her arm linked with mine, her head on my shoulder. "Is it weird that this doesn't feel weird?"

I smile to myself. She's so candid. I don't meet many people who speak without a filter.

"I know what you mean." I glance down at her and catch her eye for a quick moment before I stop and cup her face in my hands. "It's not weird at all. Maybe that's why we think it should be weird."

She nods. "Right. Exactly." She swallows audibly, and her pretty, pink tongue darts out to lick her lips.

I dip my head and my lips capture that moisture. She opens for me instantly and my tongue takes advantage, sweeping into her mouth and dancing with hers. This was just meant to be a place-holder. A reminder of what's to come, but it's quickly morphing into so much more. Into me running my hands through her hair and holding the back of her head so I can deepen the kiss. Into me pressing her soft, warm body up against mine. Into sliding one hand down to the crest of her gorgeous ass.

My cock is straining through the silky material of my suit, and right now, I have a full-on tent going. "Hmmm," she hums into me, the sound vibrating through my body. At this rate, I won't make it out of my pants without embarrassing myself.

"Please tell me you live really close," I mumble into her, nipping at her bottom lip before I suck on it.

"I live close," she echoes, pointing behind me. "Right here, in fact."

"Thank God," I groan, and her laugh flows into me.

I kiss her again, moving us in the general direction of the building she mentioned. We bang into the glass door, our bodies still pressed together. I lean into her, my tongue practically fucking her mouth and coaxing the most incredible sounds out from the back of her throat.

I greedily swallow every sound.

Suddenly, the door behind Halle opens without warning, and we go tumbling into the building. I fall forward, my feet and arms unable to keep up with my descent as momentum and gravity take over. Halle falls back, her eyes wide and startled, a half-shriek passing her lips as we stumble, desperate to remain upright. I reach out to grab her, but Halle's ass hits the floor hard, sliding back a foot.

Before I can react and pick her up, someone else is there. "I'm so sorry, miss. Are you hurt?"

Halle brushes her long burnished red strands out of her face and looks up at an older man who is redder than she is at the moment.

"I was just trying to open the door for you and your friend. My apologies."

Christ, this night.

"I'm okay," she murmurs, staring down at her hands nestled between her spread legs, the fabric of her dress gathered around her thighs. She laughs lightly and shakes her head like she can't believe this happened, either. "I swear. I'm totally and completely fine."

"She's brilliant," I chime in, bending down and grasping her hand in mine to hoist her up. "Don't worry," I say to the poor chap, who looks like he's ready to crawl in a corner and hide. "I've got her from here."

Halle is now fire engine red, but she's also amused. At least the slight upturn of her lips suggests so. She lets me wrap my arms around her waist and walk her over to the elevator, all three of us now completely silent. The silence is deafening and uncomfortable.

The poor bloke mumbles under his breath, something along the lines of, "I'll just go then," before exiting the building.

We press the button and the doors immediately open—thank fuck—and the moment they close behind us, she bursts out laughing, covering her face with her hands and shaking her head.

"Oh my God," she gasps, still cackling a bit. "How am I ever going to face him again? That was the worst."

"It's my fault," I say, gently prying her hands from her face. "I should have been looking where I was going. Are you really all right? You hit the ground rather hard before I could stop you."

"Yes. I'm just mortified. I've only been living here a month and that's the first time I've met him. But I guess he'll be easy enough to avoid, right? Big building and all that?" I raise a skeptical eyebrow and she throws her hands up in mock aggravation. "Just lie to me, Jonah. For once. I need to hear that I won't run into the man who —" She holds up a finger as if making a point "—is old enough to be my grandfather—caught me making out with the random guy I'm bringing home."

"You won't run into him again." I can't stop my grin. Damn, she's adorable.

She peers up at me. "Did you know that you still have a touch of an English accent?"

I chuckle lightly. "Sort of like your southern accent. I do have one, but it mostly comes out in my mix of American and English expressions. And after a few drinks of course."

"Not fully British. Not fully American. I like it."

I turn her in to face me, my forehead dropping to hers. It's perfect that she's so tall. I don't have far to go to kiss her. I'm six-four and not many women can handle that. "We've had an interesting night so far." She nods against me. "Are you ready for what's next?"

Chapter Five

Halle

THE MOMENT we step off the elevator, Jonah's all over me. He rakes a hand through my hair, tugging on it just enough to adjust my head so he can crash his mouth to mine. His other hand is on my ass, running across the left cheek and then the right before he gives me a tiny smack and a squeeze.

He thrusts me into the wall of the hallway, pressing his hard cock into me and I go nuts. Something in me just clicks on, and suddenly I'm on fire in a way I've never been before.

I'm an explosion of sensation.

A visceral grenade.

So helplessly turned on, my panties are soaked and I'm yanking on his suit jacket, desperate to pry it from his broad shoulders, angry at it for keeping me from my prize.

And lord, what a prize this man is. I don't even mind that he has this scary, dark, damaged side. It fits into mine perfectly. Like two jagged pieces of glass that can never fully be fused together or fixed.

"You feel so good," I moan against his mouth. I mean, I knew

Jonah was godly. I caught that in the bar, but now as my hands explore the hard ridges of his chest and abs through his thin button-up shirt, I can't get enough. I had no idea men in real life could be this stunningly sexy.

And I haven't even undressed him yet.

My mind is in a frenzy. Like a short-circuiting electrical wire, shooting out sparks in every direction. I'm thinking about his full lips on mine. About his rock-hard body covering me. About his fingers and mouth exploring me in ways I instinctively know he's more than capable of.

"We're in the hall," he murmurs.

"I don't think I care."

He draws back, smiling broadly, and it's breathtaking. As dazzling and colorful as the sunrise over the Atlantic on a summer's morning. "Which apartment is yours, Carolina?"

"There." I point down the hall, wishing it wasn't such a far walk. Wishing my bed or couch were right here in the hall. Or that the meager hallway wall wouldn't wake the neighbors if he fucked me against it.

It would.

The way I need him to take me would wake the whole building.

Clutching my hand, he leads me in that direction, his unrelenting grip practically crushing my fingers. But I don't care. I want him to take charge. To give me everything I never knew I needed.

Where has a guy like this been all my life? Why didn't I meet someone like him in college or graduate school instead of Matt? I could have been fucking men left and right. I could have been exploring every aspect of my sexuality, but instead, I wasted years on a man who never even put his face between my legs, and only touched my clit when I specifically asked him to. And then it was lacking enthusiasm and rarely did much for me. It got to the point where I'd have sex with Matt and then while he was showering the scent of us off his body—because he always freaking showered immediately after sex—I'd get myself off.

But Jonah here is kissing me like he has plans for me. For my body. Like my pleasure is just as vital to him as his own. At least, I'm praying that's what his kisses mean.

God, I didn't think I needed this, but I do. I really freaking do.

I wrench myself away from Jonah long enough to unlock my apartment and shove the door open. Once we're inside, I toss my keys on the table next to the door and click the lock into place behind us. Then I stop, absorbing the magnitude of this moment. Of this decision.

I have a stranger in my apartment and I'm about to have sex with him.

I wait for the feelings of regret or trepidation to flood me, but they never come. No second-guessing. Just good old-fashioned, lust-saturated anticipation.

Jonah glances around my apartment, taking in the furniture and the few stray boxes I have yet to unpack from my move last month. His focus shifts over to the window and then he crosses the foyer into the living room to get a better look. "This is incredible."

"Thank you," I say softly, my nerves suddenly getting the better of me. I want this. More than my next breath. But I've never had a one-night stand before. I've never brought a man I didn't know home with me, so I have no idea what the protocol is. Do I ask him if he wants a drink? Do I show him my bedroom and have us get right to it? Do I strip down and strike a sexy pose? I'm suddenly wishing I could run to the bathroom quickly to brush my teeth and hair.

Freshen myself up a bit.

But Jonah saves me from worrying over that. He spins around, desire-laced determination blazing in his eyes, as he marches toward me with long, purposeful strides. His arms encircle my waist, yanking me into his hard body.

A moan catches in my throat as he devours my mouth with a searing kiss. The kiss is demanding and powerful and so goddamn raw I'm instantly dizzy with it. I can't get enough of the way he tastes. The way he smells. The way he touches me.

More.

I want—no, I need, more.

I tear off his suit jacket, tossing it in the general direction of the couch. My fingers frantically attack his shirt, clumsily undoing buttons. One or two snap off, thudding dully on the floor. But again, I don't care, and it's evident he doesn't either since he laughs at my overzealous and less than graceful approach.

I tug at his shirt, desperate to pry it from his body, but it gets stuck at the wrists. "Wait," he rasps, clearing his throat. "Cufflinks."

He steps back, flipping the gold toggle and disengaging the cufflink from his shirt sleeve. First one, then the other. They're nice. Engraved with initials on the face and on the flipside a tiny scripted message I can't make out. He sets the cufflinks down on the counter with care, then lets his shirt drop to the floor.

He pauses, staring at me. Watching me. Waiting me out. Every beat that passes increases this insanely delicious rush that's thrumming through my ears. Heat slowly creeps up my skin, leaving warm tingles in its wake. No one has ever looked at me like this. Like I'm the most beautiful woman in the world. Like I'm sexy and desirable. Like they're going to feast on me, eat me whole, and give me the kind of pleasure I've only ever read about.

Before I can come to grips with that reality, he launches at me again, flattening me against my living room wall. I bump my head from the force of his action, but his hand is there to protect me as if he anticipated it. And hell, why does that make me like him so goddamn much? It's such a small gesture and yet so significant. He's protective and considerate and thoughtful.

Shit.

I don't want to like him. In fact, I have zero interest in it. But if I did, if I were interested, I could see how a girl would like Jonah . . .

I don't even know his last name. Wow, that's a smack in the face, isn't it?

Reaching around, he finds the zipper of my dress and glides it down so achingly slow, as if unwrapping something special, something delicate. As if he wants to savor his time doing so. It's driving me insane in the best possible way. I'm panting though he's barely touching me at this point. His entire steadfast focus is on that zipper, his eyes caressing mine as he lowers the damn thing inch by inch.

Once he finally has it undone, he steps back like a painter intent on studying his masterpiece. I nearly whimper at the loss of his warmth.

"Take it off," he commands, low and husky. I'm desperate to clench my thighs, squeeze them together to release some of this tension. "Do it, Halle. I want to see you undress for me."

Oh. My. God. My eyes flutter closed on their own accord.

"Open those gorgeous blues. Look at me while you take it off. I want you to see how turned on I am. How fucking hot you make me."

Jesus. He needs to stop all this talking or I'm going to combust.

I open my eyes and find his once again. All of that beautiful green I like so much is eclipsed by black, carnal and dark. Standing up straight, I reach up and slip one strap off my shoulder, followed by the other. The dress slowly cascades down my arms, past my breasts and hips, the silky material slinking down my legs before it lands in a pool at my feet.

He stares at me through hooded eyes and long lashes. Mine are returning the favor, feasting on his sculpted abs and that oh-so-perfect V leading to the only place I want to be right now. I freaking knew this man was an Adonis without his clothes on, but I can't find it in me to gloat.

I'm too keyed up for that.

"Halle," he whispers almost to himself before he crosses the small space between us and picks me up off the ground, forcing my legs to wrap around his waist. The muscles in his shoulders ripple and stretch as he adjusts me, and I relish the feel of them under my hands as he maneuvers us. "I take it the bedroom is this way?"

I nod. I don't know if I can formulate words right now.

Unable to stop myself, I grind on his hard cock through his pants. A low groan rumbles through his chest. His hot wet mouth kisses a trail along my collarbone, over to the base of my neck. I tilt my head, offering him better access and his tongue swipes out, dipping into my suprasternal notch, his teeth grazing my sensitive flesh.

We breach the threshold of my bedroom, and he strides to my

bed, gently laying me down on it before he dips down and kisses my mouth again. This man is a full-contact sport. There is no separation, no close enough.

His weight presses me firmly into the mattress, and I swallow down the moan Jonah breathes into my mouth. Everything about him is so fucking delicious. Large, strong hands slide up to cup my lace-covered breasts, and his moan morphs into a low growl as he gives me a firm squeeze.

Jonah's nose glides along the crest of my breasts as his talented hands knead me, his fingers twisting and tweaking my pebbled nipples through the fabric. Scooting lower, he nips at my flesh, before kissing the smooth expanse of my abdomen. He stops at my navel, his breath warm on my already overheated skin. A whimper slips through my swollen lips as he continues to squeeze my tits with just the right amount of pressure.

My back arches off the bed from the sensation of it.

"God, you're perfect."

I grin. I can't stop it. That's the perfect thing for him to say to me right now.

"I need to taste you, Halle."

Oh hell. I moan, arching farther into him. I was wrong. *That* is most definitely the perfect thing to say to me. I squirm as his mouth trails just a bit lower. I can't stop my reaction to his lips against my flesh. It's been far too long since a man has done that to me.

"I want to see if you taste this sweet everywhere. Can I do that, love?"

I nod my head desperately. "Yes," I pant, my eyes cinching shut as he continues to slither lower and lower. "Oh, hell. Yes."

When he reaches the top of my panties, he pauses, staring down at my red-lace-covered pussy. It's intense. And hot. Not enough, yet too much. His eyes find mine. He lowers his face into the lace and inhales deeply. *Oh, holy fuck.*

"Mmmm," he hums, shooting the most delicious vibrations straight to my clit. "So lovely." He grins and it's wicked and sexy and I think I might come a little just from that. "I'm going to make you scream my name over and over tonight. I'm going to make up for all those orgasms you said you were missing. And only after all of that has happened, only when you're begging me, will I fuck your tight cunt."

My eyes close again, my head rolls back and my mind clears, going someplace warm and light, because slowly—so goddamn slowly—he pulls my panties down. I feel them slide across my feet, and then he's spreading my legs wide open.

Soft lips kiss me, right on my bare mound like he's introducing himself, asking for permission to take what he's about to give. He licks me from my opening up before sucking my clit between his lips. My hips shoot off the bed, my head flies back, my fists ball up my sheets.

Two fingers slide into my soaking wet heat, pumping in and out in a slow tandem compared to the fast pace his tongue has set on my clit. I whimper, biting my lip. Sounds I'm positive I've never made before explode from my mouth as he finger fucks in and out of me.

"So sweet," he purrs against me. "Just like I knew you'd be. I could do this all night."

I had no idea dirty talk could make me this hot. No freaking clue. And the way he's touching me? Caressing me? Watching my reactions to everything he's doing? It's just so *much*. I feel like I've been perpetually hanging out with the minor league and suddenly I graduated to the majors. And now that I've discovered what pleasure and desire are truly meant to be like, I never want to go back.

"Come, Halle," he demands, sucking on me until my head spins. "Come on my face."

His words unleash something inside me. He commands it and I come so hard I see flashes of color splattering behind my eyes. My mind splinters along with my body, and there's a damn good chance I'll be screaming his name soon. Just like he said I would. I've never done that before. Never said anyone's name during sex. It always felt a bit cliché, to be honest, but Jonah's name flies unrestrained from my mouth, as if to remind me who is making me feel this incredible.

One night, Halle. It's just one night.

Right.

Why does that thought make me so goddamn sad? It's not even

Jonah necessarily. It's the sex. I don't need confirmation that I chronically pick the wrong men, but if I had any remaining doubts, they're gone now. How can I have this one night and not any after it? How can I experience this, feel this pleasure, and know I might never have it again? It literally makes me want to cry like *that* girl. You know, the one who cries after sex and we haven't even *had* sex yet.

But Jonah buried a piece of his soul—whatever that means—and I'm just getting out of a horrible relationship with a man who consistently lied to me. I just . . . I don't even know what.

I want more of this.

Is this what happens to girls like me?

We think we're all big and tough, and cool shit, can handle whatever sexual adventures are thrown at us before we move on, only to find out just how wrong we are. I don't want to be that girl. I want to be the one who can handle it when he walks away from me tomorrow—or tonight. Who can reminisce back on this night with a smile and an air of satisfied joy instead of regret and heartache.

Christ, I get all this emotion from just one orgasm? I mean, it was a phenomenal orgasm, but it doesn't have to be life-changing. It doesn't have to reign this sort of power over me. Right?

"You all right?" he asks warily, noting the shift in my demeanor. I wish he weren't so observant and in tune to what my body is doing. I love it, but as a result, he's everywhere.

"Yes," I say, forcing a smile. But I'm not, and I wonder why. Is it because I'm giving him exactly what I said I wanted? Why can't I have this one night? Why can't I enjoy it and him for what this is? "I'm fantastic," I add. I think I might mean it. I can do this. I *want* to do this.

"You sure?"

"Absolutely. Please don't stop. I want this."

He climbs back up my body, hovering over me and staring directly into my eyes. Reaching up, I run my hands across his smooth, angled jaw and into his hair, drawing his face down to mine and kissing him with everything I've got. Showing him—and me—

just how okay I am with this. I taste myself on his lips and that only seems to spur me on.

Jonah breaks the kiss to remove his pants, his boxer briefs slipping down with them. I can't stop myself from staring at him, drinking in the sight before me. Marveling at how big and hard his cock is as it stands at attention, begging for my mouth to wrap around it. I lick my lips at that thought, a fresh wave of moisture pooling between my legs. God, this man. He's impossibly tall, crazy, sexy gorgeous and cut like Zeus.

"What are you thinking about?" he asks, leisurely stroking himself as if he knows exactly what I'm thinking and wants to have some fun with my limits.

I can have some fun too. "My mouth on your cock."

"Fuck," he hisses, and I sink my teeth into my bottom lip, loving how unnerved I can make him with a simple threat. "You're going to do that later. I'm dying to see that pretty mouth wrapped around my cock, those eyes staring up at me as you take me down your throat. But for now . . ." He lets the sentence hang, coiling up into the musty, sex-scented air as he grabs a condom.

After sheathing himself up, he's back on me, kissing me like he's in no hurry to be inside me. The kiss is passionate. Languid. Toe-curlingly decadent. I could live and die by this man's kisses.

His fingertips glide down my thigh all the way to my calf before he lifts my leg and tucks it over his shoulder. And then he's inside me, massaging secret, hidden places within. We're nothing but desire mixed with passion and longing. Holy hell, the longing is incredible. Years of pent-up everything are somersaulting out of me like a prison break, being absorbed by the electricity that's swirling around us, unable to be restrained.

He thrusts into me, his eyes on mine the entire time. His hands fist my ass, holding me up, angling me just so as he sets a pace I'm helpless to do anything but take. My tits bounce, swaying every which way. Jonah pulls back, watching himself fuck me like he can't believe we're doing this either.

"You feel so good," he groans, beads of sweat coating his forehead. "So tight. So perfect."

"Don't stop," I moan desperately, not even caring that I'm begging him.

He shakes his head, his lips coming down to nip at mine. "I won't go over the edge until you do."

Thank God.

I drag him down until my knees are on his shoulders and our chests are practically touching, deepening the angle. Grasping his shoulders, my nails dig in with each push and pull. His hand squeezes my breasts, playing with my nipple and bring it up to his mouth to flick with his tongue.

"Ah!" I cry out.

"You like that?"

"Yes," I moan so close to losing my mind. The sounds of skin against skin, of my wetness all over him is driving me wild. He twists my nipple and sparks of pleasure shoot through me.

"You're so beautiful, Halle. Like a dream." He grunts, lifting me up once more by my ass so he can increase his rhythm. "I want to fuck you all night."

"Harder. Deeper."

With a growl he pounds into me, drawing me closer and closer to something I have no name for. It's more than just a climax. It's more than a peak. It's consuming. Engrossing. By far and away the best thing I've ever experienced.

Seconds later, I shatter, coming apart at the seams as he slams into me relentlessly. He follows me over, growling out my name as his body stills and shudders before he collapses on top of me, both of us panting for our lives.

"That was . . ."

He nods against me and I can feel his smile. "Yeah. It really was."

I run my fingers up the muscled contours of his back, and regretfully, I realize I didn't explore his body the way I would have liked.

The way he explored mine.

But that thought gets pushed to the back of my mind when he props himself up on his elbow and leans in to kiss me. When our lips slide apart and the moment has passed, he climbs off me, heading for the bathroom attached to my bedroom.

And all I can do is lie here, staring at my ceiling, reminding myself over and over again just how awesome a one-night stand actually is.

Chapter Six

Halle

SUNLIGHT STREAMS THROUGH MY WINDOW, bright and unrelenting. My eyes shut against it, cinching tight as I turn my face back into my pillow with a small groan.

I'm sore. In a million different places I never knew existed on, or in, my body. That makes me smile like the post-orgasmic-drunk girl I am into my pillow.

Jonah. My fingers glide across the smooth sheets, seeking that spot, that spot that was most assuredly occupied by him when we fell asleep in the wee hours.

It's now empty.

And cold.

Like it's been empty for a while.

For a moment, I tell myself he's just in the bathroom. Or maybe in the kitchen. Or maybe he ran out to get us coffee and breakfast. But no. He's gone.

It takes me a solid five minutes to convince myself it's a relief. I can avoid the morning-after awkwardness and bullshit phone number exchange, which neither of us will ever use. I got exactly what I was after—asked for—last night and anything more would be too much more. Unwanted even.

But it sorta sucks to wake up alone after the night we had.

We used a lot of those condoms—at least three of them—and then after that last time, he spent more time going down on me. My stomach flips as I recount it. Hours and hours of sex. Intimate words and acts. Mind-numbing, soul-awakening pleasure.

Being dominated in a way I never knew I'd enjoy.

My phone rings from somewhere in my apartment and slowly, remorsefully, I drag my sorry ass out of bed and shrug on my robe. As I'm tying the belt, I see my phone.

Aria. I stare at her name, wondering whether I should pick up. It stops ringing only to start again almost immediately. I groan, but a smile stretches on my lips. Smiling can't be helped when your friend is annoyingly and endearingly worried about you.

I've barely answered when her voice screeches in my ear. "It's twelve-thirty!"

Oh shit. Seriously?

"I cannot believe you're just waking up! You were supposed to call one of us by now, Halle Jane. I realize you're new at this whole hooking up thing, but that's what girls do. We let our friends know we're not dead in an alleyway, or worse, in The Fens."

I'm silent, gnawing on my bottom lip while I try to come up with a response.

"Is he still there?"

I shake my head, looking around my apartment just to confirm what I already know. "Nope. He left some time ago. No idea when, I was still asleep."

"Did he leave you his number? A note?"

"Nothing," I reply, but I'm still searching around just in case I'm wrong. "Wait." A piece of paper catches my eye. "Yes," I breathe out, surprised. "Holy crap, Aria. He left me a note."

"Oh," she exclaims, just as surprised as I am, though her tone is more pleased than mine. "That's good, right?"

I don't know.

"What does it say?"

I read it over and then sag down onto one of my barstools, because this feels like a copout. I almost wish he hadn't left anything at all. I clear my throat, then read the note aloud. "'Sorry to run out on you, but I had an emergency that could not be helped. Last night with you was everything. Jonah.'" I sigh. I don't even know what that means. *Everything* is such a vague word. I think I might have preferred the word perfect. He peppered me with that one a lot last night. Couldn't he have used that one last time?

"Did he leave his number?"

"Yes. He did. But it's probably fake, right? I mean, who leaves in the pre-dawn hour with an *emergency*?" I emphasize sardonically. "That has to be a total bullshit excuse to escape the morning-after stuff. I bet he left his number out of guilt and if I tried to call it, he'd blow me off." I sigh again and stare down at the note he'd scratched out on the back of the convenient store receipt from last night.

Aria is silent, and I hate her silence. It's confirming everything I already know. I should not feel like this. I should not care. I don't think I would have cared this much if he had just disappeared into the night like a sex apparition or spirit. This note is throwing me.

"I guess I shouldn't be surprised. We both agreed to one night." Even if our chemistry was better than anything I've experienced before. Better than the sort of magic drug dealers cook up in their basements. There was nothing forced or manufactured about it. It was the kind that only occurs naturally when two people really click.

I crumple up the receipt and toss it in the vague direction of the trash, annoyed that it hits the floor about three feet away, just as a flash of gold catches my eye. His cufflinks.

"If that's what you agreed to—"

"He left his cufflinks," I interrupt her.

"What?"

"His gold cufflinks. He took them off last night and set them on my kitchen counter. He must have forgotten them in his haste to escape."

"Or he did it on purpose to have an excuse to see you again."

I shake my head automatically. I know that's not the case. Even in the half-minute it took him to remove these last night, I could see they're special to him. I pick them up, admiring their weight and smooth, cool texture.

"No way," I tell her. "These are real gold. And they've got his initials on the face and on the bottom"—I flip them over and gasp—"Oh, Aria." My voice fails me.

"What? What's on the bottom?"

My eyes glide across the tiny script of the message engraved. Half on one cufflink. Half on the other. "One says: Bravery. Kindness. Strength. The other says: Love. Laughter. Joy." I sink back into my unforgiving barstool, staring at the words. *I buried a piece of my soul*, he had said. "I need to get these back to him."

I knew they were special, but somehow, it feels like whatever piece of his soul he buried gave him these.

"Are you going to call him?"

"I have to," I whisper, my ire at his having run out on me ebbing. He did leave his number, even though neither of us are looking for anything serious. I already know I don't have it in me to be a booty call for that man.

"Christ." I laugh, shaking my head. "I don't even know his last name. Just the letter on the cufflink. H. I have no clue what he does for a living, or where he lives, or whether he kills stray cats and cooks them up for dinner parties. I let a man repeatedly inside my body and I know nothing about him."

"Brunch. At our usual spot. Thirty minutes. I'm calling Rina and Margot now. Neither of them are working today. And Halle?"

"Yeah," I say absently, my gaze still on the cufflinks. I can't seem to look away from them.

"Bring the cufflinks and the note."

The phone beeps in my ear, meaning she hung up without saying goodbye. I set my phone down on the counter, still staring at the cufflinks. Heaving a sigh, I set them next to my phone and head toward the shower I so desperately need.

I survey the aftermath of last night as I enter my bedroom. My dress is still on the living room floor, but my bra and panties are on the floor in here. My sheets are a tangled mess, and I know if I were to press my face into the pillow he used, it would smell like him.

Which is exactly why I set to work on stripping my bed and carrying all my linens down the hall to my laundry closet. I stuff the sheets into the washing machine and start it, then head directly to the shower. Just because I am going to seek him out to give him back his cufflinks, doesn't mean I want a do-over. The sex was just sex. Sure, it was fun and seriously hot, but that's as far as it will ever go.

But here's the problem—I think I might be ruined. At least as far as sex goes.

Seriously. I think the sexy bastard ruined my vagina for all future men.

I mean, I've slept with six guys, not including Jonah. Okay, so that's not exactly a lot. But still, I feel like that should be enough of a sample size to understand that not all men fuck the way Jonah I-don't-know-his-last-name does. That they don't take the time to understand and pleasure the woman they're simply hooking up with.

Because that's what he did.

I don't even know how many orgasms I had last night because I freaking lost count.

All-night sex with one man, and I just know I'm going to be comparing every future guy to him. And most likely be disappointed with the results. Fabulous. Just fabulous.

Okay. Moving on. It was one night, and this is Boston. The majority of men are not like Matt. Or the douchebag before him, or the douchebag before that douchebag. And so on.

I turn on the faucet and wait for the water to reach my preferred temperature before I step in and wash Jonah off my skin. I let the hot water release the ache in my sore muscles and scrub my mind and body of him.

I want to give him those cufflinks. If only there were a way I could do it without having to see him.

Half an hour later, I'm strolling into our usual brunch place, walking through to the back where the small courtyard is. It's a beautiful day to eat outside and Margot already texted me to let me know she got us a table out here. The brick walls are lined with a thick layer of ivy. Coupled with the large tree in the middle of the outdoor space, it makes it feel like we're dining in a garden instead of a Boston restaurant.

They smile, standing up to hug me. The moment we sit down, however, Rina lays right into me. "I want details. Sexy details. Tell us everything."

This is not a position I am used to being in. Typically, I'm the one listening to their stories, not the other way around. Margot has a habit of sleeping with random men and hating herself—or them—for it afterward. Rina occasionally hooks up, but her dating life is more about small bursts of relationships. Aria is coupled up with Drew, a doctor at the hospital Margot, Rina, and I work at. Well, where I used to work. Drew is the one who introduced us to Aria. She's not a nurse. She's a famous artist.

"It was fun. He was great."

My friends exchange glances and I know I'm not getting away with that.

"Aaand?" Margot draws out, nudging me in the shoulder.

I stare down at the wood table, twirling a piece of my hair around my finger. I can feel my cheeks starting to burn. Being a fair-skinned redhead sucks sometimes. "The sex was fantastic. Best I ever had. We did things I've only ever read about in my bath time smut collection. But it was just the one night so . . ." I trail off with what I hope comes off as an indifferent shrug.

The waiter approaches us and we order our usual breakfast because we're in our usual brunch spot. The moment he leaves, Aria holds her hand out, wiggling her fingers impatiently. "Let's see 'em."

"Okay," I agree, fishing through my purse for the baggie I put the cufflinks in. "But just be careful, y'all. I want to return these the way he left them."

"The note, too, doll," Rina reprimands. "You're not getting off that easy."

I roll my eyes and pull out the crumpled piece of paper I fished off the floor, handing that over to her first. Rina scoots her chair over closer to Aria, the metal feet scraping against the hardscape, so she can get in on the action as I empty the baggie with the cufflinks into Aria's anxious hand. Margot half stands, leaning across the table as the three of them hover over the cufflinks like it's the precious ring from *The Lord of the Rings*. Aria rolls them around in her palm, fingering one of them. The three of them simultaneously lift their sunglasses to inspect the cufflinks properly without the filter of a lens.

I roll my eyes. "They're not some rare or magical diamond. They're just cufflinks."

They ignore me. Rina snags the note and proceeds to examine that next.

"Very nice," Rina says with an approving nod before her discerning gaze shifts to me. "It's a good note. Very solid. And I have to say, hot sex agrees with you. If I knew an orgasm or two would give your cheeks this glow and your eyes this light, I'd have told you to dump Matt years ago and find another guy."

"You did," I state flatly.

"Right." She snaps her fingers in an aw-shucks way. "I did. And you didn't listen until you discovered the dickless wonder was more into computers than your vagina."

"Thanks," I grumble. "You're an awesome friend." I take a sip of my much-needed coffee and close my eyes as the caffeine enters my blood stream. "They really need to find a way so you can main-line caffeine." I open my eyes and find my three best friends staring at me. "What?"

"So many things, I hardly know where to begin," Aria says, sipping her latte. "I'll get to these puppies last." She holds up the cufflinks, before palming them again. "First, Rina is correct. Good sex does agree with you. I'm not so sure it has to be a one and done. Maybe he's interested in a repeat."

I shake my head, downing the rest of my coffee. I signal the waiter for more, before turning back to my friends. "I don't think so. He made it clear that he's not looking for anything more. I think the note is him feeling guilty about running out. Besides, I'm not inter-ested in a repeat. Next."

"You should go out with someone you have a potential future

with," Margot says, concern etched in her expression and tone. "I don't see how one-night stands will help anything."

"Says the chick who only does one-night stands."

Margot points at me, brushing her chestnut hair behind her shoulders with a shake of her head. "Exactly. You don't want to end up like me. At least your one-nighters give you orgasms."

"This was my first one, Margot. It was a 'get Matt, and every other miserable man, out of my system' thing. I don't intend to make it my new standard."

"There's always Oliver," Rina offers, a bit too casually.

I glare at her. "I'm not dating your brother."

"Oliver likes you, Hal," she pushes, ignoring my comment. "Just roll it through your mind. He's very excited that you're going to be working together."

"He's a friend, Rina. That's all. I'm grateful that he got me the new job. Lord knows I needed it after the FBI showed up at the hospital. But that's all it should be."

"Fine. I get it. Has Matt tried to call you?"

I nod, staring down into my still-empty mug of coffee. "Twice. I didn't talk to him. Thankfully, he doesn't know where I'm living."

Aria puffs out a nervous breath and I know why she's nervous. Matt is a hacker. The reality is, he could very well know where I'm living. It wouldn't take much for him to find out.

"When do you start work? And please tell me Matt doesn't know where your new place of employment is, either."

Our food is delivered, and she shuffles her potatoes around her plate before digging in.

"Next week. They're finishing up my credentialing, but it's nearly done. My start date is a week from tomorrow. And no, Matt has no idea." *Let's hope.*

Rina points her fork at me. "Good. Great. A new job is just the thing you need. Even though they're paying you less, you'll like it more."

I snort out a laugh, shoving forkfuls of eggs into my mouth like I've been starving for a decade. Sheesh, all-night sex really builds up an appetite. "How would you know?"

"Because you've always liked straight-up family medicine, and women's health is your favorite. Now you get to do both."

I shrug. Can't argue with that. Truth be told, I'm excited for my new job. Hughes Community Health is a huge health system with three different branches in Boston alone. I'm based at the one down in Copley, and I get to do everything—women's health, adult medicine, and pediatrics. Being a family nurse practitioner might just be the greatest gig ever. Best of all, this new job feels like a fresh start.

"Next," Margot continues without missing a beat. "Did you google your sexy man yet?"

I shake my head, taking another bite of my eggs and forcing myself to swallow them down. All this talk about Jonah and Matt has made me lose my appetite. But honestly, they're not worth my starvation.

"I don't know his last name, remember?"

"Okay then." She rubs her hands together like the evil mastermind she is. "Let's call him. Right now."

"No freaking way. I'm not doing that in front of you guys. I'm hoping he'll stop by for the cufflinks, so I can avoid the awkward as fuck phone call altogether." Taking a sip of my newly refilled coffee, I lean back in my seat, done with my greasy breakfast. My stomach is starting to churn.

Aria grins widely, showing her white teeth. "It's an excuse for him to find you again. For him to seek you out. If they're that important to him, he wouldn't have left them like that. It had to be intentional."

"Yes," Margot agrees mid-chew. "Totally. God, this is so good. It's a shame this meal is like two days' worth of fat and calories, otherwise I'd eat it every day. You have to try it. I swear, these pancakes get better every damn time I eat them."

She holds out a forkful and I take a bite, trying to ignore the way Rina's eyes are glued to me. "Wow. Those are good."

"Right?" Margot asserts with wide eyes. "My advice? Wait to call him. He'll find you, like Aria said. And in the meantime, you got some hot sex out of it and you're getting ready for your new job and new life."

"I was thinking I'd text him tomorrow if he doesn't show up before that. This morning feels desperate. Anyway, I have a busy week of getting things done. I have EHR training tomorrow and on Tuesday I have a gyno appointment to discuss getting an IUD. Thursday I'm having lunch with Oliver to thank him for getting me the job and it just keeps going from there."

"Perfect," Rina smiles broadly. "And when mystery Jonah comes to collect his prized possession, maybe you two can have another romp and roll."

I shake my head. "No. I don't think that's a good idea. I need distance from men. At least until I figure out how to stop choosing losers, assholes, and criminals."

Aria shrugs, shoveling food into her mouth like she's a starving woman eating her last meal. "I still think you shouldn't give up so easily. Maybe he really did have an emergency and it had nothing to do with you or the night you spent together. He left a note with his number, Halle. He even said your night together was *everything*. Men don't do that if they don't mean it. They're nothing if not direct."

"Maybe," I whisper, but even as I let her words seep into me, I know that's not the case. He wanted a quick and easy escape, which he would have gotten if it weren't for the cufflinks. I just hope I can get them back to him with minimal effort. I'm anxious to close the book on him forever. But with my luck, I know I won't be so lucky.

Chapter Seven

Halle

I HAVE YOUR CUFFLINKS. I hit send and sit back and wait, staring at my phone like that will somehow make Jonah respond faster.

It doesn't.

With each second that ticks by without a response, I begin to doubt my text. Surely, he knows who it's from. Surely, he hasn't left several different cufflinks in several different women's apartments and is now trying to figure out a polite way to ask who this is texting him.

Right? Or maybe I should have led with, "Hey, it's Halle."

This is why I stayed with Matt so long. Dating sucks ass. But of course, when that text comes in, I'm assaulted with a jolt of traitorous butterflies.

Stop it, body. Stop responding. He's not here. No more mind-blowing sex to be had.

Jonah: Is this a ransom demand? If so, you should know I don't negotiate with terrorists.

Damn him. I laugh. Out loud in the middle of my gynecologist's waiting room. He left my apartment on Sunday and today is Tuesday.

I haven't seen Jonah.

He hasn't come for the cufflinks that I know of, but then again, I haven't exactly been home much. I can't remember the last time I had any real time off. I think it's been years. I should be away somewhere exotic. I should be on a beach, sipping a multi-colored daiquiri with an umbrella in it that an Adonis with a perfect, golden tan delivered to me.

But no, that's not my life. My life consists of doing a four-hour EHR—electronic health record—training so I can start my new job next week and spreading my legs for the freaking gynecologist.

Me: Actually, I'm charging them for rent and utilities. I don't take kindly to squatters who don't pull their weight and like to throw loud parties.

That message bubble appears instantly, and I sort of wish I hadn't waited so long to text him. I love text messages. They're the universal safety net when used appropriately. I can say whatever I want, be flirty or cheeky, and I don't have to look the other person in the face or hear their voice when I do it. And no one around me is the wiser. Good stuff.

Jonah: Are they staying up all night watching tele and eating through your kitchen? They can be unruly bastards. FYI: A little discipline goes a long way with cufflinks like those.

I smile. And it's the first genuine one I've had all day. *I don't want to smile at your adorable banter, Jonah!*

I'm in a foul mood and it has nothing to do with the EHR training or the gyno appointment. Or even Jonah.

Matt's lawyer called me this morning. He wanted to know if I'd be willing to testify on my ex-fiancé's behalf. Like a character witness or something if the case goes to trial. I told him no. Flat out.

But the prick threatened to subpoena me, even going so far as to mention that the DA or other law enforcement agencies could still charge me with accessory if they believed any part of my statement to the FBI was inadequate or false.

I hung up on him and immediately called my lawyer.

He wasn't much help in that department other than to say he hadn't heard any mention of me being charged with anything, and that my statement was more than adequate.

Great. Not all that reassuring. I ended it with Matt *before* I knew about everything he had been doing, but we're only talking a few days, which doesn't look all that great from an outside perspective.

Oh, and on top of that, I've been getting strange calls a few times a day from random numbers. No one ever speaks on the other end. Just a lot of heavy breathing into the phone. It's creepy, and part of me wonders if it's Matt. I don't see how it could be, but I can't think of anyone else who would do that.

So yeah, shitty mood.

Jonah: **Seriously though, thank you for not throwing them out the window or donating them to a needy investment banker. They mean the world to me, and since you're never home, I haven't been able to retrieve them.**

He came by! And I wasn't home. *Stop smiling, Halle. He came for the cufflinks, not for you.*

Me: **Sorry, I meant to get in touch sooner, but things have been busy.**

Jonah: **Terrible excuse. I'm trying not to take it personally.**

God, that does sound lame. Really, I've just been a wimp. After leaving Matt, I promised myself I would never be a doormat again and I feel like I'm regressing a bit with that. My life is in such a state of upheaval. Newly single, new apartment, new job, and now these legal threats and phone calls.

Things will be easier once I start my new job next week. I know that. And I genuinely love my new apartment. And I'm not sad at all about being single.

Just as I'm about to respond to Jonah, Oliver, one of Rina's older brothers, texts me. **Just confirming we're still on for lunch tomorrow? Looking forward to seeing you.**

I text him back telling him that we are. He's a resident doctor at Hughes Community Health Center and he's the one who helped me get my new job. The pay isn't nearly as good as it was at my old job. Like, I went from making hospital money to community health center money.

The pay drop is significant.

I have plenty of money saved and some I inherited from my parents' life insurance when they died. Not a lot, but enough that I can do this gig for a couple of years and float along comfortably. But I have to look at this as a temporary gig instead of a permanent job.

In any event, I'm excited to get started, but these things take time for medical professionals. We have to be credentialed through insurance companies and government agencies for each specific place we work at. That can take weeks. Longer for doctors.

But between giving my notice on my old job and the paperwork with my new job, this is the first week that I won't have any work. Which is why I'm using this small burst of freedom to get everything I need done.

Like seeing the gynecologist.

I was on the pill forever but had a couple of pregnancy scares with Matt. I'm also tired of having to remember to take a pill daily, which is why I'm interested in getting an IUD.

Ironically, my doctor's office is with the same community health-care chain I'm going to be working in, just in Brookline instead of in Copley.

I start to type more to Jonah when the medical assistant calls my name. Tucking my phone into my bag, I follow her back into an exam room.

"Here's a gown," she says, handing me what is essentially a large piece of blue paper. "Opening goes in the back. Take off everything and then cover yourself from the waist down with this drape." I take a white paper drape from her outstretched hand and then she adds, "I'll be back in a few minutes to check your vitals before the doctor comes in."

She shuts the door behind her with a soft click and I blow out a breath before I strip out of my clothes, setting them on the lone chair in here. After covering myself in the meager paper gown, I hop up onto the exam table, the white paper crinkling beneath my bare bum. I place the drape over my lap, and before I can even shift my position or glance around some more, the door opens with a knock, like the medical assistant was waiting for that telltale sound of crinkling paper to enter.

"Okay," she says, grabbing my arm and slapping a blood pressure cuff on it. "Let's check those vitals. I have to warn you, though"—she meets my eyes for a flicker of a second before returning to the meter on the vitals cart—"Cameron Powers, your regular provider, isn't here today. She's being covered by another doctor."

"Oh," I say, a little disappointed. I've been coming to Cameron since I moved to Boston. I even followed her when she moved to the Brookline location. My phone buzzes in my purse and I can't help but wonder if that's Jonah again or someone else. I hate that I'm thinking about him.

"You're welcome to—"

The door opens again with a knock, interrupting the medical assistant. "Sorry," a rich male voice says from behind the assistant. "I saw the flag was up outside the door. I thought that meant you were ready for me."

Oh. My. God. The world just fucking stopped spinning. I blink. Then blink again, positive that I'm hallucinating. *It can't be.*

Jonah. My one-night stand who was just flirt-texting me is standing in front of me.

My eyes bulge out of my head and my jaw drops and my heart takes off into a sprint, trying to run for the door to get me the hell out of here, but my body can't seem to catch up. I'm rendered completely immobile.

He stares me down for a long minute, a world of thoughts and emotions flittering across his handsome face. Surprise. Confusion. Anger. Lust. Frustration. And everything in between. It's like watching an action film where the scene continuously changes.

Visions of the other night crash into the forefront of my mind.

His kisses. His touch. The way his eyes sparkled with dirty mischief as he peered up at me through my spread legs. The way he held my gaze as he slid inside of me. The feel of his body as we moved together as one.

Dear lord, the way he held me after it was all over.

My breath stops.

Time stops.

The air in this tiny room shifts, becoming thicker, more congested. Jonah is wearing a white lab coat over light blue scrubs. His green eyes pierce into mine, looking me over in my barely-there paper attire.

I want to die. My face is a ball of flames. He glances down at the encounter form in his hand, reads my name on it, stares at the phone in his other hand and then returns to me.

"Sorry," the medical assistant says, completely oblivious to the little stare down I have going on with the doctor. *The doctor.* As in *my* doctor. The person about to give me a breast and pelvic exam.

A small incredulous giggle escapes before I quickly stifle it. I mean, what the actual fuck? What are the goddamn odds that my regular doctor isn't here and in her place is my one-night stand? You can't make this shit up. But that doesn't make it any better. If anything, it feels worse.

"I'm almost finished, Doctor Hughes. I thought you'd take longer with that other patient. She was a talker, that one." My eyes widen in astonishment. What a bizarre comment to make in front of another patient. "This one's just about ready for you, though."

"I, uh . . .," I trail off, so uneasy that my fingers are knotting in my lap. I don't know what to say.

My face must betray my level of embarrassment because the medical assistant smiles at me as she releases my arm, ripping off the cuff at a deafening decibel.

"Oh, it's okay, honey, Doctor Hughes here has the gentlest hands around." She laughs, actually freaking laughs. "Believe me, we have patients who wait months just to see him."

Of that, I have no doubt.

The good Doctor Jonah Hughes mercifully looks as mortified as I am, but his gaze locks on mine. "Do you want to reschedule?" His tone is dripping with genuine concern and I think I love that. I think I love that he's just as thrown off by this situation as I am. If he were all cocky swagger, or God forbid, excited, I might slap him. "I understand if you feel more comfortable with your regular provider."

"I can't," I puff out, rubbing my damp hands across the thin paper covering my thighs. "I start a new job next week and I won't be able to take time off." And I'm here, sitting on this table, already undressed. The idea of getting dressed again and running out of here with my tail between my legs is possibly more unappealing than the exam he's about to give me. Possibly.

"Would you like Beverly to stay?" he continues, gesturing to the medical assistant. I look over to her. She smiles. I look back at Jonah. He doesn't. I shake my head, because even though I don't actually want to be alone with him like this, I really don't want an audience.

"I don't mind, honey," she says, taking my silent turbulence at the predicament I find myself in for discomfort with my provider. "You've seen one vagina, you've seen them all."

My eyes widen once again as I try to muffle my laugh. Jonah's lips twitch as he, too, fights an amused grin. I shake my head at her and clear my throat. "No, thank you. I'm fine with Doctor Hughes. These exams always make me a bit nervous."

"Don't blame ya one bit. Who knows what he'll find. Am I right?" I can only stare at her. Yet, her inappropriate comments are somehow slicing some of the edge off this. "Holler if you need me." And then she walks out, leaving me alone with Jonah. Or should I refer to him as Doctor Hughes?

His eyes flit around the small room for half a second before he steps forward to the side of the table where I'm seated. I'm hit with the scent of his woodsy aftershave. With the warmth of his body. With the delicious memories of the night we spent together. Before I woke up alone.

Right. Need to remember that. Nothing sexual going on here. Nope. Not at all.

"This is not how I pictured seeing you again."

"What? Naked and covered in medical grade paper?"

He chuckles awkwardly, moving in closer to me and twisting around so that he's half sitting on the table next to me. His eyes search mine. "Do you want to reschedule? I don't have to examine you. I realize how bizarre this situation is and honestly, it's not the most appropriate."

I sigh. It's a loud sigh. One that speaks of the mania that is my life. "No. I really don't. I'm already naked and here, so we might as well get this over with."

He shakes his head at me, the corner of his mouth bouncing up. "I hate it when a woman says that to me."

"That happen to you often, Doctor?" I quirk an eyebrow and laugh, relaxing a little into him, even if this moment hits the top ten for most ridiculous.

"Only with the really beautiful ones. Seriously, Halle, if you really can't reschedule, then I'll examine you. It's my job and I'll be one hundred percent professional. But if you're at all uncomfortable, then I'll go out there and squeeze you in with the first available provider who is not me and then we'll leave here, and I'll buy you dinner."

"Okay, but it has to be this week. And it has to be a really nice dinner."

He smirks at me, pushing off the edge of the exam table. "Done and done. Get dressed and meet me out front."

Jonah leaves the room and I blow out the breath I feel I've been holding since he stepped foot in here. It is a universally acknowledged truth that if something can go wrong, it does. Murphy's Law, I believe it's called. I think I'm going to rename it. Whitcomb's Law —that's my last name. Because I can't even do a one-night stand the right way. It's called hit-it-and-quit-it for a reason.

Evidently, I missed the part where you're supposed to quit it, aka, never see them again.

Well, that happened. I snicker to myself. The room is bigger without him in it. He seems to suck up all the available oxygen and space wherever he is. I noticed it when he stepped into my apartment.

I liked it then, and admittedly, I like it now.

Which is why I force myself to remember that liking anything about Jonah Hughes is not an option. Not now. Not ever.

Chapter Eight

Jonah

I LEAVE Halle's examination room, shutting the door softly behind me when what I really want to do is slam it. Actually, what I really want to do is slam my bloody head against the wall. Repeatedly.

I'm such a goddamn bastard.

Instead, I go for storming down into my borrowed office, ripping off my lab coat and chucking it against the wall.

"Shit!" I half-yell, mindful of ears outside the office door. One fist comes down on the hard surface of the desk while my other hand runs roughly through my hair.

I knew I'd have to see her again. I just never imagined it would be like this, naked and on my exam table. Ready for a breast and pelvic exam. I feel like a fucking creep. Like a pervert.

Like I'm taking advantage of my position and of her.

I miss my wife. I haven't been with a woman in two years, and now it's like I can't escape. I knew this moment would come. I never figured I'd be celibate forever. But . . .

I'm sick from it.

From everything.

From sleeping with Halle on the anniversary of Madeline's funeral. From leaving my cufflinks at Halle's. From running out on her after our night together.

I really am the worst sort of wanker. The worst type of man. I didn't think my self-loathing could hit a new low, but evidently, I was wrong.

Scrubbing my hands down my face, I growl out just as there is a knock on the door. "Come in," I clip out, trying to get control of myself—something I haven't been able to do whenever I'm around Halle.

"Sorry to disturb," Beverly says, her head the only thing visible as the rest of her is tucked behind the door. "Halle Whitcomb is waiting for you at checkout."

"Can you have someone schedule her in this week with another women's health provider?"

"Oh." Her eyebrows hit her hairline, but she regains her composure quickly when she realizes I'm not going to give her the answers she's after. "Of course."

"And please let her know I'll be right there."

For once, Beverly keeps her mouth shut. She closes the door behind her, probably sensing the shift in my mood. I grab a small sheet of paper and scribble instructions on it, then fold it up and tuck it into my palm.

Walking out the door and down the long corridor, I head past patient rooms and offices toward the front. Halle has her back to me, her body wrapped in a pink sundress with delicate spaghetti straps hugging her narrow shoulders. Her long copper hair is down, flowing in unruly waves to her mid-back.

She's lovely. Every perfect inch of her.

I can't remember the last time I was this drawn to a woman. Madeline was different. I had known her for what felt like ages before we became more than friends. It's difficult to feel that sort of pull with someone you already know so well.

"Miss Whitcomb?"

She twirls around, her expression guarded as if she's not sure what I'm about to do. I peek down at her dress and smile. It has a heart-shaped neckline. It's sweet. Demure. Pretty.

"I didn't think redheads wore pink," I comment before I can stop my musing.

She glances down at her dress before looking back up at me with a small smirk playing on her equally pink lips. "It's too pretty a color not to wear."

"I completely agree," I murmur, not wanting others to overhear even though we're in a private patient area. "Were they able to reschedule you?"

"Yes. I'm all set. Thank you."

We stare at each other for a quiet moment. And I feel it. That same warmth when I first gazed into her eyes that night at the bar. She's unwittingly awakened something inside me. Something I'm not sure I want resurrected.

"Well then, Doctor Hughes. It was a pleasure to meet you."

I reach out my hand for her to shake, and when her small, warm hand is engulfed by my much larger one, I slip her the piece of paper. "Same to you, Miss Whitcomb. Best of luck at your new job next week."

Her eyes widen when she feels the paper transfer to her hand, but she doesn't say anything. I leave her standing there, forcing myself not to peek back to see if she's read the note, even though I'm dying to catch her reaction. She was my last patient, and except for some administrative business, I'm done for the day.

The office door shuts behind me and I drop into the oversized chair, spinning around and staring out the window that directly faces another building.

I don't know what I'm doing with her.

I tell myself I'm just meeting her to get my cufflinks back, but I know better, because just the thought of seeing her again in less than an hour shoots a thrill through me. I haven't been able to stop thinking about Halle and how responsive she was to my touch. How her touch made me feel like I was alive, burning with a long-forgotten fire. The way she looked beneath me, above me. The way she smelled and tasted.

Fuck, I couldn't get enough of her.

I hated leaving her the way I did. And now? Now I have no clue what I'm after with her.

I feel sick all over again, but for entirely different reasons. I'm a mess of a man. Hung up on a woman who is gone forever. I'm riddled with guilt because it's all my fault. And I hate myself because I wasn't there when it really counted. I have nothing to offer a woman like Halle.

Nothing of worth anyway.

I dictate Halle's chart as well as two others, and in under half an hour, I'm out the door. The clinic closes at nine every night, but after five-thirty it's solely urgent care. Thankfully, I'm not filling in for that tonight. Especially when I wasn't even supposed to be here today. I took this week off, thinking I'd need it.

Madeline died two years ago, and this time of year is hard on me. I didn't want to work this week. The thought of getting into my routine, knowing I could no longer ring her, or go home and see her, is still too much to bear. Knowing she's no longer part of my world, no longer where I need her to be, is the worst sort of pain.

Knowing I'm at fault? I have no words for that.

But when the clinic called me this morning in a panic, I couldn't say no. Women's health has never been my favorite part of my career, but I was getting through the day without a hitch. Halle texted me about the cufflinks and it was like air finally managed to find its way into my lungs.

I could take a breath that didn't feel like it was lined in lead and soaked in bleach. Then I walked into that exam room and caught sight of that wild hair and those pretty blue eyes. My heart stopped. But not in the way you'd think. Yes, I was surprised to see her there, but that's not where the sensation came from.

Right now, I'm jogging up the steps at the T-station, sweating and regretting not taking an Uber to the restaurant. Rush hour in Boston is a nightmare. I take a minute to cool myself down as I run a hand through my now-damp hair. I don't know if she's here yet or not. I don't know what this dinner will lead to—if it will lead to anything at all. More importantly, I'm tragically torn.

I want to see Halle again. I don't want to see Halle again.

I want to spend the night with her. I don't want to spend the night with her.

It's the best and worst sort of push and pull.

As I yank open the tall glass door of the restaurant I picked, I'm instantly enveloped in a welcome blast of cold air-conditioning. I glance to the right where the main bar is located, but I don't find Halle's bright hair or pink dress amongst the after-work fray. Soft, hypnotic jazz hums through the background, kissed with the din of patrons laughing and talking and blowing off a day of heat and stress.

The last time I came to this restaurant was two months before Madeline died. I watched her smoke a joint to alleviate the pain and ease her stomach, so she could actually eat something, and then we came here. I held her hand all night, because in my gut, I knew it might be the last time we'd be able to go out to eat together. So why am I torturing myself now by coming back here to meet Halle?

To keep myself focused.

To remind myself where my head and my heart lie rather than my dick.

But as I catch sight of Halle sitting in the far corner booth, her angelic, porcelain face upturned as she smiles and talks with the waitress, I realize it's going to take a hell of a lot more than a restaurant to keep me focused.

I want this woman. Again. That unwanted thought has me frozen in place, staring at her, knowing just how dangerous this game could get.

The brain and the heart rarely agree on anything. Especially when you desperately want them to. When you truly need them to absolve you, to make you whole instead of divided. Madeline has held my heart in one capacity or another for over a decade. Which is why, when I woke on Sunday morning, guilt consumed me and nearly crushed me alive when Madeline's baby sister, Erica, rang me.

I'd left the after-cemetery party without saying goodbye or checking that Erica was all right. She wasn't. Erica called me, plastered beyond reason, sobbing uncontrollably into the phone. I left Halle's to get her. What else could I do? But I didn't wake Halle up. I left her a rubbish note and my number. A number I very nearly didn't write down. A number I talked myself in and out of giving a dozen times over.

And just as I think that, my phone vibrates in my pocket and my heart inflates in my chest for half a beat before it shrivels back up into nothing. It's not Madeline—naturally—but it is Erica.

Thank you again for saving my sorry ass the other morning. Dinner this week? With Mom? She's really struggling.

Thick grief clogs my throat and I swallow so hard I can barely take a breath. I glance over at Halle again and seriously consider turning around and walking out. Why did I suggest dinner? Why didn't I just ask to meet her outside her flat to get my cufflinks back?

You know why.

I do, and I hate myself more and more for it. I text Erica back, telling her to pick the day and place and I'll be there. Then I refocus on the woman I lost myself in.

Even if it was just one night.

Stepping into the dining area, I bypass the hostess who attempts to stop me by asking if I have a reservation. I walk directly over to Halle's table, watching her before she spots me. As I pull out the chair across from her, I admire the way her baby blues flash over to me.

She doesn't smile. She's all caution.

And now I want to laugh at myself. Halle doesn't want anything with me. I'm not hurting her. She was quite clear about her desires and intentions. I'm such a daft, arrogant fool.

"I have your cufflinks with me," she says by way of a greeting, her eyes struggling to hold my steady gaze. "In case that's what you were expecting by asking me to dinner. I mean, you didn't have to go through all this just to get them back."

I stare at her, blinking rapidly as I try and process what she's actually trying to say to me. She thinks I'm feeling obligated to her?

That I only asked her to dinner so I wouldn't come off like an asshole when I asked for my cufflinks back?

Shit. I hate that her mind went there.

I reach across the table and touch the hand that's delicately resting on the base of her wine glass. Her gaze drops to my hand before returning to mine. "That's not why I asked you to dinner, Halle."

"Oh," she breathes out, a bit surprised, her cheeks turning that gorgeous shade of pink. "I wasn't expecting that. I was expecting a swap and ditch."

I grin at her honesty before I lift her hand from her glass and intertwine our fingers. I like holding her hand, which makes me want to smile and cry since it was never all that appealing, even with Madeline.

"My running out Sunday morning had nothing to do with you," I tell her. "You were—are—lovely. I had an amazing night with you." I squeeze her hand. "I don't regret any of it for a second, and I sincerely hope you don't, either."

"I don't," she says firmly, those winter-sky eyes piercing into mine, making my heart beat just a bit faster. "I assumed you were trying to avoid the awkward morning-after thing."

I shake my head as the waitress approaches us. I throw out a drink order, and Halle takes the brief pause in our conversation to guzzle down half of her glass of wine before ordering another one. The waitress leaves and I focus on Halle again. She's blankly staring down at our linked hands. She's so honest, so open about what's on her mind, yet right now, it feels as if she's holding everything back.

I should swap and ditch, as she put it. I should let go of her hand, take my cufflinks and head home. But all that's waiting for me at home is emptiness. A void so thick and heavy I can hardly hold it up.

"I wasn't trying to avoid the morning-after awkwardness. That's not why I left."

"We don't have to do this—"

"I buried my wife two years ago," I interrupt her. Her eyes widen into baby blue saucers. "But she was so much more than that.

Madeline was my"—I search for the right word, my chest tight, knowing that there isn't one to describe her—"world since I started university." I blow out a harsh breath. There is no sugarcoating it if I want her to believe me and forgive me. Even though I shouldn't care about her pardoning my sins, I do.

"A piece of your soul," she whispers the words I had uttered Saturday night.

I nod. "Yes. And that piece of my soul has a younger sister, who I callously disregarded when I left her mother's early for my own selfish reasons. She's why I left Sunday before you woke. She was a mess and she needed me, and I feel responsible for her. I'm sorry."

Halle releases my hand and stands up. This is it. She's going to walk out on me. But she doesn't. Instead, she steps around the table and wraps her arms around my neck. It catches me completely off guard. We're in the middle of a crowded restaurant, but she doesn't care, just clumsily bends over, pressing me against her.

Fuck it.

I stand and hug her back, dropping my face into her neck. Her scent overwhelms me, and I swallow down the lump that forms in my throat along with the comfort she so willingly gives me.

"I'm so sorry about your wife." Her voice is thick with emotion.

"Thank you." I press my lips to her cheek. I might just be a bit overwhelmed by her. Her skin warms beneath my lips and it only makes me want to do it again. To do more than just this. I pull back and give her a lopsided grin despite myself and my better judgment. "Am I forgiven?"

"Yes." She laughs the word. "You're forgiven. I'll even give you back your cufflinks without the ransom I was ready to place on them." She steps back and retakes her seat as I do the same.

"Did it come with one of those letters with mismatched news-paper text?" I ask, taking a sip of the scotch the waitress set down on the table.

Halle scoffs at me, dramatically rolling her eyes. She's holding her wine glass up, the large round bowl lolling to the side as she appraises me in mock indignation. "What sort of kidnapper would I be if I didn't have a ransom note with crazy mixed-media text?"

She reaches into her large purse and pulls out a plastic baggie. My cufflinks are nestled inside.

I take it from her with a nod of gratitude and tuck them into the pocket of my scrubs. When I'm sure they're safe, I find her staring at me with an indiscernible expression, her playful smile all but gone.

"Your last name is Hughes. As in Hughes Healthcare. As in the very community health center we found ourselves in today."

"Yes." I watch her for a moment, trying to read her, but she's giving nothing away. That bothers me for some reason. Typically, she's quite expressive. A heart-on-her-sleeve type of girl. This is not a conversation I enjoy having with women, but she's already put it together, so I might as well tell her.

"My father was a surgeon back in England before he died. He was very philanthropic and donated a lot of his time and fortune to helping underserved populations, primarily women and children. My mother founded the clinic in my family name when we moved here from the UK. It's grown from there."

"I didn't think you were a gynecologist," she blurts out, shifting in her chair, her wooden features finally giving way to—is that apprehension on her face?

"Pardon?" My eyebrows pinch together in confusion.

"I figured you for a lawyer or investment banker. Especially with those cufflinks and that bespoke suit."

I chuckle lightly. It's the way she's looking at me—like she's never seen me before—that incites the chuckle. "I'm a family medicine doctor. As I said, I was just filling in for Cameron today."

She nods her head in quick, jerky motions, taking a sip of her wine and staring off into the restaurant. Something just happened. I don't know what exactly, but she's like a different woman suddenly. All nervous jitters and uneasiness, but I can't determine if that uneasiness is for me or my profession.

"Can I still buy you dinner?"

She finishes off her wine in one impressive gulp, before handing it to a random passing waitress. Her full glass is waiting on her, but she doesn't touch it. She tucks her bottom lip into her teeth, sawing back and forth across the soft flesh. Bollocks. I nearly gave her a pelvic exam and now I'm asking her to dinner. She probably figures I'm the ultimate creep.

"I work for you," she blurts out.

"I'm sorry?"

"My new job," she admits, shifting in her chair some more, though her steady gaze doesn't waver. "I'm working for Hughes Health Care. In the Copley Place clinic. I'm a family nurse practitioner."

"Oh." My stomach drops to my feet. I lean back in my chair, taking my glass of scotch with me. I take a sip. Then another as I absorb her words. She works for me. *With* me. Motherfucking hell.

"Yeah," she continues on, oblivious to the disappointment coursing through my veins. "I wasn't going to say anything, but I thought you should know since I guess you're technically my boss now, even though we'll never see each other since you work in Brookline, and I work in the city."

"I work at the Copley Place clinic." My voice is barely above a whisper, but she hears it.

I can't work with this woman. I want her.

I'm inexplicably drawn to her. I can't see her on a regular basis. My name is on the goddamn building. I'm technically her boss.

Shit. Double shit. Triple motherfucking shit.

I run a hand through my hair, squeezing the back of my neck to try and release the stifling tension. It doesn't help. I take a healthy gulp of my drink. That doesn't help, either. What the bloody hell am I going to do now?

Her eyebrows knit together, and she tilts her head like I'm speaking to her in German. "But I just saw you——"

"I was filling in. I occasionally do that when it's needed."

Her eyes widen, and her mouth pops open ever so slightly at this. It would be an adorable reaction if I didn't despise everything about this conversation. "So you're saying——"

"We're going to be working together, yes."

I stare at her. Watching. Waiting. For what? I don't know.

Maybe for her to tell me that this, whatever this is, cannot happen. I don't think I can do it. Even though it can't happen. Even though my mind is a mess and I'm in no shape to offer anything of value to a woman right now.

Even though . . .

"I have a hard and fast rule about not dating or sleeping with people from work. I never break it." I cringe inwardly as I say this. Honestly, I was never tempted to break that rule before. I was married to the love of my life. After Madeline died, I was the wrecked widower.

I've had women make advances, so I created that rule and hid safely behind it. But now?

Halle nods her head like she gets it, like she agrees. "It's like we said Saturday night, Jonah. I'm just getting out of a terrible relationship and you buried a piece of your soul. And now you're my boss. And you have this rule."

"I have this rule." A rule I suddenly find myself hating.

"Then I don't think we should have dinner."

My stomach drops. "No. Probably not. Next week we're strangers once more. Work colleagues."

"Seems like the only way. Nothing else could possibly work."

I nod, giving her a tight smile, though I don't feel any of it. She's right. Nothing else between us could ever work. And now I'm stuck working with her.

Chapter Nine

Halle

"WHAT DO you know about Jonah Hughes?" Oliver pauses mid-chew to look up at me before he resumes his chewing, then swallows down the bite of his sandwich he was just pocketing in his cheek. He washes it all down with a sip of his coconut water. Freaking health nut.

"What about him?"

I hate that question. I wish he had just said something specific or even vague, because for the last twenty minutes of my lunch with Oliver, while he was casually chatting with me, I've done my very best not to ask anything about Jonah when really, he's all I've wanted to ask about.

"I met him the other day at the clinic in Brookline. Seemed like a good guy, but you've worked with him, and I'm going to be working with him, so . . ." I trail off, feeling ridiculous for even asking.

Especially when Oliver frowns ever so slightly. I take a bite of my Cuban, wiping the excess grease from my mouth with my napkin. Freaking Oliver is eating roasted turkey breast on multigrain with sprouts, avocado, lettuce, and tomato. I'm eating fries with my sandwich and he's eating a salad. It's sort of aggravating.

But maybe that's why he looks the way he does.

Oliver is a tasty piece of biscuit smothered in gravy. If he weren't Rina's brother, an unapologetic player, and if I weren't working with him and generally regard him as a friend, I might think about going out with him.

Oliver sits up a bit straighter, eyeing me in a way that makes me want to blush. Damn perceptive bastard. I forgot how astute he can be. How quick he can read someone. I school my features as best I can and shovel some fries in my mouth. I have no poker face. It's why I don't play—or lie, for that matter.

"He's a good guy," Oliver offers slowly, his tone measured. "A great doctor. He's the medical director and the CEO, which you would think wouldn't work, but it does. He listens to the providers and even goes out when the staff gets together. He's also great to the residents, bringing us in on interesting cases and always there to help us when we need it."

I nod, pretending to be more interested in my Diet Coke than I am in Jonah Hughes. But the truth is, I'm insanely interested in Jonah Hughes.

Even after the drink the other night where we declared a sexual stalemate. Even knowing it will never ever happen again.

"Awesome," I say with what I hope is an indifferent shrug. "So, I shouldn't be afraid that we're working with the big boss man?" Yeah, I'm making this about work when my fascination has nothing to do with his skills as a doctor or medical director.

Oliver laughs, and the dark note he was just rocking seems to be dissipating. I know Oliver kinda sorta likes me. Or at least, Rina has been filling my head with that. She's all over that one like a fly on a horse's ass. I think she has visions of one of her brothers—she has five—marrying her best friend.

I don't share that same vision.

"No. You'd never know who he is or the fact that he's a billion-aire if you didn't know his last name."

"I don't know how you people handle all those zeros. The taxes alone," I jest.

Oliver rolls his eyes at me. He's a trust fund baby himself. So is Rina. They're Fritz's. Boston royalty. I'm not poor, but I'm hardly hanging out in the three-comma club the way they are.

"You know, this is not how I wanted to celebrate your new job," he says.

I raise my eyebrows and he gives me a dopey grin, his green eyes soft and slightly vulnerable.

"I wanted to take you out for dinner. Take you out somewhere nice. Use some of my zeros on you."

I smile at that. *Why don't I want you, Oliver? You're so goddamn perfect.* Especially for a man who has probably pulled that same line on countless women.

Maybe I should try. Because he is perfect.

When Jonah and I shared that drink so he could get his cufflinks back—after we declared a sex-truce—I told him about Matt and he told me about Madeline, and we both confirmed just how fucked we are.

Because the tension between us? The pull?

Holy Christ on a piece of toast was it there. And strong. Like a magnet, times a thousand. He explained more about why he doesn't date people he works with. I told him that my felon of an ex isn't even behind bars yet.

Needless to say, after that drink that lingered far longer than it should have—especially since I refused to let him buy me dinner—I got into an Uber alone, went home and touched myself with visions of him in my head, or more accurately, him between my legs.

"I know," I say to Perfect Oliver. "But you've already done so much for me that I wanted to buy you lunch instead of letting you buy me a crazy dinner. Plus, my heart can't afford your price tag." Does that excuse sound lame? Because it is.

Oliver smiles impishly as he takes another bite of his healthy sandwich, staring off out the window onto Boylston Street. I love this part of town and wish I had rented a place closer to here. I like the South End, but you don't get the same vibe that you do down here.

"What if I asked you to dinner not as any sort of celebration? Just us. Just dinner." His eyes find mine and damn him for being this perfect. "Or, you know, whatever."

"Or *whatever*?" I raise an eyebrow and he gives me a wicked grin. "You know that's not a good idea with us working together, right? And with our love of the same female who will cut your balls off at the stem if you try and fuck your way through me like you do the rest of the city's nurses."

That wicked grin turns to a lopsided smile, crooking up the side of his beautiful face. "Probably."

I shake my head, laughing lightly at that.

He throws his hands up. "You were with Matt forever. This is the first chance I've had to make my play. Is that so wrong?"

I stare at him for a moment. I'm tempted. I am. I'd have to be dead not to be. But he's offering me exactly what I tried to do with Jonah, and after one goddamn night, I'm still thinking about the gorgeous swine. Can't stop thinking about him, if we're being honest here.

"Actually, I think that idea comes with alarm bells. Big, fat, loud ones that scream 'Don't be a fool! You'll never get out alive!'"

He laughs, wiping his mouth with his napkin before tossing it lightly onto his mostly empty plate. Oliver looks away, and in this moment, I wish God was fair. I wish She made it so that you liked the people who liked you. So you could be with the people you were crazily attracted to. Made it so that sex didn't actually have the strings, feelings, and intimacy we pretend it doesn't.

I wish there wasn't all this drama when it came to trying to be with someone. To connecting with them.

It's just unfair, because Oliver is so great. And what he's offering sounds ideal. Except I know better, because screwing Oliver is a ticking time bomb. And . . . I want another man.

There. I said it.

Hi, my name is Halle and I want Jonah Hughes. Hi, Halle, you're officially fucking nuts.

So yeah, this sucks.

"You're probably right," he finally replies. "But I'm suddenly wishing I hadn't gotten you that job with me and that you didn't know my sister, and that you had never met Matt."

Ah. So perfect. Do they teach men like him lines like that in college? Is there a special course they take? How to get into a woman's pants with just the right line 101.

Damn you, God. And I don't even curse your name often. At least not directly like this, because typically, we're cool. But really, what did I ever do to you to be so screwed in the love and life department?

Oliver and I finish our lunch shortly after.

It's not awkward. It never is with us.

We flowed onto safer topics. But after he hugs me in the middle of the sidewalk and treats me to a lingering look and goes back to work, I'm on my own again. I head up toward the Public Gardens, not really wanting to waste this beautiful summer day by going home where my thoughts are the only thing to greet me.

My feet guide me without much conscious thought, and before I know it, my fingers are popping along the wrought iron fence of the entrance of the Boston Public Gardens. But I quickly stop, clutching onto a rung and staring straight ahead.

Jonah.

He's panting, sweaty, and so goddamn *hot* my chest hurts. He's breathing hard—the way he did after he came inside me—and wiping sweat from his brow with the back of his forearm.

He stretches against the fence and I can't look away. I watch as his leg muscles lengthen. I watch sweat effortlessly glide down his brow, arms, and neck because it's too hot out to run, but he did it anyway. I watch the way his biceps and abs flex when he reaches up with the hem of his shirt to wipe away more delicious sweat.

Delicious sweat?

Yeah, I think I'd lick it off him, so I guess delicious works. He glances up and catches me in the act of unabashedly staring, but I don't bother looking away or even trying to hide my blatant admiration.

"You're a runner." And for all my education and brains, that's what I come up with. I think he even told me he was a runner that first night, so that statement really is something else.

"I like running in the heat." His response isn't much better. Probably because he likes my dress. A lot. If his heated gaze and sudden chub in his shorts are any indication.

I shake my head, trying to clear all that away. *Good luck,* my subconscious teases. Bitch. "You're insane."

He smirks, stepping toward me as his green eyes eat me up for lunch. And it's nothing like the healthy lunch Oliver ate. This is a full-on I'm-eating-every-bad-thing-under-the-sun lunch. "I've been called worse."

"Like what?" I challenge, flirting in a way I know I have no business doing.

"Boss. Doctor. Friend."

I might have called him all three of those the other night over that drink after the fateful almost pelvic exam. "At least they're technically accurate."

His smirk grows into a playful grin, swallowing up our distance by half with two large steps. "Are you stalking me, Carolina?"

"Seems that way, but no. Sorry to disappoint. I just so happened to turn a corner and there you were. What are the odds?"

His grin turns crooked, playful. "Pretty poor in a city this size, but I'll gladly take them." His eyes do a big once-over on me. "You're quite beautiful in that yellow dress."

I peek down, tempted to say, *this old thing?* Instead, I go for the smile that makes my eyes sparkle.

"I like dresses when I'm not at work."

"I like you in dresses, too. You also love color."

I nod. Swallow hard. Clear my throat. "I do. I love color a lot." And then I laugh because the way he said "love" sounded just so British. Even though he doesn't sound all that British at the moment. His accent is like a game of hide-and-seek I can't help but love playing.

My laugh quickly dies on my tongue as he takes another step toward me. Now he's right here, breathing down on me with his heavy breathing and manly scent and delicious sweat and charming smiles.

"What else do you like, Halle?"

You. I like you.

"The Public Gardens."

He chuckles lightly, smiling wide and beautifully, his green eyes alight with this game we're playing. We do this well. "Have you ever walked through the whole thing?"

I shake my head, because as much as I hate to admit it, I haven't. Who has time to walk through parks anymore?

He laughs harder. "Then how do you know you like it?"

"I like parks. I like grass and green space and trees and summer."

He glances over at the fence and the hint of trees and green space beyond. "Would you like to see it? Walk through it?"

"Now?"

He shrugs, inching even closer. "Now's as good of a time as any. I know it all by heart."

I roll my eyes. "Of course, you do. But I have to warn you, it takes a lot more than a walk through the park to get into my panties." Why did I just say that? It's like our entire we-cannot-happen-and-here's-why conversation not even two nights ago never happened.

Those grass-green eyes instantly darken. "Then what does it take?"

For you? All you have to do is ask.

I open my mouth to say the most perfect thing in the history of perfect things when I'm clipped by a guy riding a bike on the side-walk. Have I mentioned how illegal that is? At least, I think it is. In any event, the guy hops the curb, hits me like he's aiming for me, stretches out to try and snatch my purse from me only to miss, and then hops off the curb and rides off in a blaze of fury as Jonah yells something I can't make out.

I fall forward, so ungracefully and unladylike. Jonah reaches out, but it's about two seconds too late, because he completely misses me. Only in romance novels and movies does the hero actually catch the heroine. But my life is neither a romance novel nor a movie, unless we're getting into Shakespearean tragedies.

I hit the ground, my knees smashing into the nasty Boston sidewalk.

Why? Why can't I just have one time in front of this god-like man where I don't make a total fool of myself?

"Bugger! Halle."

I'm on all fours, the hem of my dress is who the hell knows where, but I can tell my knees are roughed up, mostly because they sting like a bitch in heat. A strong, firm hand wraps around my upper arm, slowly helping me back into a standing position.

"Are you all right?"

I'm still staring down at the ground.

"Fuck," he hisses. "I should have gone after him. I should have tossed him off his bike and beaten the piss out of him."

I glance up at Jonah's ire, tilting my head, still a bit dazed.

"You're bleeding, Halle. Come on." He tugs on the arm he's still holding. "You're coming up to my place, so I can bandage your knees."

I glance down, taking in the trail of red as it cascades down my shins. It seems I am a bleeding mess at the mercy of the handsome hero.

Oh no. This never ends well for heroines like me.

Chapter Ten

Halle

THE DOORMAN OPENS the door to the beautiful building, allowing us to pass freely. The outside is stone and just tall enough that I know the top few floors have a fantastic view, without being skyscraper-scary tall. The inside of the lobby is everything you'd think it would be. Modern, cool, art deco chic, open, beautiful.

I don't allow myself to linger all that long, mostly because Jonah is guiding me over to the elevator like I'm a dog on a leash.

Panic swirls in my stomach. I can't go up to his apartment. I can't be alone in a confined space with this man.

"I can bandage myself, Jonah." I try to pull away, but to no avail. "I'm a nurse practitioner. Believe it or not, studies indicate that patients are more satisfied with our level of care than they are with doctors."

Jonah's lips twitch. "I believe that. It's why I value all of my mid-level providers as highly as I do."

"Then I can go. I'll catch an Uber or a cab or whatever is closest. I have a crazy-awesome first aid kit. Seriously. I'm all set."

Now he's smiling. "Crazy-awesome first aid kit?"

I shrug, because I realize it's a bit dramatic in reference to a first aid kit, but I'm grasping at straws here.

"I have a pretty crazy-awesome one myself and mine is much closer. I can't have my new family nurse practitioner risking infection by having her get into the back of a dirty Uber or cab."

I have nothing for that. I think it's his smile's fault.

"I'll behave. Professional, remember? I can be one if you can be one."

Right. Except there is nothing professional about the way he's dressed or being up in his apartment or having his hands on my body. Again! Or the fact that all I can think about is our playful flirting about getting into my panties not even five minutes ago.

We step into the dreadfully silent elevator and he punches in a code and swipes a badge, then we're zooming up to the tip-top floor. *Bastard.*

Jonah is standing really close to me. And he still smells good. And I'm so acutely hyperaware of his size and proximity that I just want to touch and kiss and lick him. It's like I've been struck down with some disease, because I don't remember ever being this physically wound-up or sexually enthralled with a man. Ever.

I like sex.

I just never knew how much I liked it until I joined the multiple orgasm club. This membership is both a blessing and curse, because now I don't see how I could ever settle for less. Honestly, for a while, I believed they were an urban legend. Something crafted by bitchy women to make others feel bad about themselves and their mediocre sex lives.

I was wrong.

The elevator doors part and we step into a large open-concept great room that feeds into the dining room and kitchen. And I do mean large. This one space alone encompasses my entire apartment and then some extra. There are two wings branching off on opposite sides, so I know this place must be epically huge.

But the view is the most staggering part.

It outshines the gorgeous, top-of-the-line kitchen and wealthy

Boston bachelor furnishings. I can see the entire Public Garden and Boston Common from up here as well as much of the city beyond.

I don't realize I'm at the windows until I touch the pane of glass with an awed, "Wow."

"It's why I bought the place."

I don't turn around as I say, "I don't blame you."

"Come here," he commands, and I turn, pressing my back into his window so I don't fall to the floor out of nerves. But Jonah is not watching me. He's not even glancing in my direction. He's back to being professional Doctor Hughes as he retrieves his first aid kit out of a cabinet and opens it up. He's removing gauze and antiseptic wipes and bandages and gloves. I'm shocked he hasn't pulled out a suturing kit. Because yeah, his first aid kit is crazy-awesome.

I stare at him for a beat before I follow his orders, moving across the great room that I refuse to focus too closely on, all the way back into the kitchen. He points to a stool and I wordlessly sit, ignoring the soft leather cushion my ass sinks down into.

Jonah walks around the marble island, slides his hands along my calves and lifts them up, propping my feet on the stool next to me so my legs are parallel to the dark wood floors.

Before he can even get the gloves on, his hands are on my skin. Like he can't even help himself. It sends a jolt of lust straight to my core.

"Does it hurt at all?" he asks, gliding the tips of his fingers near my wounds without touching them.

I shake my head. It does hurt, but I want to be brave. I think if I admit my knees hurt, he'll be more tender with me than he's already being and that might be my total undoing.

"They're not bad, just bleeding a lot. No stitches required."

I nod. I already knew that. He gives me that sexy crooked grin, complete with dimples.

Jonah takes both my feet in his large, warm hands and lifts them until he's seated in the chair they previously occupied. Then he drops my feet down into his lap. He doesn't look at me. He's laser focused on my knees, but I wonder if, from this angle, with my dress high up on my thighs, he can see my panties.

"Sorry," he mutters, his voice thick. "It's the only way I'll be able to get a good angle to clean them."

I think he's lying. I think standing beside me, hovering directly over my knees put him at a better vantage point than sitting and having to bend over the lower half of my long legs to reach. *You like touching me, Doctor Hughes.*

"It's fine." I sound like a needy hussy. When did I become this girl?

My heart pounds. Sweat slicks down my cleavage. My skin tingles. I want him to touch me. I want him to touch me other places than my knees. That is until he swipes those murderous anti-bacterial wipes on my open wounds. I hiss through my teeth and his darkened green eyes fly up to mine, a pained, apologetic look marring his features.

"Sorry. I know that must sting." Puckering his lips, he blows cool air on my wounds, and I briefly close my eyes. "That better?"

"Mmmm."

"Open your eyes, Halle." I do, but I really wish he hadn't asked that, because I remember those exact words leaving his lips that night. "Are you really okay?"

"Yes."

"I hate that you fell. I hate the fuckwit biker who jumped the curb and hit you. I'd still very much like to kick his ass." His eyes lock with mine. "But I'm glad I'm here to help you and I'm glad you were walking around in my neighborhood. It hasn't even been a week and it seems you're everywhere."

The air crackles, thickening with a dense fog. Our silence, our quiet tones, are amplified. Everything is heightened, and I know he feels it, too.

I know he does.

It's in his every move, touch, and breath. It's in the way his thumb brushes up and down the side of my knee as he examines my wounds. It's in the way he wraps gauze around them and secures it with freaking tape. It's everywhere, both swirling around this room and inside each of us.

I want this man. And I know he wants me.

But I know I can't have sex with him again. Especially since I'm going to have to endure him every day at work and pretend like he's nothing more than my boss. But more importantly, the idea of anything more than sex, the idea of actually dating him, makes me nauseous. It's something I know I'm not ready for and it's something I know he's not ready for.

So, I guess I'll have to live with this. I'll have to do my best to ignore it.

Jonah clears his throat and meets my eyes, his hand leaving my bandaged knees and returning to my feet. He removes my sandals one by one and begins to massage the soles of my feet.

Wow, that's so good.

"You have a beautiful place. How long have you lived here?"

Why aren't I leaving? Why did I let him remove my shoes when shoed feet are my best hope of escape? Why am I bothering with small talk when my knees are good to go?

"Five years. It belonged to a friend of a friend's grandmother. I got it at a bargain and fixed it up."

"I don't think the word bargain belongs anywhere near Boston real estate. The two are polar opposites."

Jonah chuckles, pressing a little deeper into my feet. I moan at the pressure before I can stop myself. "Probably true," he concurs, rubbing my feet harder and watching my face as he does. "London is worse. I briefly looked into returning, but it wasn't practical, and I was needed here."

"Because of Madeline?" I have no idea why I just asked that, but I did and it's too late to take it back. Though, I try. I shake my head quickly and say, "I'm sorry. That's none of my business." Even though I secretly want to know about her.

"No," he blurts out. "This was after she had already passed. I thought it might help. You know, fresh start and all."

I nod because I know what it's like to need a fresh start.

The bleeding expression on his face cuts me to the quick. I wonder what it felt like to be her. And I don't mean the illness, because that's horrible and no one should know what that feels like. I mean being so loved by someone.

Someone like Jonah.

A deep, powerful ache slices me, cutting a path of jealousy and longing straight through me. I've never experienced that sort of devotion, and I was engaged to be married for over a year.

But I do know with absolute certainty that I want it. One day. With the right man.

It makes me question whether I've discounted Oliver too quickly, knowing that I'll never, ever be able to have Jonah like that. He's already given his heart and soul away and I'm not so sure a man can fully do that twice. Can they?

"I should go."

Jonah nods in agreement, but he doesn't release my feet and he doesn't move to show me out. Instead, he continues to rub me like he doesn't want to let me go.

Let me go, Jonah. Don't do this to me.

"What if I don't want you to go?"

That look he's giving me is making my resolve falter. I want more time with this man, I realize. More of our banter and easy conversation. More heated looks and flawless touches. I want more of Jonah Hughes.

But I can't have more of him.

"That's exactly why I need to."

He blows out a breath, his head dropping back, his chin pointing to the ceiling. He knows I'm right. He knows we're a lost cause surrounded in too much chemistry and sexual tension.

"I'm trying so hard to remember my rule. To remember why you and I aren't a good idea. And I'm failing. I'm failing big time." His chin drops and when his eyes meet mine, my insides quiver at the intensity I see in his. "What will it take to get you to stay even when you need to go?"

My heart pounds against my ribs and my breath catches in my chest. How easy would it be to lean in and kiss him? To open my legs just a little wider so he could see everything I'm offering him?

"A little white lie. One where you're not my new boss and I'm not your new employee. One where I'm not coming out of a wreck and you're not buried beneath the earth."

He jolts back like I slapped him. He stares me down with slightly narrowed eyes, and I hate my words. Hate them. But that doesn't make them any less true.

He knows it. I know it.

It's our reality. One he was adamant about just the other evening in the restaurant. *"I have a hard and fast rule about not dating or sleeping with people from work. I never break it."*

So, whatever this is here in his apartment, it's not real. It's a tease. And if I didn't like being teased as a child, I hate it even more as an adult. Especially when so much is at stake.

I have to protect my heart from this man, because he has the power to claim it. To destroy it for good. I hardly know Jonah. Barely even at all. But I can tell all that already and it scares me. Downright terrifies me. The urge to lose myself in him is real. Calling, even.

But then what?

What happens when I wake up naked next to him and he remembers that he doesn't sleep with employees and the woman he's really in love with is dead? What then? Then Halle gets shoved to the side. Halle gets forgotten and overlooked and hurt.

I get hurt.

That's how this story would go for us, and I'm so very tired of getting hurt.

Jonah raises my feet off his lap and stands up, taking a step back away from me. I stand up, too, and slip my feet back into my sandals. I need out of here ten minutes ago. I should have never come up in the first place.

"You want to know the ultimate white lie, Carolina?"

I stare at him expectantly, but my brain is screaming at me to walk away.

"That I didn't find an incredible woman in a random bar in the middle of Boston when my heart was crushed into gravel and hers was formed into solid steel. That we're not so absolutely right and yet so very wrong for each other. That I don't want to say fuck it all to my carefully crafted rules."

He takes another step back and I'm hit with a crushing pang, desperate to reach out and grab ahold of him. To haul him close and never let go. Instead, that pang morphs into an insurmountable level of regret. Of loathing.

Fuck you, life. I walk around him, going for the elevator, my back to him as I press the down button.

"I'm just trying to save us from more pain, Jonah."

"I know. And I'm grateful for that. If you can lie to yourself, Carolina, I can as well. I'll see you at work on Monday," he finishes when the elevator door opens for me and I step inside.

"You'll think of me before then."

I didn't say that loud. Barely even above a whisper and he's far enough away from me that he should not have heard me unless he's Superman. But I already know he is, so maybe that's why he turns back around and faces me, taking a few small paces in my direction, his lips arching up into a sardonic grin just as the doors begin to close.

"That's the thing, love. I haven't stopped thinking of you. Not once."

And then he's gone. The doors close and I'm descending back down to ground level. Back down to earth.

Fuck you, life. Fuck you, love. Just fuck you. Because I'm about to get my heart ransacked and I don't remember giving it the freedom to do so.

Not again.

And never like this.

Chapter Eleven

Jonah

MONDAY MORNINGS ARE for large jolts of caffeine. For obnoxiously small breakfasts you eat on the run because you hit snooze on your alarm twice. For hours of groaning and lamenting work.

But this Monday morning is the day Halle starts in my clinic.

I've been appropriately sequestered in my office for the last two hours, catching up on paperwork that really could wait. I don't have a patient for another hour because the staff was reluctant to book too early after my week off.

But I came in anyway.

She was right when she said I'd think about her.

It's been a little more than a week since I met her, and she's occupied more of my thoughts than I care to admit. All weekend in fact.

I didn't go out. I didn't see people. Not even Erica. I stayed in, ordered takeout, and drank alcohol by myself. And thought about Madeline. And Halle. I thought about the two of them. I thought about the difference between lust and love and I thought about fucking versus making love.

I thought about all of those things.

All while fighting the urge to text Halle.

I haven't seen Halle since she walked—more like ran—from my flat. White lies, she spoke of. It felt like a sucker punch to the gut. Even if she wasn't wrong.

Do I want her because she's forbidden or because I simply want *her*?

My head drops into my hands. I'm a bloody mess.

"Have you seen the new hire?" Rex Fox asks, popping his head into my office uninvited. I can't stand Rex. Partially because his name is Rex Fox—no one has two *X*'s in their name without being a supreme wanker. Partially because he's a charming wanker who's always rubbed me the wrong way. And partially because he just asked me about Halle in a tone that was nothing if not suggestive.

"No."

I stare at my computer screen, reading over the same patient information like it's somehow going to change, and miraculously, this man will no longer have a meth problem while poorly managing his Type 1 diabetes.

"You should come check her out," he encourages, like she's some sideshow, there for his viewing pleasure. "But I'm calling dibs, so don't get any ideas."

I glare at my screen, my jaw clenching. He laughs. He knows I don't date people from work. I've refused to be his wingman at work gatherings on numerous occasions.

"Go see a patient, Fox. Go earn your community health center paycheck."

He laughs harder, and I would very much like to punch his smug face. He's another wealthy doctor who works in this system for the challenge of the patients we see here, as well as to do good.

Poor, students, medically disinterested.

Those are the three primary types of patients we see in this branch and they generally lend themselves to some interesting cases.

Why else would doctors agree to be paid markedly less while taking shit from patients and the system?

Rex, Oliver, and I are all loaded with family money, so our paychecks don't mean a whole lot. For me, it's more about helping underserved populations obtain quality healthcare. Probably is the same for them as well, though I've honestly never asked. It's how I was raised and why my mother started this place.

Rex opens his mouth to say something sexist I'm sure, when he's interrupted by yelling, followed by screaming, followed by rushing footsteps. I bolt out of my chair, the wheels rolling back until it collides with my office wall. I push past Fox, who appears more curious than anything and hasn't so much as moved a muscle.

"Code Blue. Pediatrics registration area. Code Blue. Pediatrics registration area," sounds through our overhead PA system.

Fuck.

I sprint down the hallway and burst through the door that leads to the waiting room of the Internal Medicine area. Pediatrics is on the other side, the distance frustrating me to no end.

I catch two of the pediatric nurses running, holding their stethoscopes so they don't bounce against their chests as they head away from the employee break room. I follow after them, one swiping her badge on the keypad on the wall to give us access to the pediatric area. The second the light turns green and the door unlocks, the three of us race through it.

The pediatric waiting room is full of wide-eyed, stunned patients watching us run to registration. And when we reach it, there's a crowd of people three layers deep standing in a circle around what I assume is the patient on the ground.

They're all vying for a better vantage point of the scene below, but I can't make out much of what they're saying. It's a cacophony of noise and yelling, saturated with scared cries and shocked gasping.

A pediatrician rolls in with the code cart, a nurse helping him weed through the spectators as she demands everyone step back. But as I push myself through the crowd, I catch that flash of copper hair.

Halle has a toddler folded over her arm as she slams the butt of her palm into the boy's back, directly between his shoulder blades. The boy's lifeless body lurches with each thrust as a woman stands in front of them, her hands covering her mouth as she screams and cries in petrified agony.

On the last thrust, something comes flying out of the boy's mouth and hits the floor, followed by a small amount of vomit. He chokes, coughing violently as he begins to squirm restlessly in Halle's arms.

Halle lets out an audible sigh of relief, dropping to her knees and rolling the boy onto his back. He's awake and blinking, his color turning from a pale bluish-white to beet red as he begins to howl, flailing and crying. The boy's mother follows Halle down onto her knees, profusely thanking her as she tries to cradle her son into her embrace.

Halle stops her, holding her back with soft comforting words and hugs, while the pediatric team comes swarming in, assessing the boy further.

Jesus Christ, Halle just saved this boy's life. And on her first day.

I can't stop my small, incredulous grin.

Providers surround the boy and Halle rises back to her feet, stepping away to let them do their jobs. She appears astonished, her head shaking back and forth ever so slightly. Her cheeks are flushed and her eyes bright as she plants her hands on her hips and continues to wordlessly watch the team.

Once the boy is stabilized, one of the pediatricians lifts him up into his arms, talking with the mother as he holds the boy.

The crowd begins to disperse now that the action is over, and the pediatric team is bringing the boy and his mother back to an exam room. I watch as a few of the nurses and doctors converse with Halle and congratulate her, then go back to their waiting patients.

And when Halle is standing all alone, she covers her mouth with her hands and lets out a small squeak like she can't believe that just happened.

She spins around, catching me observing her, and her hands

drop to her sides with a small slap. Pale blue scrubs match her pretty eyes, her wild hair pinned up on top of her head in a bun that was probably more put together before she worked on the choking boy. She steps forward and I do the same until we're standing directly in front of each other in the middle of the registration area of pediatrics.

"You all right?" I ask.

She shakes her head and then nods, a small bubble of a laugh escaping her lips. She's so beautiful.

"You were incredible."

"I've never done that before." She shakes her head again, a reluctant smile curving up the corners of her full pink lips. "It wasn't even proper technique, but I had him standing to Heimlich him and he just couldn't do it. I wasn't able to get a good hold on him and instinct took over." She reaches out, almost absentmindedly and grasps my shoulder, the contact warm and wonderfully unexpected. Her hand drops with a self-deprecating shrug. "You think he'll be okay?" Her southern accent is quite thick right now, completely unfiltered.

"You saved his life."

Halle glances back and forth around us, ensuring no one is within hearing range. Leaning in, she cups her hand around her mouth like she's got a secret. And like a moth to the flame, I lean into her right back. "Is it considered unprofessional if I tell my new boss that I was scared shitless?"

I laugh, wanting to reach out and tuck a wayward strand of her thick, silky hair behind her ears. "No. I think I would be, too. You want to know a secret?"

Her eyes widen, and she grins so big I can't help but step into her just a bit more, our bodies so close that I catch a hint of floral shampoo and can see each of her pinpoint freckles along the bridge of her nose.

"Tell me." She bites her lip, desperate to hide her widening smile. "I'm dying here, waiting with bated breath and all that good stuff."

"I've only ever been in a few codes and I was never by myself during them. The first one I was ever in was during medical school and after the poor chap made it up to the OR, I went outside and threw up."

"That's not the best secret, Doctor. But I get you wanting to keep that one to yourself. You know, being the great and powerful Medical Director and all."

"You've been checking up on me."

She nods, tilting her head and tucking that loose strand I'd been eyeing behind her ears. "I have, but you're not supposed to know that. I'm too high on endorphins and adrenaline to care right now, but I'll care later, so pretend I didn't say that."

"Your secret is safe with me," I say on a laugh.

She sighs. "Back to work, I guess." She shrugs, glancing around before returning to me. "I was supposed to meet the HR lady here when the mother ran in screaming about her son choking."

"What do they have you doing today?"

Halle opens her mouth to reply, but before she can get a word out, Janet, the resident HR person, comes traipsing up to us, her small fists clenched as she marches. "There you are, Halle." She grins at her, a streak of red lipstick on her teeth, her salt-and-pepper hair standing on end in tight frizzy curls like she was just electrocuted. "And I see you've already met Doctor Hughes. Perfect." Both Halle and I stare down to the five-foot, small woman who appears almost child-like next to our much taller frames. "I just heard about the boy. Fantastic work. What an awful situation to walk into on your first day."

"I'm just glad he's going to be okay."

"As we all are," Janet exclaims, ushering both of us off to the side and away from the registration area. "Halle, we're going to need you to fill out a report of the incident. But after that, I was hoping you could shadow Doctor Oliver Fritz." I swallow hard, an unwelcome surge of jealousy creeping up my spine. "His schedule has been adjusted accordingly. Oliver thought it might be the perfect way to get Halle acquainted with the way we work here," Janet finishes, eyeing me with a gleeful, lipstick-stained smile, hoping I'll give my blessing.

I stare at Janet for a beat, grinning at her as I reluctantly nod my head in agreement at Oliver's clever scheme. "That's wonderful." Wonderful is a bit of an exaggeration. I'd rather match up with Rex Fox and drink rubbish beer at a frat party than have Halle spend the entire day working closely with Oliver.

But maybe this is the right way forward? The best path for me to keep my distance from Halle?

"Sounds great," Halle says, but I can't tell if she means it or not. Her tone and expression give nothing away. Her accent is all but gone.

"Perfect." Janet claps her hands together like the world isn't the imperfect mess that it actually is. "Okay. I'm loving the vibe here. Let's heal people."

Seriously? Halle suppresses her grin and I take a modicum of relief in the fact that I'm not the only one.

"Jonah, I'll catch up with you later. Halle, come with me." Janet grabs Halle's arm, squeezing her tightly and dragging her away from me.

Halle turns her head over her shoulder and catches my eye. "See you later, Doctor Hughes."

I don't reply. I just watch her go. Right now, one question continues to loop through my mind. How am I going to stay away from the woman I can't seem to get out of my head?

Chapter Twelve

Halle

"SO YOU'LL COME?" I ask Oliver, just a bit desperate at this point. I'm stuck going to a party an old college friend planned for tomorrow night. A party that has been planned for two months and is most definitely a couples' dinner. And since I'm no longer with Matt, I need a date. And since my friend called me early this morning to tell me that I was not getting out of attending and that she could set me up on a blind date if I needed, I took matters into my own hands.

I don't have it in me to suffer through a blind date. Not at this point. And lord knows who she would find for me on such short notice.

"I said I would." Oliver laughs, nudging my arm just before I pour coffee into my mug. A second later and I'd be covered in the boiling hot black stuff. "But you'll owe me. Something big for dragging me to a couples' dinner party at that psycho Miranda's house."

"She's not a psycho." He throws me a dubious look and I can only shrug. "She might be a bit . . . pushy." I get a raised eyebrow this time. "I don't want to go, either. I seriously don't, but I promised her months ago and I've known her forever. I don't break my promises."

Oliver grins the grin of the devil at me. "Oh, I know. I'm planning on using that to my advantage."

Fucking Oliver. He's lucky he's hot and nice and charming, because if he weren't . . .

"What did you have in mind?" I ask, suspicious of this man and his gleam as I pour sweetener and cream into my coffee. After stirring it, I take a small, hesitant sip, so it doesn't burn my tongue and ruin the taste of food for the rest of the day.

"If I'm your date tomorrow night, you need to be my date for Friday."

"Friday?" I scrunch my eyebrows.

"At the bar. There's a nurse I can't seem to get rid of, but if you're my date . . ." He leaves the sentence hanging.

And again, fucking Oliver.

This is why you don't pee where you sleep. Or is it fuck where you work? Whatever the saying, it's true all the same. Though, I wouldn't mind making an exception with one person in particular.

Not gonna happen, Halle.

Right. I need to remember that one.

"Yes," I agree, with a slight measured tone because I have a feeling this is going to come back to bite me in the ass. "I'll be your date if you'll be mine."

Oliver smiles at me like sunshine after a storm. Warm, bright, and welcome. His sparkling green eyes bounce around my face a time or two and then he leans in and kisses my cheek. Slowly. Softly. Like it has purpose and meaning, and for a moment, my heart kicks up a beat. But more out of nerves than anticipation and more out of apprehension than enjoyment.

And when he pulls back, he grins at me like he knows exactly the game he wants to play and how to play it to win.

"You smell good, Halle."

He's testing me. This flirting isn't real, right?

I open my mouth to give him just a little bit of hell for that kiss when the sound of someone sharply clearing their throat startles me back.

But not Oliver. No, fucking Oliver winks.

Bastard did know what he was doing because Jonah is standing in the doorway of the break room. His jaw is clenched tight, but otherwise, he appears unaffected.

"Sorry," he grumbles in a frozen tone. "Didn't mean to *interrupt*."

Heat climbs its way so high up my face I'm positive my hair is turning a brighter shade of red. Oliver could care less about Jonah being in here. Nor does he seem to notice the heavy shift in the atmospheric pressure.

Jonah goes about making himself a cup of coffee as Oliver, oh so helpfully, places his hand on the small of my back to shift me aside to give Jonah room.

"What time am I picking you up tomorrow?"

Dammit, Oliver! But seriously, I shouldn't care. It shouldn't matter if I'm making plans with Oliver in front of Jonah.

Jonah who doesn't date or sleep with people he works with. Jonah who has been blatantly avoiding me like I've brought the plague into his clinic. He hasn't even asked how things are going for me in my first week. I mean, I get that it's only Wednesday, but still. He could ask.

"I think Miranda said we should get there by six-thirty. Does that work for you?"

"Whatever you say. Like I said, I'm yours since you agreed to be mine." He most definitely did not say it like that. I would have remembered. "Catch you later, Halle. I've got a patient to see." And then he kisses my cheek. Again. When he steps back, he smiles warmly at Jonah. Like kissing the new girl in the break room is all just so normal for him. For us. "See you, Jonah."

Jonah doesn't return the pleasantry. He just rewards Oliver with a curt nod and cold eyes.

Silently, I draw in some much-needed air. Men, right? I'm starting to think the world would be a less dramatic place without them.

Or maybe it's hormones. Or those icky bastards called feelings.

I turn around to pick up my mug of coffee that I set down at some point during my mini mental explosion, only to find Jonah casually leaning with his back against the counter and his eyes on his phone, his eyebrows pinched like he's focusing really hard on something he's looking at. Like I'm not even in the room.

It shouldn't bother me. But it does.

I shouldn't care. But I do.

Mostly because I still want this man. I'm like a dying plant and he's the first few drops of rain after a drought. Is it too much to ask for me to meet a normal, sane man? One who isn't gay? Or an obsessive gamer? Or a cheater? Or a criminal? Or in love with his dead wife? Or a relentless flirt who sleeps with every female he encounters?

I mean, think about that for a moment.

Seriously. That right there sums up the extent of my love life.

And the last one, being Oliver, isn't even part of my love life. He's just the guy friend who likes to flirt and would no doubt take advantage if I dropped my panties to the floor in front of him.

I think there is a lot to be said about staying single. I am the queen of my ship. The most powerful player on the board. The king can only move one space at a time and is dead in the water without the queen. So, what does that say? It says they need me more than I need them. It says I'm the one with all the power. Right?

Right.

Only, half the time, it feels the other way around.

"Excuse me," I say softly. Does he know he's standing in front of my coffee? Is it intentional?

Jonah slowly—so freaking slowly it's ridiculous—raises his head to meet my eyes. "Pardon?"

"You're standing in front of my coffee." He shifts maybe a centimeter to the side. I reach behind him, since this seems to be what he's after, and slide my fingers along the porcelain of my mug, lifting it up and stepping back away from him.

I don't get far. I'm a caged mouse when he pivots until he's directly in front of me, his green eyes slaying through me, drawing all the air from my lungs.

Didn't I just say I have all the power? But I make no move to leave and he sees that.

Oddly enough, I don't care. I want him to see me. I want him to acknowledge me. I want him to feel me, feel a streak of desperation when he looks at me this deeply. I want his helplessness at our situation to match my own. I'm raw with this man and I hate it as much as I love it. I want it to stop as much as I never want it to stop.

"Oliver fucks around."

I shrug.

His jaw tics. I'm tempted to reach up and smooth the tension away. But this Jonah, the jealous one, is too perfect to mess with. "You deserve better than that, Halle."

"Is that what this is, Jonah? A warning? A friendly chat to build up my self-esteem? Or is this something else?"

He steps forward, his body crowding mine as I press myself against the counter, the sharp edge digging into my back. The zing is almost welcome. It somehow grounds me, which is good, since I feel like I'm outside my body, watching this madness as a spectator.

"With you, it's always something else. But just because I can't have you doesn't mean I want to watch you get hoovered up by a man who could care less about what you need."

"And you think you know what I need?"

"I know I do."

I shake my head, just a bit pissed off, a lot incredulous and possibly, horribly, incredibly turned-on. "Oliver's known me a hell of a lot longer than you have. And he's as available as they come."

Now I'm just taunting him, but I don't care enough to stop. If this is all I can have with him then I want it all. His fire. His jealousy. His passion. His goddamn lust, because it's all flowing from him like water free-falling off a cliff. It's like screwing without touching. That's what this look from him is.

It's so hot I completely forget we're in a break room at work. That anyone can walk in here at any moment. That this man is, in fact, forbidden. But the temptation of him . . . God, this temptation is so great. I'm teetering on the precipice of it, balancing as I go, knowing that if I fall, I'll get burned. But you can't force affection.

You can't force love, and you sure as shit can't change someone else's reality.

Jonah snakes his arm around my waist and jerks me into him, forcing me to feel just what I'm doing to him. A soft moan slips past the edge of my lips. I want to drop to my knees and take his huge cock in my mouth. I want to rip off his clothes and lick every delicious inch of his body. I want him to prop me up on this counter and devour me the way I know he can.

Our faces are inches apart when he smirks, his green eyes nearly black with his anger and desire. "And if you didn't want me as much as I want you, I might be worried about you with Oliver. But you're not that kind of woman, Halle. I know this, because, I. Know. You. Inside and out. Every perfect inch. So, go on your date with him, Carolina. But you'll be thinking of me and not him."

"And you'll be thinking of me, Jonah. The girl you want but refuse to have. The girl you're desperate to stay away from, but don't know how to accomplish that."

He nods roughly. "You're right. You're all those things. I have no explanation for it. Maybe I should sack you and put us both out of our misery."

I roll my eyes, and he smiles, dropping his forehead to mine as if the minuscule distance between us was just too much to handle any longer.

"You think I'd let you fuck me if you fire me?"

"You could find another job. I'd give you a fantastic recommendation."

I laugh, dropping my head back and trying to clear myself of him. Instead, he runs his nose up the column of my neck. I shudder as he breathes me in.

Oh, Jonah. Why does this have to be so . . . much?

"I have no right to ask you not to date Oliver Fritz," he whispers against my neck just under my jaw, his warm breath causing me to erupt in chills, "but I *really* want to. It's driving me mad, Halle. It's making me want to nip at your neck until I redden it, so everyone can see the mark I leave."

I close my eyes, my voice coming out on a needy whisper. "I already told you what Oliver and I are."

"Doesn't mean I don't want to snap his neck like a twig every time I see him near you. You're turning me into a man I don't recognize."

I smile at that. Something tells me Jonah needed to come out of his shell some. "Good. I like this man."

"Me too," he says softly.

That surprises me enough to drop my chin and open my eyes to look at him. He's still holding me against him, but our mood has shifted once again.

"I both hate and love the way you make me feel in equal measure."

"Funny," I remark. "I was just thinking the exact same thing about you. Maybe one day we'll figure out how to either get over it or embrace it."

"Until that time . . ." He trails off, then steps back and releases me, filling me with an unfathomable emptiness. I want his arms around me far more than I should, so I push off the counter, take my now ice-cold mug of coffee and leave Jonah without so much as a backward glance.

He's already in my head.

But as I turn the corner and release the breath I was holding, I wonder just how long we can continue like this before one of us snaps and gives into everything we're trying to resist.

Chapter Thirteen

Jonah

I'VE SUCCESSFULLY AVOIDED Halle all week. Ask me how, because it wasn't easy. Sure, there were moments when seeing her was unavoidable. Like in the hall down by the lab. Or in the break room when we both went for a cup of coffee—she likes hers sweet and creamy, just like she is. Or when we were both coming out of a patient room and nearly slammed into each other and I had to wrap my hand around her to make sure she didn't fall.

All right, maybe I didn't *need* to wrap my hand around her, but it just seemed to happen.

But in any event, I've avoided her.

Until now.

She's walking down the long, narrow hall toward the patient area, a young girl beside her. I'm heading up the hallway, toward the exam area, alone.

"Doctor Hughes," Halle greets me as I get closer to them. "Are you heading in to see a patient?"

"Not at the moment. I have a few minutes if you need something."

"Perfect." She gleams. "I'll be right back after I take Kaylee out to her mom. Wait for me?"

Absolutely, I think before I can hold it back.

"I'll be in my office. I have to send a prescription for a patient."

"That'll work."

As she passes me, our arms brush. I swallow at the contact and then go directly for my office at the back. Today is Friday. I know the staff is planning on heading over to a pub after work. I haven't decided if I'm going to join them or not. I can't figure out if this is the night to switch up what's become my new routine.

I've gone home every night after work, stared at the cufflinks and my wedding band that I no longer wear, as I think about the two women I can't seem to get out of my head.

Madeline and Halle.

How this happened with Halle, I have no idea. I've been blaming it on the sex and the fact that I had gone so long without it. I'm not sure how sold on that I am.

What would Maddy think of me now? The torment of my thoughts is profound. But I can't let Madeline go. Not yet.

The way things ended, the way she left, pulverizes me.

It's my fault she's gone in the first place. I miss her so much. I don't know if I'm using thoughts of Halle to distract myself from thoughts of Madeline. That's precisely what I did the first night I met Halle, but since then, I'm not sure.

I can't explain it. It just feels different.

"Knock, knock," Halle says as she raps her knuckles twice on my door in sync with her words. She enters my office when I glance up, catching her eye. She's wearing black scrubs today. I've never seen her in anything other than color. The lack of color accentuates her hair and eyes. I rather like her in black.

But there is something behind her eyes that distracts me from how stunning she looks. Nerves? Apprehension? Fear?

I stand automatically and shut the door behind her, but instead of sitting back down the way I know I should, I move across the small room and perch myself on the edge of my desk as she sits in front of me in the chair. "What's wrong?"

She lets out a nervous laugh, her eyes scattering every which way that avoids me. "How can you tell something is wrong?"

"It's all over your face, love. You have one of the most expressive faces I've ever seen. And your accent is thicker."

Another nervous laugh, but this one is hollow, the sound forced, and it has my heart rate bumping up a beat. "That sucks. It would be nice to have a solid poker face, at least. The accent I can't do much about, I guess."

Her head drops as she leans forward, intertwining her fingers and resting her forearms on her parted thighs.

"Halle." I reach out and clasp her shoulder, lowering myself to one knee directly in front of her so I can see her face. If someone walked in here right now, this would look bad. But I don't care enough to worry about that. What if she tells me she's pregnant? That's a likely scenario, right? A bit soon to know, but possible. My stomach sinks and lifts all at the same time. "Talk to me."

Her face slowly raises up to meet mine, her eyes glassy and her cheeks pink. "Do you remember what I told you about my ex?" I nod. "About how he's a piece of shit scumbag who stole from people?" Another nod. "I got subpoenaed to testify against him."

I blow out a breath, blinking a few times as I stare into her eyes. "When?"

"Next month. I'm only telling you this because you're the medical director and I will need the day off. I know I just started and I'm sorry."

I lean forward and wrap my arms around her, cupping the back of her head and drawing her face into my shoulder. Her body sags into mine, her arms encircling my back. She squeezes me, holds me as tightly as I'm holding her. I inadvertently lower my face into her neck and can't help but breathe her in. This shouldn't feel as good as it does.

"Do you want me to go with you?" I ask after a few quiet beats. "You don't have to do this alone."

She pulls away, blinking back tears as she stares at me. "You'd do that? You'd come with me and sit for hours in court while I testify?"

She's incredulous and I understand that. We don't know each other well and certainly not for very long, but I don't want her there alone. She told me about her ex and the things he's accused of doing. She told me how he ignored her in favor of his computer.

But more than that, I'm hit with a flash of nonsensical possessiveness. I want to protect her.

I've never had this before. Madeline was so very different. She was mine and I was hers. Our world, our relationship, was built on a different foundation.

With Halle, everything feels new and jumbled up.

"Yes. I'll come with you," I promise her.

"But—"

"I'm your boss?"

She nods, swallowing audibly with something resembling hope in her pale eyes.

"I'm also your friend." I cup her face, rubbing my thumb across her silky cheek. Something so very un-friends-like. "And you look like you need someone to go with you."

She closes her eyes, a small tear leaking out the side. I wipe it away with my thumb. "I don't understand why they want me to testify. The DA said something about a piece of evidence." She shakes her head. "I don't have anything. I never wanted to see him again. If I went the rest of my life without seeing him, I'd be happy. But not only do I have to see him again, I have to answer questions about our relationship in court. In front of him. And . . ." She trails off.

She looks so lost and vulnerable that I can't stop myself from dropping my forehead to hers. I don't kiss her. I do everything I can to keep my lips away from hers because if I give in to that, into the tiny inches separating them, I'll give in to everything.

Right now, I'm comforting her.

I'm already crossing the line with that. I know I am. But Halle is more than just a woman who works for me. When you develop a preoccupation with someone—the way I have with Halle—and they come to you like this, it's not possible to maintain boundaries you already hate on principle.

"And?" I encourage when she doesn't follow it up.

"And he's been calling me, Jonah. Matt has been calling me for the last two weeks. It started right after . . .," she trails off again, swallowing as she closes her eyes before they reopen and lock on mine. "It started right after our night together." Her finger wiggles back and forth between our chests. "I have no idea why. The number is always different, and he never leaves messages. But when I do pick up, I know it's him. I know it. There is no way they're all random and yet all the same. He breathes into the phone before hanging up. I have no idea what to do. I told my lawyer, but he intimated that aside from recording the calls and hoping he somehow reveals himself, there is no way to prove the calls are from him. As long as he's not threatening me, there isn't a lot the police will do."

Shit. A cold chill runs up my spine. "Does he know where you live? Where you work?"

She lifts one shoulder in a half-hearted shrug. "I don't know. He's a hacker. How difficult can that be for him? Even if he's technically not allowed to use a computer."

"I'm going with you next month. And if you want to stay at my place, you can. I have a spare bedroom," I add so she doesn't think this offer is about anything other than trying to keep her safe.

She smiles, brushing her nose against mine. "I'm not moving in with you, Jonah. That would be an epically bad idea. But thank you. That means a lot."

For a moment, I want to fight her on this. I want to object and explain how it would not be an epically bad idea. That in some weird, twist of fate or reality, it makes perfect sense.

But she's right.

I would never be able to resist her if she were living with me. And resisting her has become a daily struggle. One where I neither win nor lose.

It's why I keep my mouth shut, even though it feels wrong to do so.

Halle sits up in her seat and I slip myself off the ground, finding myself perched back on the edge of the desk. Just like that, our little encounter is over, the intimacy dulled. I don't want it to be. I still want this woman as much as I did that first night. More. I want her more.

But that want doesn't obliterate our realities.

Soon enough, memories of our night together will fade. I'll revert to solely torturing myself over Madeline. And Halle will transition into nothing more than a work colleague.

But until that point . . . "Do you feel unsafe?"

She shakes her head. "He's never hurt me, and I've never known him to be violent. I think he's just out of sorts, scared and doesn't know what to do." She heaves a sigh. "I'm sure I can talk Rina, Aria, or Margot, or even Oliver, into coming with me to court. You don't have to trouble yourself."

Oliver? Is she taking the piss? No way Oliver is going with her.

"I already told you I'll be there. Text me the information and I'll pick you up. We'll ride together, and I won't leave your side except for when you're up there. And after it's done, I'll take you out for dinner or ice cream or the biggest dirty martini in Boston. Whatever you like."

A soft smile pulls up the corner of her pink lips. She stands and I love how tall she is. How beautiful she is. Especially when she smiles. "Okay, Jonah. Thank you."

I open my office door for her like the gentleman I feign to be. I'm officially running behind now, but she's worth it, so I don't care.

"I'll see you tonight," she says.

"Tonight?"

She steps out of my office, pivoting back around to face me, tilting her head with a playful smirk. "The bar. Aren't you coming out with the rest of the staff?"

"Are you going?"

"I am."

"Aren't you Oliver's date?" I most definitely overheard that when they were in the break room on Wednesday. Before I cornered her, of course.

Her nose scrunches up. "Sorta. But it's . . ." She laughs. "I'm just doing him a favor. It's not a *real* date or anything." Her cheeks pink up. "Are you coming?"

No. Say no. Don't do it. Go home, drink scotch alone, and forget about her. "I'll see you there."

She smiles the most breathtaking smile that lights up everything inside me like fireworks.

I'm so screwed.

Chapter Fourteen

Halle

LET'S start this off by saying I haven't been in a bar since my night with Jonah.

I get it, it's only been two weeks, but by Boston single-girl standards, that's a long time. Especially when my best friends promised to buy all my drinks for a month. Yeah, I need to start cashing in on that.

But seriously, in the immortal words of Yogi Berra, it's like déjà vu all over again. Because here I am, at a trendy bar—this one in the Financial District instead of the South End—and Jonah is once again sitting at the bar, nursing a scotch.

I'm on the opposite side of the bar, drinking a martini and trying not to watch Jonah drink his scotch. It's not going so well since the gorgeous bastard is like a magnet for the senses.

I went to his office today with the best intentions. I got that subpoena last night, and when I told that HR chick, Janet about it this morning, she explained that I had to let Jonah know since he's the Medical Director and therefore my boss.

I didn't expect to get all emotional when I informed him about the court date. I didn't expect for him to touch me in the most perfect of ways. I didn't expect him to use soft, commanding tones that turned my already fragile-girl self into a helpless mush. I tried to be strong, I really did, but sometimes strength crumbles when someone else offers to take on some of your burden.

That's what happened today.

It's Matt's fault.

Nothing makes a woman feel more vulnerable than having her ex repeatedly calling her. I know it's him. There is no one else it could be. When you've been with someone for two years, you get to know their breathing. Sense things about them. I have no idea if he's going through disposable phones like they're M&Ms or what, but he calls from a different number at least two or three times a day. The call this evening, just as I stepped into the bar, was another silent one.

And I can't take it. I can't.

Partially because I sorta, kinda feel bad for him. I mean, he's facing prison. That blows. If it were me, well, I might consider putting my passport to good use and disappearing somewhere because I'm chickenshit like that.

But part of me wonders what he thought would happen.

Was he so completely arrogant that he truly believed he'd never get caught? That spending hours upon hours on your computer instead of with your fiancée would gain you a happily ever after?

I don't know. What I do know is that I don't miss him and that has nothing to do with his criminal activities.

"Here," Oliver says as he hands me my second martini of the night. He's insisted on purchasing my drinks even though I told him I was fully capable of buying my own. He isn't buying anyone else their drinks.

Oliver is another issue. I don't know what to do about him. The other night he accompanied me to my friend Miranda's house. He was charming—as he always is—and afterward we went our separate ways without a hitch.

But tonight? Tonight, he's touching me. My back. My shoulder.

My face. He's also looking at me. My legs. My tits. My legs. My tits. My face. And the way he's looking at me . . .

"Thank you," I say as I take a sip, careful not to spill the very full beverage. "Is Rina coming? I texted her like an hour ago and she gave me a maybe."

He shrugs, running a hand through his chestnut hair. "Don't know. Don't care." *Oh. Okay.* "I like it better with just the two of us." He takes a sip of his drink. I'm not really sure what. It's some sort of mixed drink with a peel of lime. "Oh shit. That nurse is here."

I glance across the bar in the direction he's looking, and sure enough, a pretty little blonde thing is staring at Oliver with come-fuck-me eyes.

"One and done. Why is that so impossible for women to understand?"

Poor Oliver. He had his heart broken and since then, he views dating like it's toxic waste attempting to pollute his life.

I laugh, nudging him in the side. "Maybe you should try keeping it in your pants when it comes to people you work with."

His head swivels back in my direction, his eyes alight with playful mischief. "There is no fun in that, Halle. Especially when the women I work with are as hot as you are. Dance with me."

I peer over at the dance floor that is actually moderately crowded with Friday night grinders and then back to him. "Eh—"

"It'll be fun. Come on."

He tugs my free hand, dragging me into the clearing on the outer rim of the small square floor. His hand skims around my waist, settling right on the crest of my ass. I blink up at him, a little stunned by the position of his hand, but then he starts to move, holding me close to his body as we sway and drift to some tripped-up version of a Rihanna song.

I don't know many people from work yet, just a few of the nurses and other providers, but none of that matters right now. Because all of their eyes are on me and Oliver. It makes me both self-conscious and uncomfortable.

"Oli," I start, wondering just what the hell I'm going to say. Mostly, I want him to move his hand up without my being rude.

Since I still have my stupid half-full cocktail in one hand and my other hand is on his shoulder to maintain my balance, I'm at a loss. Like a one-legged man at an ass-kicking contest, as my father used to say. "I'm not much of a dancer."

Yeah, that wasn't all that compelling. I wiggle a little, but he doesn't take the hint. Actually, his hand dips lower, his fingers most definitely grazing some of my ass cheek. I open my mouth to tell him to move above the Mason-Dixon line before he gets a knee to the balls, but he starts speaking before I can.

"In case you missed it, Halle, I don't care. I'm not, either." He draws back enough to catch my eyes. "Do you still love him?"

I scrunch my eyebrows in confusion.

"Matt," he clarifies when I don't reply.

"Oh." I laugh nervously, slightly taken aback by the shift in conversation. "No. I don't." My gaze drops down to the small space between us, I don't like talking about Matt. Just his name sets me on edge. "I don't think I have for a long time."

"Good. Because Jonah Hughes has not taken his eyes off you since we started dancing."

"What?" My head springs up to find him staring down at me with a determination I haven't witnessed before from him.

"Yeah. I noticed it the first time in the break room the other day. He was standing there watching us talk about our dates like he was ready to grade-school kick my ass. Jonah Hughes is not typically that juvenile or interested."

"I met him before I knew he was going to be my boss," I explain, unwilling to admit to our night together.

He nods, like it's all starting to make sense. "That's why you asked me about him that day at lunch."

"Yes. Does that make me totally pathetic?"

He chuckles lightly, leaning down to kiss my cheek. Oliver is nothing if not touchy-feely. Sometimes I like it. Sometimes I don't. But right now, I think I like it. It feels brotherly. Protective.

"Are you into him?" he whispers in my ear. "I mean, do you have feelings for him?"

"Jesus, Oliver. Have you always been this blunt?" I puff out some air, taking a ginormous gulp of my drink and doing my best to dodge his pointed question.

"He lost his wife, Halle. A woman he was very much in love with. I never knew him with her. I've only been a resident here a year, but the rumor mill is that he was devastated when she died and hasn't dated anyone since."

I stare at him, unsure what I'm supposed to say, supposed to think. It hurts, and yet, I love that about Jonah. I love that he loved his wife to the ends of the earth and back. It gives me a deranged hope. Not for Jonah and me, but for life and love in general.

"I know about that. He already told me. But I'm not exactly rocking out on relationship street, either. Besides, it was only one night and once we realized my current employment situation, it was definitely done."

"It's none of my business if there's something going on between the two of you," he continues like he's gearing me up for a long speech. "But I care about you. You're my friend and I don't have many female friends I haven't slept with." I'm treated to a wink for that. "So, I particularly don't want to see you get hurt." He glances over my shoulder in the direction of the bar. In the direction of Jonah, I assume. "I'm not boyfriend material. You know this, but if you want me to tell him you're mine so he'll back off, I will."

"Oli, I—" I start and then pause, genuinely giving his offer some thought. I want to say no, and I want to say yes. I know I need to stay away from Jonah, and if Oliver tells the world we're in a relationship, Jonah will absolutely back off. Jonah is dangerous for my heart. I know this, too. I'm relationship-phobic and so very damaged.

And yet, I like the man I have no business liking. My ex is wreaking havoc on my brain and I can no longer determine night from day and day from night.

"This could benefit both of us, now that I think on it," Oliver says. "It will get Jonah off your back and the nurse off mine."

Jonah may offer to come with me to my court appearance. He may offer me a place to stay, but it's in his guest room.

Oliver's right, he's in love with a dead woman and I can't compete with that.

The fact that he's my boss is another piece of cheese in the spread. So why can't I say yes to Oliver? I should say yes. But I really don't want to. I want Jonah's heated looks. I want Jonah's soft touches and tender words and dominant encroachment.

I want Jonah. Even if I shouldn't.

"Oliver."

"You want him back," he interrupts. I stare up at him and he grins knowingly down at me. "It's okay, Halle. Just make sure you know what you're getting into. You're not really the hookup type. I joke with you, and honestly, I'd love a night or six in bed with you, but you wear your heart on your sleeve."

"I'm not getting into anything. Nothing is actually going on between us."

I cannot stand his you're full-of-shit expression, so I wrap my arm around his neck and we slow dance. The song shifted to something slow during our little heart-to-heart and Oliver is taking full advantage, his hand especially as he moves us around in a slow circle.

But I hardly notice anything, because as we turn, I find Jonah.

And he's most assuredly staring at me from across the bar, his eyes vacillating between Oliver's hands and my eyes.

His expression is the hottest combination of lust-fueled jealousy and some form of passionate anger. It could set this whole building ablaze if he so desired. His eyes bore into mine. Hold me captive. Tell me a million different things while asking a million different questions.

"Oliver, I'm sorry." I pull back, staring intently into his eyes, but try as I may and try as I might, my heart is not into Oliver Fritz or his half-baked offers.

"Don't say no yet," Oliver quickly interrupts me. "You might find you need me. And I'm here, Halle. For whenever, if ever, that happens."

I give him a slim nod, a kiss on the cheek, unsure what else to say or do about it. I finish my drink off, setting it down on a nearby table and then I put my arms around Oliver's neck and finally, he brings his hands up to my waist and off my ass. I silently sigh out, trying to avoid looking at Jonah as Oliver and I continue to move and sway.

I want Jonah, and those searing looks are muddling with my resistance until it's nothing more than pulp.

Jonah stands up and tosses back the last of his drink before he slams the empty glass on the bar top. He says something to the person seated next to him, and then eyes me hard, forcing me to see him. To acknowledge him.

I do. I'm helpless against the pull.

My whole body comes alive when he looks at me like this. Every aching inch of my insides are a smoldering pit of embers. He stalks over to the bathrooms in the back, the message in his eyes clear, *come meet me.*

A bolt of erotic jitters skirts through me at the prospect.

"I need to use the restroom," I say to Oliver.

I suck at life. I truly do. I know the fire I'm playing with. Oliver just fucking warned me. But if I don't go, then I'll always wonder. And if I don't go and eventually say yes to Oliver's scheming, I'll always wonder.

In the two weeks I've known Jonah Hughes, my desire for him has not dissipated. Not even a little. It might have actually grown into a reluctant crush.

Oliver steps back and smiles softly. "Sure. But don't do anything I wouldn't do, Whitcomb."

"That doesn't include much."

He shrugs a shoulder. "Exactly. But in your case, I should probably say don't do anything I *would* do."

I have nothing for that. He's right. I'm wrong. But the temptation . . . Oh boy, the temptation.

I leave Oliver on the dance floor, and as I turn into the back hallway where the bathrooms are, I spot a nurse—not the blonde with the come-fuck-me eyes—eyeing him before invading his space. Oliver gives her a slow smile and the two begin to dance together. Don't do anything he would do. No kidding, Oliver.

"Are you making sure your date is situated before you sneak off to join me?"

I smile to myself before I turn and face Jonah. He's tucked back amongst the dark, leaning casually against the far wall, his piercing green eyes on me. He's wearing a dark shirt and dark jeans and his light hair is tousled.

He looks so freaking hot I can barely contain my panting. My panties are totally soaked and all he's done is look at me. "Maybe. Would that bother you?"

His eyes are emerald fire. Even in the dark, I feel the heat. They do a slow, languid sweep of me, traveling down my body, all the way to my purple heels and back up to my eyes. In those few seconds, I feel like I died. Like there is no way I'll survive him.

He doesn't answer me. He doesn't have to.

"I hate how much I want you."

That's not what I thought he was going to say and I feel myself frowning. But when I think about it, I realize the feeling is mutual. "What do we do about that?"

"It's funny you ask. It's a question I've been debating all day. For two weeks, if we're really keeping track."

I lean against the wall, bathing myself in shadows. A woman exits the ladies' room, but she doesn't notice Jonah, who is too far back, and all I get from her is a compulsory polite grin.

"Have you come up with any answers?" I ask, once we're alone again.

"Just one."

"And what's that?"

He runs a hand through his hair before he squeezes the back of his neck like he's trying to release some of the tension that's building up there.

Jonah is so many things. Sometimes he's this in control, cool, composed man. A triple-C threat. And then other times, it's like he's hanging on by a thread, ready to unravel at any second.

I like both sides of him.

But I get off on his discomposure the most, simply because I like to believe I'm the cause of it. At least it feels that way right now.

"I can't stay away from you, Halle. I can't get you out of my head and I'm tired of fighting this." He wiggles a finger back and forth in the empty space between us.

"It's only been a couple weeks, Doctor. You'll get over it."

He shakes his head, a wry smile bouncing on the corner of his lips. "I went home after work tonight and sat in my flat as I contemplated just that. I thought about not coming here, because you're a temptation I can't seem to resist, but should." He lets out a mirthless chuckle, sweeping a finger across his lower lip, his focus dropping to my dress. "And then I tortured myself about what type of dress you'd wear. Would you put on something sexy, thinking I was coming tonight? Or would you be wearing it for Oliver since you're technically here with him and not me? The punishment of both those options was acute and I knew I had to come and see either way."

"And?" I prompt when he falls silent for a beat, my heart racing around my chest, desperate to keep up with the butterflies that are swarming in my stomach.

"It's lovely. Everything I thought it would be and more."

I laugh, and he joins in. I'm so grateful for the lift. The tension was eating me alive. I could hardly look at him without coming on the spot. No foreplay required. It would be a first in the history of womankind.

"Don't laugh yet, I'm hardly done with you." *Oh fuck.* "After I decided upon coming, I thought about whether it would make a difference if I moved to a different clinic to avoid you? I came up with no. Would it help if I never saw you again? I came up with I'd always wonder about you and regret not seeing you again. In two weeks, Carolina, you've managed to get under my skin. I think I'm the same way for you, because I catch the way you look at me when you don't think I notice."

"What are you saying, Jonah?" My heart is pounding faster now, my stomach is coiled low and tight. He's over there and I'm over here, and yet, it doesn't feel like that. It doesn't matter, because I feel him everywhere. It's like he's touching me with his words, and hell, it's so damn good.

He pushes off the wall, taking slow, deliberate steps in my direction. "I'm saying, I can't let you go home alone tonight. Or with Oliver."

Oliver who? "Why not?"

Lord, why does it sound like I just ran around the entire city of Boston. I'm winded and breathy and my cheeks are flaming. My body is on fire and I just need . . .

Him.

Fuck.

I need him. I have never had anything remotely close to this level of heat for anyone else. And now that I feel it, own it, I don't think I can accept anything less. I don't want anything less.

"Because the only person you're going home with tonight is me. You know it. I know it."

I shake my head, and bite on my lip to tamp down the fierce tension. It's consuming. I can hardly breathe through it, let alone continue sexy banter. But he comes with a minefield of heartache. A heartache I am intimately familiar with because I've experienced it, lived it, breathed it, been fucking blown up by it before.

How many times can a woman get hurt before she shuts herself off for good?

"No."

"No?" he parrots, slightly taken aback by my blatant rejection.

It's good for him, I remind myself. I doubt a woman has ever been so stupid as to reject him before.

Another head shake, my teeth sinking so deep into my lip, I'm starting to taste blood. This staying strong stuff when your body is screaming at you to be weak is not easy. "You'll be gone when I wake up."

"Not this time."

My chest is tight. My breasts are heaving. My palms are sweating.

He swallows up the remaining distance between us, and suddenly, I wish someone was here. Someone from work or Oliver or anyone.

But no one is around.

This seemingly crowded bar could care less about peeing apparently. Forever my luck, because Oliver's words from before slam into me with the impact of a Mack truck. *He lost his wife, Halle. A woman he was very much in love with.*

"You'll regret this when we wake up. You like me the night of, when your dick is hard, and your mind is ready, but you run from me the morning after." *And I'm scared how I'll feel when you do. Again.*

Jonah blanches and that's all it takes for me to take a step back, my heart in my feet. He recovers quickly. Too quickly. And the expression he's skewering me with? Christ, I'm already melting into something non-solid. Something so very weightless and soft and sweet and pliant. Something that no longer has a backbone or can stand firm.

"I want to take you home, Carolina. Right now."

I shake my head, blowing out the breath I'm holding and blinking my eyes rapidly to focus better on him.

"I'm dying to fuck you again. Hard. Fast." He reaches out, running his hand through my hair and tugging gently against the roots, forcing my steady gaze to meet his headstrong one. "I want to pin you down and kiss you until you can't remember your name. I want to look into your beautiful eyes and fuck you like you've never been fucked before."

I swallow so hard it's audible, my knees trembling, ready to give out at any moment.

"I don't care about work. I don't care about right or wrong. I only seem to care about, and notice, you." I open my mouth to object, but he quickly cuts me off. "Yes, I'm a mess. Yes, you're a mess. But we want each other. And I can't think of any other way to stop it. Maybe two wrongs finally make a right." He pauses here, searching my eyes, his filled with a feral heat, but maybe some vulnerability, too? "Say yes, Halle. Say yes to me. To tonight and tomorrow and next week and however long we allow this madness to consume us. Say yes."

Chapter Fifteen

Jonah

I'M STUCK in that moment where you know everything that's coming out of your mouth is wrong, but you can't help yourself, because it's like you're outside your body looking in. Yeah, that moment. The one you're afraid you might regret. But either way, I'll have regrets. Either for doing this or not doing this. It's a no-win.

But that appears to be my life when it comes to this woman.

I want her.

I crave her in a way I'm not completely comfortable with, nor do I understand.

But what's worse? She wants me in return.

And *that's* what drives me wild. Makes me rock-hard and ultimately buggered. I think about her. I fantasize about her. I daydream about her. I obsess about her. And now, I'm desperate to get her into my bed.

She's eyeing me hard. Like her trust for the male gender resides in the bottom of her feet. Like I turned her on, but she still wants to slap me for my naughty words and tempting offer. I've jumbled her up, so I suppose that makes us even.

Even though I had come to all of those startling conclusions this evening, I was still holding off, wondering if I was wrong. Wondering if I was being hasty and allowing my dick to run the show for me.

So, I came and sat at the bar and tried not to notice her.

Clearly, that didn't work out so well for me, because I allowed my overwhelming jealousy—over one dance, might I add—to force me to corner her into a hallway and lay my cards on the table. To explicitly explain how I want to fuck her. To promise her that I won't disappear after I have my wicked, wanton way with her.

But I didn't lie to her.

I don't care about right or wrong or work or anything else. Halle and I are a mutual mess. But the future? That's the one promise I can't make. Then again, that wasn't something she was too interested in exploring, either.

"What happens when Oliver no longer cares, Jonah? What happens when he takes home the nurse he's grinding against?"

"I won't notice. I'll have already taken you home."

"And tomorrow?" she challenges, tilting her head and meeting me word for word. Promise for promise.

She doesn't believe me. And who can blame her? I left her that morning before she even woke. I tell her I don't date or sleep with my staff only to beg her for a fling after one drink, one wrong dance and a sad story in my office.

And if life were that simple and easy, I wouldn't be back here. But it's not. Because as I said before, I can't stop thinking about her.

I. Cannot. Stop. Thinking. About. Her.

Time seems to hold no bearing on that. No domain. Time could give a toss. Maybe people really do walk into each other's lives at the right moment. Maybe there is a purpose and a meaning to the universe. To life and death. Or maybe it's all one big game of chance.

But Halle doesn't feel like chance. She's not a game I won. And she won't be something I lose. Mostly because I will not own her. There will be no possession. No love and absolutely no forever.

I crowd her with a purpose I can no longer ignore. With a purpose my body is already aware of even if my brain is five minutes behind. "Tomorrow morning is Saturday and neither of us have work."

"You don't sleep with people you work with," she reminds me, trying to stay firm when her demeanor has already slipped into compliance.

She's right. I know she's right and she knows she's right. So where is all of my vigor from earlier? My hard and fast rules that I never, ever break?

"I don't care," I say more to myself than to her. I do not care. It's only been one week of working with her, but that one week was enough to push me over the edge. "You're worth breaking the rules for, Halle." I cup her jaw, much the way I did earlier today, though this one has far more meaning. Far more heat.

"You will, Jonah. When you remember that you love someone else, you'll care."

I pause. Her words stun me, and I freeze, staring into her baby blues. I love Madeline. That hasn't changed. That will never change. My body, my heart, still aches for my wife. My best friend. I still miss everything about her.

"Do you need love?" I ask her. "Is that what you're after? I thought you didn't want a relationship right now? That you were just getting out of something awful and you weren't ready to jump back into anything serious."

Halle breathes in. Then breathes out. She dips her head to the floor and steps forward into me, her heat pressing against me.

"I'm not looking for anything serious right now. It's the only reason I'm still standing here. But I might eventually." Another deep breath. "I want love, Jonah." Her gaze finds mine. "I won't lie about the things I'm looking for just because I think you're hot and want you to want me. I'm too old for that shit. I want love in my life. I've had men who've told me they love me, but I can't speak to whether or not I've ever fully had love before. If we're just hooking up, well, I can do that. For *now*," she adds, and it's a warning I don't miss. "But when I'm ready to move on or you're ready to move on, that's it. No looking back. No regrets. I need honesty and openness and no bullshit. Because as I said, I'm going to want more eventually, and if you're not the guy for that, then fine. I'm cool with that."

"As long as you know before this turns into more?"

"Exactly." She smiles at me like I'm finally getting it. Like we've reached some sort of mutual understanding.

Have we? I don't know.

I hate everything she's saying. I hate the implication of a commitment when my head is still wrapped around someone else. I hate the implication of her walking away. I hate that she's so cavalier that I'm not the guy for more. Buggered seems to just about sum it up.

But where can we possibly go? We're terminally mismatched. So actually, her mindset on things seems to be just right.

Honesty. She wants openness and honesty.

I can give her that.

I stare into her eyes and brush my thumb across her lower lip. I've already broken so many rules with her. So, so many rules. "I want to break more rules with you, Carolina."

She shakes her head. "They need to be shattered, Jonah. Breaking them isn't good enough."

My mouth crashes against hers. Halle steps back against the force of my mouth, of my body. I don't care, I just wrap a hand around her waist and pull her firmly into me. She moans at the contact and my tongue takes full advantage, entering her mouth and tasting her.

Our tongues dance, our lips meld and sway. It's hot and sweet and spicy. And my body sighs out in relief. Like it's been waiting two goddamn weeks for a repeat of this kiss. For a repeat of this moment. And it's everything I remember, but nowhere near where we need it to be.

"Never enough," I say against her and I wonder where the words stem from. Just how true they are.

"It's going to have to be. Because I will not fall in love with you, Jonah Hughes."

I grin against her. It's a dare. It's a promise. It's a bloody challenge.

I stay silent. I have nothing for that.

She's in no place to agree to my terms and I'm in no place to accept them. I'm all bravado tonight. All lust and passion and desire. She's my ultimate temptation. But I won't lie to her. I may be a lot of things, but a liar is not one of them.

"Come home with me."

She nods against me, her forehead rising to mine as she draws back to catch her breath. "Yes. I'll come home with you."

I step back, take her hand, and stare into her eyes. "It's going to be more than just tonight."

"I know."

"I have old condoms at my place, so we don't have to stop this time."

She smiles, the light finally returning to her eyes. "*Old condoms?*"

I nod. "They're the best sort."

She laughs and squeezes my hand. "Lucky for you, I'm on the pill and have recently been tested for STDs."

"Sexy. Did all that come out well?"

"No. I'm like the Typhoid Mary of Boston."

I pull her into me and kiss her. She laughs against me, bouncing on her toes.

"You're wasting time. My carriage turns back into a pumpkin Sunday at midnight."

"Don't worry, Cinderella, I know the magic spell to keep us at the ball way past bedtime. There is no expiration date in this land of fairy tales."

She eyes me again, knowing that neither of us is the stuff of magic or fantasy. I pull her hand and lead her out of the pub. I don't spare a glance in Oliver's direction and I don't care if she does or if he notices what I'm up to.

For once, I don't care who sees.

I've lived so much of my life under everyone else's law. Under a litany of expectations. And I was fine with that. It was never something I thought about pushing against. Until now.

Now, I'm ready to put myself first.

Ironically, it was something Madeline was always encouraging me to do.

I tug Halle onto the sidewalk, holding her hand tight. She stares at it, as if she's wondering what all this means. But right now, there are no explanations. I feel like I'm on the clock. Like I only have a finite amount of time with her. I don't plan on squandering a second of it. I press her into the bricks of the building and kiss her, much the way I did that first night. She giggles into my mouth.

"Déjà vu."

"Except this time, no one is leaving after. I don't plan on letting you out of my place."

"I have to go home at some point, Jonah."

I shake my head, my nose rubbing against hers as I do. "Not happening. At least not until you have to. Until reality takes over and our lives catch up with us."

Her eyes instantly darken, and she blows out a breath, covering me in its warm sweetness. "Not tonight, okay? I don't want to think about anything serious tonight."

"I've got you, Carolina. And until the Uber gets here, I plan on kissing you until you're so worked up, you're begging me to finger fuck you in the back of the car."

"Hmmm," she hums against me. "If there weren't freaking video cameras in Ubers, I absolutely would. But knowing our luck, we'll end up on YouTube or some obscure internet site."

I laugh into her, pressing my body deeper against hers, but I'm quickly interrupted by the honking horn of our Uber. I take her hand again and lead her over, opening the door and helping her in. She smiles up at me, light and easy and when I sit beside her, instead of kissing me, she rests her head on my shoulder, her hand clasping mine. Like lovers do.

It might be better than the kissing.

I had women in my life before Madeline. Some of them lasted

135

longer than others, but none of them hit me on the same level as Halle. None of them made me feel a tenth of the passion and heat and jealousy and rage that Halle gives me. Madeline was different. She was my wife, and I refuse to compare her to anyone else.

But Halle is a woman I've never encountered before, and I plan on worshipping at her altar until she forces me to stop.

Ten minutes later, I'm spinning her into my apartment, twirling her around and around as she giggles into the dark air, her head thrown back, hair flying wildly around, a breathtaking smile spread across her lips.

"Have I ever told you about my history as a ballerina?" she asks and I shake my head no and she catches the gesture as she twirls. "I was the prima ballerina for my town, and every year we put on our own makeshift version of The Nutcracker. I was Clara, of course." She curtsies, holding out her white dress and I return her curtsy with a bow. "So, the night of the first performance, I was all excited, right?"

I draw her into me, and her chin rests against my chest as she gazes up into me, her expression alight with the wonderment of memories past. I hold her steady, my arms around her lower back as we sway to no music in the middle of my great room.

"I was wearing the nightgown that Clara wears and I had my pink ballet slippers on. I was dancing and then suddenly, I felt like I was going to puke. I assumed it was nerves and powered through it until it became too much for me to handle. I started puking back-stage while the Sugar Plum Fairies were dancing. It was humiliating."

"Why? Surely, you weren't the first person to throw up during a performance."

She grins at me, sinking her teeth into her bottom lip, her light eyes practically glowing against the street pollution filtering through my windows. "You could hear my retching all the way in the back row. Even over the orchestra."

I chuckle, cupping her face in my hand. "So, you decided to become a nurse practitioner instead of a ballerina?"

"My father was the mechanic for our town and my mother was

a waitress in the diner. Ballet lessons are expensive, and I felt bad asking for them, so I told them I didn't really like dancing. After the vomiting incident, they believed me."

I lean down and kiss her. Softly. Gently. "Did you love it? Dancing, I mean."

"Not enough to have my parents stretch thinner than they already were."

"Was?"

She furrows her brow.

"You said was. Are your parents retired?"

Her lovely smile slips into a heart-wrenching frown. "No. They're dead. Car accident on Christmas almost three years ago."

I kiss her. Just a sweet peck. I understand death. So does she, it seems, and our hidden pain is yet another thing we have in common. "I'm sorry."

"Yeah. Sorta ruined Christmas for me." She blinks away her sadness and forces a smile. "What was your family like?"

"I grew up in a very wealthy family. We had a large flat in London and a country estate, which my mother still owns and maintains, though she hasn't been there in over a decade. My father loved it there, and she doesn't have the heart to sell it. But when he died, she couldn't handle staying in rainy old England, so she moved my sister and I back here. My mother was born and raised in Weston, a product of private schools and trust funds. She's a rampant philanthropist and sits on the board of at least a dozen charities. She met my father during a college semester abroad and didn't return until he died. I have a younger sister who I don't see all that often."

And my dead wife's family that I love like they're my own blood.

Halle's hand comes up, her fingers running through the side of my hair to the back. She cups my head. Just holding me, playing softly with the ends of my hair in her fingertips. I've known this woman for two weeks and this has become one of the most intimate moments of my life, with a woman who isn't my wife.

"My parents were so proud of me when I graduated college. They were front and center in that auditorium at graduation, cheering me on. I was the first of our family to do that. They died six months before I got my doctorate as a nurse practitioner. I skipped my graduation for that. I couldn't face it without them there."

"My mother and sister showed up at Madeline's funeral, but only because it was expected of them. They stayed a total of thirty minutes. Just long enough to watch me cover her with dirt and roses. They knew her as long as I did, claimed to love her just as much. But when I needed them, they weren't there for me."

I get a kiss for that. A long, passionate one. One that says she meets my heartache with her own. I have no idea why I just opened up to her that way. I never do that. With anyone. But it felt natural. Especially given we just shared some equally heavy material.

"Does it get easier? You lost your dad when you were young."

"Not really. It just changes. It becomes more about the things you wish they weren't missing in your life. But it also becomes about the good memories you have of them. When I think of my father, I no longer think of the day he died or the days following it."

She nods like she gets it. "I'm not there yet. But hearing that gives me hope."

My fingers trace the lines of her face, my eyes following the motion. "You're beautiful."

She smiles up at me. "Then you should kiss me." My fingers glide through her hair, my mouth claiming hers. I swallow her moans and press myself against her warm, soft body. She hums in response. "Harder," she breathes.

Harder? I can do harder. I can fuck her into next week.

I lift her up and her long, smooth legs wrap around me. Our mouths never break momentum as I carry her across the great room, past the kitchen, down the hallway past a few more doors and into my bedroom, all the way at the back. The lights are out, but the curtains are drawn back, and the lights of the city shine through, illuminating a path for me to see by.

"Open or closed?"

"Can anyone see in?"

I shake my head as I set her down, enjoying the hell out of the way her fiery hair splays out across my white duvet. The way her white dress gets absorbed into the monochrome she's surrounded by, highlighting the lines of her exposed skin.

"Open then. The view is perfect."

I rub my finger across my lower lip, taking her in. "I couldn't agree more." I step toward her, towering over her supine form. Tonight, there is no holding back. "Are you ready for this, Halle?"

Chapter Sixteen

Halle

"ARE YOU READY FOR THIS, HALLE?" he asks, and the first thought in my mind is no. And that has nothing to do with the physical state of my arousal, because if he caught a glimpse of my panties right now, he'd know I'm more than ready.

But the word *this* feels like he's asking about more than sex.

Or maybe I'm just reading too much into this because Jonah is still standing tall and gorgeous over me, slowly unbuttoning his dark shirt that I like too much to rip off him.

I told him I could handle just hooking up. I told him I could handle a temporary situation as long we're open and honest about what we really are to each other. I told him I could do this, because the simple truth is, I want it too much to dig deeper into the validity of my truth.

I'm not a hookup girl.

I'm not a one-night stand girl. I think I already proved that.

But that's all Jonah wants.

A monogamous hookup. And after all this bullshit with Matt, all the calls he's sending my way, I'm not all that interested in a relationship, either. Jonah feels different though. Jonah is someone I could like. Okay, that's lie one. Jonah is someone I *already* like.

And that's what worries me most. I like Jonah. He's funny and smart and sexy-as-sin, and listens to me when I talk, and fucks with reckless abandon. Like it's a sport he's out to perfect.

He might be close already.

So, is he going to turn into yet another tragedy in the Halle Whitcomb library of losers and horrible relationships?

Possibly.

Probably.

Can I handle that eventuality? Maybe. That's the best I've got. But is maybe enough of an answer to say no to the *temporary* he's offering me? I don't think so. So, I'm going with this.

I'm going with, "Yes, I'm ready." Even if I'm only sixty-eight percent sure I am. That's better than half, right?

He watches me closely, staring deeply into my eyes. I stare back, letting him see it all. If he stops this, well, then it is what it is. I can't tell if his baggage is worse than mine, so I'm going to leave this in his very capable hands.

His shirt falls to the floor, no cufflinks to remove this time. "Take off your dress."

I comply instantly, sitting up and pulling the delicate fabric over my head. He takes it from my hands. Unlike the neglect he showed his own apparel, Jonah carries my dress over to a chair in the far corner and lays it over the back, ensuring a wrinkle will not be found when I put it back on later.

"I like that you're not wearing a bra."

I also like it, because his heated eyes are feasting on my breasts like they're a rare delicacy he's about to ravage. I take him in, my eyes unable to stop as they glide across his shoulders, loving the hell out of the way his corded muscles move as he undoes the button on his jeans. He doesn't take them off, just leaves the button open and I continue my perusal.

"Like what you see, Carolina?"

I grin. "Most definitely, Jonah." I give a half-smile. "I need a nickname for you. Jonah feels so very formal. You can't even shorten it."

"Master?"

A clipped laugh flies out of my throat and I shake my head no. "God?"

"Nope. Try again."

He slides onto the bed, his bent knee between my parted thighs as he hovers over me, our faces only inches apart. "I like it when you call me Jonah. I like it when you cry it out as you're coming, and I like it when you say it softly, like it's a secret. And I like it when you're angry and practically shout it at me."

"Jonah," I say, biting my lip to hide my amused grin.

He laughs, dipping his head to run his tongue up the column of my neck. "You got it, Carolina. That's bloody perfect. Just like you."

His lips meet mine once more and then his mouth takes over, kissing my lips and sucking on my tongue like it counts. Like I'm the only thing in the world and everything else in our universe is superfluous. My tits receive the same level of worship. Jonah cups my left breast, squeezing it firmly until I moan loudly. His mouth covers my right nipple, licking and flicking and sucking and biting until it's diamond hard, so deliciously, painfully sensitive.

"Ah, yes," I cry out, running my hands back through his hair and holding him right there. *God, yes, right there.* "Don't stop."

"Baby, I don't think I ever could." He squeezes me, lifting my nipple up so he can devour more of me.

I'm lost. Succumbing exquisitely to this beautiful sensation. But at the same time, this is not where I really need him. I need him farther south.

He knows it. This sexy, irresistible man knows exactly what I crave because even though his hands and mouth are loving the hell out of my tits, he slips away from them with a wicked smirk.

Warm, hot lips glide down my stomach, kissing a wet path lower . . . lower. So nearly there as he takes his time building up this sweet, blissful torture.

I can't stop moving, writhing.

"Tell me what you need." His tongue peeks out, swiping at the top of my panties. Goddamn tease.

"More."

"You need more than just more. Tell me what you want me to do to you, Halle."

I close my eyes and arch my back, desperate to show him, but he pushes my hips down with his large, strong hand. He's gonna make me say it. Beg for it. And I'm too wound up to care.

Digging my elbows into the mattress, I prop myself up, staring down at him with an unapologetic devil in my eyes. "I need you to go down on me, Jonah. I need you to lick my pussy and make me come."

He growls out something I can't understand. It's feral and primal and I think I just reached a new level with this. Shit. I'm a fireball. Like those cinnamon ones you suck on and your lips turn red and your mouth goes up in heat. That's me. Except instead of just my mouth, my body is in flames. So hot.

"So hot."

He grins against me.

"Yes, you are. Especially here."

He slides the crotch of my panties to the side and then his mouth is finally there, eating me, licking inside me, sucking my clit between his lips like it's his last meal and he's on death row and shit just got real.

"I could do this forever. I can't get enough of the way you taste." His tongue fucks my channel, thrusting in and out of me, his thumb coming up and rubbing my clit in rough circles, dragging me closer and closer. The pleasure of it unlike anything else.

"Mmmmm. Then don't stop. Please."

"Beg me, baby. I love it when you beg."

Baby. He's calling me baby and I don't think I care enough to stop him. I might even like the cheesy endearment, even if it sounds oddly placed with his hint of an accent and strong, dominant ways.

"More," I demand, his lips taking over where his thumb just was, while two fingers slide into me, curving to find my perfect, hidden spot. My pussy is so wet, the sound of him finger fucking me so lewd.

My thighs start to tremble, my stomach quivering as he devours me, sucking and eating me out so hard it's nearly too much. My orgasm hits me hard. Slamming into me and crashing through my body without mercy.

"Oh. My. God. Yes. Yes. *Yes!*" I scream.

It's so obscenely loud, I actually hear it echo off the tall ceilings. My legs clamp around his head as my body twists and contorts. I grab onto his hair. Jesus, is this good. Like so unbelievably I-can-never-get-enough good.

Jonah draws back slowly as the last of my aftershocks wrack through me. He grins, his lips slick with my arousal. Wow, who knew that would be so hot? I think he gets where my mind is at because his lips smash into mine, his tongue forcing entrance, forcing me to taste myself on him.

"Now you can remove your panties."

I do. I slide my thong down my legs and let the lace drop to the hardwood floor.

"Spread your legs for me, Halle."

Was he like this last time? So in control? I can't remember, but I'm absolutely loving it now. Jonah stares at my pussy, my most intimate part. Instead of being embarrassed or wanting to cover myself up, I spread my legs further. I want him to see all of me.

This sexy, godlike man wants me. The sensation surges up through me like a geyser. Never before have I felt this beautiful. I feel like I could fly. That's how high he makes me.

"Do you like what you see?" I ask, echoing his words from earlier.

He grins, his dark, sex-filled eyes finally finding mine. "You're a goddess. A siren. You're it, Halle."

Out of all of the things he just said, calling me *it* makes me smile and flutter in a way that can only be trouble. Jonah rolls on one of his old condoms. I don't even care if it breaks. I trust him. I'm clean and still on the goddamn pill because I haven't been able to schedule my IUD appointment.

I gasp as he pushes into me, thrusting to the hilt. My back arches and my mind goes wild, color swirling behind my eyes. "Yes," I pant.

He pulls out, shifting my feet up until they're above my head, and then he slides in again, each thrust stroking a different sensation out of me. He fucks me like this. Slow and with deep, diving plunges.

Green eyes are locked on mine, sweat clinging to his temples as he works to control every movement. Every push and pull.

"Good?"

"So good," I pant. "I need it harder."

In one swift movement, Jonah spins me around, hoisting my ass up in the air, and slams back into me. "Harder you say?"

That's when he fucks me deep. Kneading my ass, he pounds his cock into me. Over and over and over. The comforter balls up in my fists as I hold on, meeting him thrust for pounding thrust. It's like the perfect symphony of sex. Like the ultimate concerto that only two aligned souls can create.

My eyes close, my body lost in the sensation of it all. His deep, rough grunts. My moans. The feel of his hard body against me, in me.

His hand reaches around, strumming my clit as he continues to take what he wants from me. Giving me everything in return. The feel of his fingers rubbing me, his cock fucking me, throws me over the edge.

My face falls into the blanket, my ass higher in the air as I come on a muffled cry, stars shooting behind my eyes. He comes with me, a primal growl piercing the air, his hand on my hip bruising as he empties inside of me.

I collapse down, Jonah along with me before he rolls, taking my body with him until I'm on top of him from behind, my back to his chest. We're both breathing impossibly hard, panting for our lives.

His hand cups my breast, just sort of holding me there, his other hand trickling along my hip bone.

"Jesus, you're incredible," he mutters.

"I know," I reply, a smile on my lips that explodes into laughter when he does.

"You think we can beat our record from last time?"

"I'm sure as hell willing to try."

His cock is already hardening beneath me, making my breath hitch.

"Round two?"

"Round two," I agree, just as he rips the condom off, puts on a new one, and sinks inside me again.

I have no idea how many times we do this particular dance. I lose count. His hands never leave me. His mouth is always on my skin. His words perpetually infuse my mind.

All I know is that when the sun starts to crest above the horizon and the air warms up, I fall asleep in his arms just as Boston starts to wake. With my heart full, my mind empty, and my body sated.

This time, when I wake, hours later and perfectly sore, I'm not alone. He's still here. I can't stop my smile. I. Can't. Stop. My. Smile.

Oh no. It hits me. I'm at his place so of course he's still here. Crap. Maybe I shouldn't have stayed so long? Jonah's nose runs along the column of my neck, his legs intertwined with mine, his hand on my breast as he feels my heart beat. "Will you spend the day and night with me?"

I hate that I just sagged in relief. I close my eyes against the intrusive early afternoon sun. "What did you have in mind?"

"The Public Gardens."

I open my eyes, not even caring if it's bright as hell in here since we never closed the curtains. "You really have a thing for that park."

"There are these benches in there. They're the perfect place to eat"—he leans over and checks his alarm clock on his nightstand—"a late lunch. Since we skipped breakfast, maybe we'll do that?"

"I like bacon on my egg and cheese sandwiches."

He gives me a crooked grin, hovering over me, green eyes to blue. "No gravy, Carolina?"

"Oh, do I get a southern Benedict?"

"A what?" he laughs. "That sounds oddly dirty."

I also laugh and shake my head. "No gravy then. Just a standard bacon, egg, and cheese. And coffee. Lots and lots of coffee."

"Sweet and creamy. Just like you."

Jonah kisses the side of my face. My lips. My eyes. My cheeks. My nipples. My stomach. Then he gets out of bed, walking across his bedroom completely naked as he opens drawers and puts on clothes. The sun shines through his large floor-to-ceiling windows, bathing him in a glow of light. For a second, I think about how easily I could get used to this. To him. To this feeling.

"You all right, love?" he asks as he turns around and catches me watching him. Again, I wish he weren't so damn observant.

"Yes. I'm perfect."

"I already know that. But I'm asking if you're all right." He stares at me after pulling on his green shirt. It matches his eyes making them stand out further. He resembles a god, and I'm naked under his sheets that are tucked under my chin.

"I'm scared of getting used to this," I admit because we promised honesty, and since it was my stipulation, I refuse to go back on it now.

Jonah walks over to me, his eyes never wavering before he drops to his knees and takes my face in his hands. "Me too. I'm scared out of my mind. But in a good way, I think. Last night was the most fun I can remember having in ages." He smirks. "Other than the last time I was with you." Now his eyes search mine, raw and vulnerable. "Do you think we should stop?"

I shake my head. If we stop now, I might die.

"Me either. So, how about that breakfast in the park?"

"I'm in." Because I am.

Even if this might kill me later.

Chapter Seventeen

Halle

IT RUSHES OVER me like a wave. Like an irregular heartbeat. It crawls up the hairs on the back of my neck and has my stomach doing a funny, swooshy thing. It's the feeling of being watched. Every woman in the world is intimately acquainted with it. It's something that, unfortunately, we instinctively learn. And right now, it's consuming me.

I try not to be obvious as I surreptitiously glance around. I do my best not to make my uneasiness known. But I can't shake it and as Jonah and I walk down the street, my eyes pick up their pace, searching every face we pass.

Then I spot someone across the street.

He's casually leaning back against the side of a building, his foot propped up behind him. And yeah, he's looking at me. But is he just *looking*, or is he *watching*?

And why does he seem familiar?

Matt automatically springs into my head. Maybe he's friends with Matt? Maybe that's why he looks familiar? The guy smirks at me. I don't return it. Dark hair, tall, average features. That's all I've got of him. He's too far away for much else. No eye color. No discernible stubble or scars or tattoos. Just a face in the distance— fifty yards out easily.

I'm held captive as he pushes off the building, our eyes still locked. I'm granted a curt nod of acknowledgement. Then he walks off.

That's it.

Moment over.

All that within a matter of five seconds.

Did I imagine it? Was he actually looking at me or someone near me? My breath picks up as I force rationalization after rationalization through my mind in rapid succession. It was nothing. He might not have even been looking at me. He was just checking me out. Maybe he was checking Jonah out. It was nothing. That last one cycles on repeat.

I brush it off. There isn't much else to do. Because like I said, it was nothing.

And it's over.

Glancing behind us, I can't find the guy anywhere. It's a relief, I tell myself. Just my imagination running wild. So I focus on the task, on the man, at hand.

Jonah and I started out with the intention of going to the Public Gardens, a beautiful park in the heart of the city. He's holding my hand and though I should pull mine away, we've already done this so many times that, at this point, it's futile. We meander around his neighborhood in search of breakfast—or late brunch anyway—to take on our picnic. All too quickly I become distracted by the fancy market up ahead on Newbury.

"Do you wanna get some things for dinner?" I ask. "I can cook us something."

We've been quietly chatting about nothing all that important, but for some reason, this question, this innocuous, nothing of a question makes him stop dead in the middle of the sidewalk with the city rushing around us.

His impenetrable gaze is intense. "What would you make?"

I swallow hard. Something in the tone of his voice and the expression on his face makes me nervous. "What do you like? I'm a pretty versatile chef. I eat anything except crawfish."

A half smirk breaks through his hesitant quiet. *Thank God.* "Crawfish?"

I nod, giving an exaggerated shudder. "A trip to New Orleans in my senior year of college. I won't get into the dramatics of it, but let's just say I now have a strong aversion to the small crawly things."

"No small crawly things. Got it."

He starts to walk again, my hand still clasped in his, but something is wrong. I stop us again, and Jonah pivots to face me, a puzzled V between his brows.

Without hesitation, I reach up with my free hand and cup his cheek. "You can talk about her, you know."

He blinks, shuddering back an inch. "How did you know it was about her?"

I shrug a shoulder, running the tips of my fingers through his blond stubble. "Just a guess. I'm generally good at reading people. It's the nurse in me. But I'm serious. I get needing to talk about the people we lost who are important to us. Probably better than most."

He shakes his head slightly, like he can't believe I'm offering to listen to him talk about another woman. A woman he admittedly loves. Still. "You don't think that's off-putting or awkward?"

I think on that for a moment. I'd like to believe Jonah is my friend in addition to being my temporary lover. I'd like to imagine that whenever this physical connection comes to an end, our friendship won't—even if I'm a bit overly optimistic or naïve on that. I know he misses Madeline. I don't know how many real people he has in his life to talk to. I get the impression Jonah doesn't open up much, but he opened up to me about his family last night and I'd like him to do it again.

"No, Jonah, I don't think it's off-putting or awkward. You can talk to me about her. I want to hear whatever you want to tell me. I care about you. You're my friend and my . . . whatever we are. So yeah, tell me about your life," I say, feeling a bit surer about it. "About Madeline."

He leans down and kisses me, gliding his hands through my hair before holding me tight. So tight that everything else around us—the city, the noise, the people shuffling—all fade away into nothing.

It's just him and me and this kiss. This kiss that is so very different from any before it.

There is no tongue. No lust, per se. But the passion behind his force, the emotion behind every swipe of his lips, makes my knees weak. And when he's done with what could easily be described as the simplest and best kiss of my life, his forehead drops to mine and his eyes close.

Jonah blows out a breath, the warmth cascading over my flushed face. "The last time I went to this market was three months before Madeline died. I was trying to get her to eat, which she wasn't doing much of at the time. I got her stoned." He pauses, and I feel his smirk against me even though I cannot see it. "I thought her having the munchies might seal the deal. As we approached the market, I asked her, 'Do you want to get something for supper? I can cook for us.'"

I suck in a rush of air. That's almost exactly what I just asked him. I lean up and press my lips to his nose.

"It stunned me, is all. I'm fine. I get through most moments. I know she's gone, and I know I can't call her or see her, and I know this is my reality. But occasionally, it hits me hard and knocks the wind from me."

Hell. What do I say to that? My heart absolutely breaks for him. Shreds into a million tears. *Oh, Jonah.* I do the only thing I can think to do. I wrap my arms around his neck and hug him, much the way he did when I lost my shit in his office over the whole Matt insanity.

I don't say I'm sorry. I don't offer bullshit platitudes. In my experience, they mean very little. I just hold him against me and do my best to infuse him with my . . . love?

No. Not love. With my heart?

Shit, that doesn't work, either. I'm going to give him my empathy, which doesn't feel like enough, but those other two things are not on the table to be doled out.

"Do you want fish and chips to remind you of Merry ole England, or do you want Mexican? Because I'm sorta kinda craving the latter."

His eyes find mine and he gazes at me, a small smile on his lips. "Where did you come from, Halle Whitcomb?"

"I'm assuming that's rhetorical, since you already know I'm a southern lady. But I'm going to flip the tables and say that you got lucky one night at a bar."

"I sure did."

My heart does a small skip thing in my chest as butterflies spring to life in my belly. I have to change the subject quickly before I get sucked into his vortex and am lost forever. "So which is it? Fish and chips or Mexican?"

"I rarely ate fish and chips when I lived in London. My mum——" He winks at me "——had a private chef. I can assure you that none of our food was fried."

"Did you go to elementary school there?" I assume he did since he moved to the US when he was fourteen.

"Yes, but we call it primary school. Let's just say that moving to the States was an adjustment. Especially with my posh accent."

"Is that what that is?" I scrunch my nose and he grins, big and wide. "It sounds more like a quirky combination of English and Boston."

He laughs, wrapping his arms around me. "Do you know how to make guacamole?"

I snort, rolling my eyes as he takes my hand and we head into the market. "Of course I do, though it's more of a Southwestern thing. Now, if you wanted biscuits, I'm your woman. And I make the best southern fried catfish you'll ever have."

"Is that a fact?"

I nod.

"Considering I've never had catfish, or been south of New Jersey, I don't think I'm in a place to disagree with you."

I shake my head at that. God, how can you live in this country and never experience the South or the West, or the Northwest? Or any other part of it, for that matter? I may not have grown up with a lot of money, but my parents took me on long driving trips to various places around the US for two weeks every summer.

"Then tonight I'm going to make you Mexican food. And if this sexy business between us continues, then I'm going to make you all kinds of American dishes. Ones you can't get delivered."

"Then I guess I'm going to be eating a lot of American foods."

I grin. Shit, I need to stop this grinning thing. "I guess so."

He leans over and kisses my lips chastely. We start to meander through the market, getting avocados, peppers, tomatoes and onions, and even homemade tortillas and other things that will be amazing with dinner. Just as we're stepping outside into bright sunshine, my phone rings. Fishing through my purse, I find it and groan out a loud sigh.

"What? What's wrong?"

"Nothing." I stare down at my still ringing phone, debating if I should answer. "It's one of those numbers."

"Answer it," Jonah demands, and as I do, I reluctantly peek up. Our eyes lock, his dark and foreboding. No one speaks. But I hear them breathing heavily into the phone. A chill runs along my skin. "Who is it?" I shake my head miserably. "Give me the phone, Halle. This madness ends now."

The call disconnects just as Jonah reaches for my phone and I yank it away, stuffing it back into my purse. "I'm sure it was just a wrong number."

"If your twat of an ex calls you again, I want to answer."

"Twat? I cunt hear you."

He rolls his eyes at me for behaving like a petulant child, but I can't do this with him. I can't think about what these phone calls are. Why they only happen when I'm out.

What that man watching me earlier was all about.

"I hate that he's scaring you like this. It makes me violent. I'd kill the coward if I could."

"No violence, Jonah. Let's just let this go, okay?" I squeeze his hand.

He puffs out an aggravated breath but does what I ask.

A few minutes later, Jonah pulls me into a liquor store and buys tequila, giving me a big fat wink while he does it. I have a feeling I'm going to get drunk tonight and have crazy sex again. That's all great. In fact, I'm a bit amped-up about it. But then what?

"What happens Monday morning?"

Jonah swings our interlaced hands between us, looking this way and that at the passing landscape and pedestrians. Suddenly, he turns and plants a big, sweet kiss on my cheek. "Well, we go to work. And at work, we see patients and try to help them with whatever brought them into the clinic."

I roll my eyes and elbow him in the side. He lets out a loud *oomph*, grabbing onto his flank and feigning pain. Please. I'm not fooled.

"How's this then? We go back to your place before we cook dinner together. We pack you a bag of clothes for tonight at least. At work, we keep a separate, professional presence. Does that work for you?"

"I'm not staying with you Sunday night. I don't want to go into work together."

"I'm not asking you to, Carolina. I'm asking you to stay with me tonight. Especially if you're a good cook." He grins at me and squeezes my hand. Then he does the sweetest thing and kisses the tip of my nose.

And I might be falling. That's what this feeling is, right? This giddy bubble that's so ready to burst. I know it's too soon. I know it's ridiculous and probably multiple-orgasm-induced emotions, but—

"At work we pretend, act like we're nothing more than two people who work together."

He gives me a sidelong glance. Possibly judging my expression. Likely hoping it was a statement and not a question. It was. I won't be that girl. The one stupid enough to fall for her boss. I mean, I already am, but I won't be her at work.

"I think that's the only way."

"And we're exclusive?" I don't do cheaters.

He glares at me, like he's hurt I even had to ask. He doesn't dignify my question with a response.

We head back to his apartment and after we put everything away the flank steak is marinating, Jonah strips me and goes down on me until I come on his face. Twice. He's got a real penchant for doing that, no way I'm going to argue with that. But when we're lying in bed, before we get up to run to my apartment, he holds me close. So close that our chests are pressed together, and our heartbeats are one.

"We're exclusive, Carolina," he says into the quiet. "We're a thing. A fling. A special arrangement. An affair. We're everything on the naughty spectrum. I can't classify it. I can't label it. I can't give you certainty or promises. But I can tell you that I like you. I care about you. I enjoy having you around, especially when you're naked like you are now. I want you to stay with me tonight. Longer really, since your psychopath ex is looming out there."

I ignore that last statement. "If we can keep this separate from work, I think everything will be perfect between us."

"We can absolutely keep this separate from work."

I mean, how hard can that be, right?

I know I should argue that I need to stay home alone tonight. That I need separation in order to keep my head on straight and my mind clear of him. I know I should tell him I'm staying in my apartment and that our sexy time needs to be limited. But I don't do that.

Because the moment we step out of Jonah's building, I feel it. *Again*. That damn sensation. My stomach sinks with panic-saturated dread. I glance around. I look every which way, even trying to see past the wall of the park across the street.

But I don't see anyone watching me.

Not that guy. Not anyone.

But I feel them lurking. Like the coming of a virus in my body. Or maybe I'm just losing my goddamn mind.

Why would anyone be following me? It makes no sense.

But still. I can't shake the feeling and as I glance up at Jonah, I wish he weren't with me. I wish he weren't holding my hand like we're a goddamn couple when we really aren't. And I really wish he hadn't told me he liked me. I wish he had kicked me to the curb and sent me home in an Uber I had to pay for.

"I think I should stay at home alone tonight."

Jonah doesn't respond. He's pretending like he didn't hear me as we walk over to the corner to grab the Uber we ordered.

"This is going to end ugly. We work together, and I have an ex who I think has turned a little crazy."

Again, he doesn't reply. He just holds my hand as he helps me inside the car. I actually try to shut the door on him, practically slamming it into his leg. It might even knock him off balance. *Oops.* He recovers quickly enough so it's not like I hurt him physically or anything. I mean, he's not limping.

"What the bloody hell?" he growls, rubbing the spot on his leg that the car just hit. "You've turned into some mad woman who slams car doors on men? What's going on, Carolina? You're not normally this nuts. Clumsy, sure, but not nuts. I thought we worked all of our stuff out. I thought we were on the same page about what we are and about work."

I sigh, sinking my head back against the dirty as hell seat that is probably riddled with lice. I think I might have to shower at home before we do whatever else we're planning on doing tonight.

"I'm just out of sorts. I'm sorry. I really am. I don't know what's come over me. It's the calls and the testifying and the really good sex with the hot guy who happens to be my boss. My mind is playing tricks on me. That's all this is." Jonah stares at me and I can't tell if his expression is a good one or a bad one. "Are you all right?"

"I'll live. What do you mean your mind is playing tricks on you?"

"It's nothing. Really. I think I'm just hungry and tired. We'll grab an overnight bag for me and then we'll make dinner at your place. I'll shower. I'll become my normal, less batty self. Promise."

Jonah leans in and kisses me softly. His eyes open and lock on mine. "So, we're okay, then?"

"We're okay. Sorry about your leg."

He grins against me. "You'll make it up to me."

I smile back at him and turn to search out the window. I can't help it. That feeling. It's still there.

Chapter Eighteen

Halle

THE FRONT of my building looks like a crime scene. Or maybe a bomb threat that was proven false, but the police felt the need to hang out a bit. There are three squad cars lined up right in front of my building with their lights flashing, and a couple of cops are hanging around outside, shooting the shit as they talk to a couple of random people.

"You think someone died?" I ask absently.

I feel Jonah directly behind me, staring out the window over my shoulder. "Don't know, but there's no ambulance, so I doubt it. They don't look in a hurry. Maybe just a false alarm."

I shrug, relieved that he's mirroring my thoughts. We step out the car and head for the building. One of the cops turns to look at me. "Do you live here?"

I nod and he gives me a returning nod that says I'm free to go inside.

I unlock the doors and head into the lobby. It's empty. Not a soul alive, or dead, to be found.

"Weird," I mumble under my breath as we step onto the elevator. That weird turns into, "What the hell," when we step off the elevator to find the hall lined with two more officers, all glaring at us.

It's like something out of a movie.

Jonah takes my hand, giving me a firm squeeze, but we stay silent. Partially because we're too stunned to talk. Partially because there are ears and eyes on us and no matter how innocent you are, when the police are staring you down, you feel guilty.

Then we turn the corner and my world stops.

A startled gasp flies past my lips as my hand comes up to cover my mouth. My eyes instantly water. Jonah's arms find their way around me, but I can't acknowledge him or the officer who is suddenly in my face, trying to obscure my view of my apartment.

My apartment that has the door open and more officers inside.

What could have happened?

"Halle." Jonah's forceful tone breaks through my rattled haze and I blink twice, clearing the tears that haven't shed from my eyes. "Did you hear what he said, love?"

I shake my head and look at the officer. He's about my height with a bald head and a kind smile that I'm in no place to return. "Are you Halle Whitcomb?" he asks.

"Yes. What happened?"

"We've been trying to reach you."

"I left my phone at your place." I glance in Jonah's general direction, but I don't see him. I don't see anything. The calls had been getting to me and I just wanted a break. Stupid.

"I'm sorry, but your apartment has been broken into."

Jesus motherfuck. My heart that was already working overtime takes this moment to stop dead before taking off at a full sprint. My vision sways and I feel like I'm going to pass out. Jonah holds me tighter against him and I'm so grateful that he's with me because otherwise, I'd be on the floor.

Nothing makes you more discomposed, more exposed and vulnerable, than finding out your apartment, the place where you live, and sleep, and shower has been broken into.

"If you'd come in and have a look around, we'd like to know if anything is missing," the officer continues.

I blink again, trying to stare over his shoulder in the direction of my door, but I can't see anything other than his navy-blue uniform.

"Of course," Jonah answers for me as I hear him and the officer talking more, but I can't focus on what they're discussing.

Because all I can think of is Matt.

He did this.

My suspicion only grows when I step into my apartment and gasp again.

"He trashed everything," I whisper, my voice barely above a breath.

"Who, ma'am? Do you know who did this?"

I shrug because I don't know for sure. I mean, it could be random. The calls could be random, too, as well as that eerie sensation of being watched. That guy today and the biker in the park who knocked me down like he was aiming for me.

The biker in the park? Was he the same guy I saw earlier today? I don't know. He might have been. The guy who went for my purse. Everything is jumbled up right now. It could all be random or unconnected. Right?

My couch cushions are strewn all over the living room, some of the stuffing removed from a couple of them. My large chair by the window is flipped on its side. My kitchen cabinets are all open, the contents spilled across the counters and floors, including the flour and sugar, leaving a thick white coating.

Clothes. There are clothes everywhere. From my front closet. From my dressers and bedroom closet. My work desk is knocked over. My laptop is on the ground, half open and more than likely broken.

All around me there are sounds. Police talking. Jonah talking. Questions being asked. They need to stop asking me questions. I have no answers.

I push past all of it, stepping over discarded items, and heading for my bedroom. And when I reach the precipice, I lean against the frame of the door as that seems to be the only thing in this whole fucking apartment that hasn't been trashed.

My mattress is hanging precariously, somewhere between the floor and the bed frame. My pillows look like they've been slashed, the feathers scattered. My blankets and sheets are thrown in every corner of my room. More clothes. Jewelry. Perfume. All of it on the floor. The doors of my dressers hang open and empty.

Before I can make sense of anything, I reach into Jonah's pocket and pull out his phone. He raises a questioning eyebrow, but I don't have time to answer it. Instead, I dial Matt's number. It rings three times and then he is there, on the other end of the line.

"Did you do this?" I ask softly. Suddenly Jonah and an officer in a white dress shirt and dark slacks are standing before me.

"Halle?" Matt questions, as if he's shocked to hear from me.

"Did. You. Do. This? Did you break into my apartment and trash it, Matt? Or pay someone to do?" I scream the last sentence, no longer able to hold back.

"Halle," he says like he's trying to calm me down. Like he's the sane, rational one of the two of us. Maybe he is. Maybe my life really is just a clusterfuck of bad luck and poor timing. "I have no idea what you're talking about. You're scaring me, sweetheart. Your voice. What happened? Are you okay?"

I know Matt. At least I think I do. I mean, I was with the man for two years. So, I feel like I should know him. Know his tones and whether or not he's lying. But I had no idea he was hiding years of criminal activity from me. And right now, I can't tell if he's lying. If he really has no idea what I'm talking about.

"Did you break into my apartment, Matt?" I ask again.

"No," he protests adamantly. "I'm home. In *our* home. I'm out on fucking bail, Halle. I've been giving you the space you asked for. I swear, sweetheart, I have no idea what you're talking about."

Tears fall from my eyes, one after the other. There is no stopping them. Jonah reaches out, snaking his arm around my waist and draws me into his large, warm chest. Sucking in a deep breath, I extract comfort in the smell of his cologne as I close my eyes.

"Are you the one who has been calling me? Was that you?"

"No. Halle, Jesus Christ, all of this is getting out of hand. How can you question that? You know me. We lived together for almost two years. We were engaged. I loved you. Then you suddenly broke up with me and the FBI was arresting me for things I haven't done. And now your apartment is being broken into and you're getting calls? I don't know what's going on, but it's like someone is after us. I swear, I'm not doing anything. I need you. Come home, to our home, and we'll figure all this out. *Together*," he stresses.

I shake my head. Nothing is adding up. Nothing is making sense, and yet . . . "I'm having the police come and speak to you."

"Fine. Whatever you need for me to prove to you that it wasn't me. That I would never do anything to hurt you. I love you, Halle. I miss you. I want you back—"

I disconnect the call and the phone slips from my fingers, clattering against the floor. Is it possible? Could Matt really be innocent? Could the FBI have gotten the wrong man? And could someone be after both of us? Maybe framing Matt? Maybe stalking me? How? Who? Why?

What could they be looking for that would make them tear through my apartment like this?

"It's like looking for zebras instead of horses," I say, sinking further into Jonah.

"How do you mean, love?" he asks softly, his hands running down my hair. There is an expression in medicine where providers should look for horses—more common diseases or illness processes —before looking for zebras—the rare stuff—because nine out of ten times, it's horses we're dealing with and not zebras.

I pull back enough to catch Jonah's eyes. "He said it wasn't him. That he's out on bail and that he's home. That the calls, the breaking in, none of it is him." The man who tried to grab my purse, who was watching me today...

Jonah's eyes darken with concern. They're asking the same thing I am. If not him, then who?

"Miss Whitcomb," the officer interrupts, coming to stand beside me. I slide my head to the side, still wrapped up in Jonah, unwilling to let go. He doesn't seem bothered by it. "I'm Detective Simson. I overheard your conversation. You believe you might have an idea who did this to your apartment?" he asks gently, like he's afraid of pushing me back over the edge. Too late. I'm so far over the edge that I'm flat on the ground.

"My ex-fiancé, Matt Lyons, was arrested about six weeks ago by the FBI for cybercrimes. I broke up with him prior to that and had no knowledge of anything he's accused of. But in the last week or so, I've been receiving strange phone calls. Just someone breathing into the phone. The calls are from random numbers. I assumed it was him"—I half-shrug—"doing something crazy with the phone. I don't know."

"Write down his address and I'll have someone question him."

He hands me a notepad and a pen, and I do just that. I write down Matt's address. My old address. And then I meander around my apartment, but I'm unable to determine if anything specific is missing.

The police ask me two dozen more questions as I search. According to them, a neighbor called the police when they heard crashing inside my apartment. Unfortunately, they didn't witness anyone entering or exiting. And no one is in here hiding. Not that that's all that reassuring. It's not.

Nothing about this is.

The door was not kicked in or even showed signs of a break-in, which means they either knew how to pick a lock like a pro. Or had a key. My stomach churns at that thought, bile climbing up the back of my throat. First thing I'm going to do is change the locks and have an alarm installed.

Not that I want to stay here any time soon.

The police leave Jonah and I to deal with the aftermath, reminding me how I need to come in and fill out a bunch of paperwork. Whatever. I can't even mentally get there. I'm stuck on the mayhem before me.

"What could they have been after?" I whisper, almost to myself.

"Don't know. Do you have anything your ex, or anyone else, might want? Anything you can think of?"

I shake my head as I wrack my brain, but I come up empty.

What could someone like me possibly have? I'm a nurse practitioner. I'm a normal girl suddenly living in a not so normal world.

"I think someone's following me."

Jonah stares at me, his eyes grave and piercing.

"I got the sensation that someone was watching me earlier today and when I looked up, I saw someone. It was just some random guy leaning against a building across the street from us. But . . ." I lick my dry lips. "It felt like he was watching me." Jonah swallows hard. "Then I felt that sensation again tonight when we left your place to come here. I didn't see anyone that time. And I know I'm nuts. I know it probably wasn't anything. Those hang-ups from random numbers could be anyone. But what if they're not?"

I turn away from the destruction that is my apartment and face him, staring into his green eyes. They're so beautiful it almost hurts to look at him.

"If it is Matt behind all this, then I don't want him to see you. He could be walking the scary side of crazy street. I can handle him, but I don't know how dark crazy street gets. And if it's not him . . .," I shake my head. "You shouldn't be mixed up in this. It could be some random psycho or something. We don't know each other all that well and this is just a whatever between us. You should run away now while you can."

Jonah stares at me for so long I start to squirm, desperate to look away. I can't handle his intensity. "So, you wager that if your ex, or someone else, is actually physically stalking you, following you on the street and breaking in to ransack and demolish your apartment, that I'm going to let you do your own thing alone and run off?" He raises his eyebrows at me, his eyes widening.

Dammit. I shift my position, glancing down at the mess on my floor before meeting his eyes once more. "When you put it like that, it sounds bad."

"No, it doesn't sound bad. It sounds preposterous. It sounds impossible. It sounds fucked-up and dangerous."

"Don't yell at me, Jonah!" I stomp my foot like a small child.

"Then don't ask me to do something you know I won't do, Halle! Did you miss the part where I told you I care about you? Do

you honestly believe I'm going to let you stay alone in this deci-
mated apartment without me here to protect you from a man who is
mentally questionable? You're grabbing as many suitcases as you
own. You're going to pack all your work clothes, shoes, makeup,
your pretty dresses that I like on you, whatever you've got, and then
you're coming to stay with me. If you have sexy lingerie, that's
getting packed, too. If not, then you can go without panties. And if
you argue with me, Halle Whitcomb, I swear to God, I will throw
you over my knee and spank your ass red before I pack your stuff up
myself."

I smirk.

"Don't smirk, I'm dead serious."

"I can see that."

Now he's smirking.

"Are you trying to drive me insane?"

"Possibly. I've never been spanked before."

His eyes darken before me, and I'm instantly wet, which is something I did not realize was possible given the situation I find myself
in. I won't even think too deep on the diversionary tactic. I've never
been good at facing this sort of hard reality, why start now?

"I've never spanked anyone before, but for you, I'm going to
make an exception."

I bite my lip and he licks his. "Promise?"

Jonah breaches the space between us, slamming my body into
his, his hot breath fanning against my ear. "Promise. Now pack up,
baby. I can't handle being here another moment. Don't worry about
the mess, I'll take care of everything. You don't have to worry about
any of this."

Jonah's hand finds my ass and mercifully, my mind momentarily
clears of this horror. I can't focus on anything other than his palm
on my ass, while I mentally categorize all the slutty lingerie I own.
That is not sprawled out across my floors. Dammit, I can't handle
this.

"Do we have a deal? You'll stay with me?"

"Yes. But I don't know for how long. I don't think staying with
you indefinitely is a good idea."

"We'll discuss all that later. For now, let's pack you up and get out of here." Jonah doesn't say anything else and I don't follow that up. I start shoving things into suitcases and he helps. But inside, I'm reeling. Over my apartment. Over Matt. Over the possibility of this being some unseen entity. Over staying with Jonah.

I'm scared on so many levels that I hardly know how to make sense of them. Everything feels like it's coming at me all at once and I have no idea how I'm going to make it through any of this.

Chapter Nineteen

Halle

"YOU LIKE HIM," Rina declares, a stern finger pointed in my direction.

I totally do. "I do not," I protest with a derisive snort and a dramatic roll of my eyes.

"You're blushing." That's Aria, and she's right, I am blushing.

"It's hot in here." It's not hot in here. This restaurant is actually on the cool side.

"You're living with him and you like him and you're having naughty, hot sex." Margot shakes her head, clicking her tongue at me like my mama used to. "What are you thinking, Halle?"

I sigh, sagging back into my seat and taking a sip of my mimosa because this morning felt like the morning for some alcohol with my OJ. I hate it when my friends are right. For once, couldn't they just keep their relentless honesty to themselves? Allow me to enjoy the glow I should not be enjoying?

"I'm not living with him. I'm just staying there for a few days until this nonsense with my apartment settles down." And that's when I finish my first mimosa and order another one as our waiter passes. I haven't had anything to eat yet, and I'm already feeling that warm fuzziness that only accompanies champagne. "It's fine. Jonah and I have been talking. We're open and honest. We both understand and appreciate that we're not looking for anything more than what we have going on." I wave my hand at them like I'm shooing away a fly. "Temporary. It's all so temporary."

Aria purses her lips, raising a dubious eyebrow at me. "You've been staying there for over a week." Now it's my turn to purse my lips. "And there is nothing non-relationshipy about the two of you. In fact, everything about you and Jonah screams relationship."

"Relationshipy is not a word."

Aria rolls her eyes at me. "At some point, you are going to have to admit you have real, legit feelings for each other. He watches you like he can't take his eyes off you. His absurdly handsome face lights up whenever you speak. He hangs on your every word and touches you whenever he can. He's falling for you, Halle, and you're falling for him. And Drew totally agrees with me. He was talking about it the whole way home after we left your—I mean *his*"—she smirks knowingly—"place the other night." She finishes that lovely speech with a sip of her non-alcoholic OJ.

"He's in love with another woman." Now I'm getting defensive and I hate that I'm getting defensive. "And what does Drew know? Your boyfriend is one of the least love observant men I know." I get another eye roll for that. I hate that I'm already having to remind myself, and others, that he loves Madeline. Not me. He cares about me, but that's as far as it will ever go.

The truth is, I should have left his place by now. I shouldn't have agreed to go back to his home with my suitcases that first night. But every time I mention it, he shuts me down.

And his reasons are valid.

I mean, sorta. Like he said he's this big, tall guy and can handle himself. If someone dangerous is lurking about, then I'd be putting my friends at risk by having them take me in. That he likes to know I'm safe and if I'm staying with him, then I am. That since we're having so much sex, it only makes sense for me to continue to stay with him. In his room. In his apartment. Indefinitely.

But it couldn't possibly mean anything more than that. Right?

"Oliver told me that Jonah has never dated or openly slept with anyone from work. That he's most definitely never left a bar with a woman when there were work people present at said bar. Oliver *also*," Rina points a stern finger at me to go with her raised eyebrow, "said whenever he speaks to you at work, Jonah looks like he's going to rip his arms off and beat him to death with them."

"I never would have pegged Oliver as a gossip, Rina." I lean back in my seat, my flute in hand as I fold my arms over my chest, trying for attitude and imperviousness. "This is good to know. Did he tell you all this while braiding your hair and painting your toenails?"

"You're being a bitch." That's Aria again, and I nod my head because I know I'm being a bitch.

"I know and I'm sorry. But I don't want to hear all this crap. Just let me enjoy this." My pleading gaze bounces between my friends. "Let me enjoy this," I repeat a bit more adamantly. "I know the score. I'm not some stupid, delusional woman. I'm having fun. A lot of fun. I don't want it to stop. I don't want to overthink it. I don't want to analyze it. I can't go home right now, and I need you ladies to be supportive and understanding. And when it all falls apart and I'm a sniveling mess, I need you to be there for me and not say we told you so."

They exchange looks. The sort of looks that question whether or not they can actually do that and call themselves my friends. I get it, because when you believe your friend is making a mistake that will eventually get them hurt, your instinct is to try and stop it. You want to object, and you want them to listen to your all-knowing wisdom.

But sometimes, people don't want to be warned. We want to do the stupid thing because it feels too good not to. And we need our friends to be supportive, no matter what.

"Fine." Margot sighs. "But our thoughts on the subject have officially been added to the record."

"Officially." I nod, taking a bite of my breakfast. "Lord, I'm starving." I groan at the first bite of food. "I could probably eat a horse, a cow, and all the chickens in the hen house."

"That's what happens when you're busy fucking the farmer all night," Margot supplies around a mouthful of food.

I choke on my omelet. I'm about to throw myself over the back of my chair and give myself the Heimlich maneuver, but somehow, I manage to dislodge the obstruction and swallow it down. "Now, tell us about your apartment and testifying against Matt."

And now I choke on nothing. "Do you remember when we were in nursing school and our biggest worry was not failing, not killing patients during our clinicals, and seeing if we could get random men to buy us drinks we couldn't afford?"

"Are we getting nostalgic now?" Rina asks mid-chew.

I pick up my flute and finish off my drink, holding the empty glass in my hand and staring at the remaining trail of orange pulpy liquid as it slides down to the bottom.

"I'm happy. I'm scared. It terrifies the hell out of me because I can't remember a time when I felt two strong opposing forces simultaneously. I like Jonah way more than I should and I don't know what to think about my ex. Is he a psycho criminal? Is he being framed by some obscure force in the shadows? My apartment was in shambles, y'all."

I stare each of them down in turn, suddenly wishing my empty glass would magically refill like it does in Harry Potter.

"Like, no surface was spared in the making of that disaster. I know I should be freaking out more about it. But I'm not and that scares me more. Jonah had the entire place professionally cleaned and put back together. He had an alarm installed and had the locks changed. He took care of every last detail and not only wouldn't tell me how much it all cost but forbade the companies he used from telling me. I haven't felt this calm with someone before. This taken care of." *This adored*, I don't add aloud. "Not in the years I was with Matt. Not with any of those other losers. And I hate this calm. I resent the fuck out of it, because it's going to disappear. It's fleeting and mocking and cruel. I feel like for the first time in my life, I'm having fun and hell is hanging out on the periphery, like a cat playing with yarn, only in this scenario, my hair is the yarn. Does that make any sense?"

And for the first time in my life, I think I've silenced my friends.

"So, don't let the bitch win," Aria says after a very long contemplative minute. "You're having fun with a seriously hot man who wants you just the way you want him. Maybe even more. Stop waiting for the other shoe to drop. It doesn't have to. You said you're being open with Jonah?"

I nod, picking at my potatoes, my eyes unable to quit the sad state of my plate. This being turned inside out stuff is not for the faint of heart. We're open. We discuss everything. Hell, most days we can't shut up and end up talking for hours. But I also feel as though I'm hiding everything from him.

At least the one crucial, consuming element.

I'm crazy about him and that's just so very wrong. I'm lying to keep him, to keep this going, and that's also so very wrong. But most importantly, I'm breaking my cardinal rule about us. I just never expected to feel like this.

"Then you're good. And as for Matt, I can't think of anyone else it could be. It has to be him, right?" She shrugs helplessly. "He's going to go to prison soon enough. He's never been the aggressive type. This phone call nonsense, the apartment, they're just his way of being petulant. In a rather destructive, prickish way."

I nod again, because I don't have it in me to tell them that I think he's following me or having me followed. They'll tell me I'm overreacting, which is entirely possible. The police called the other morning to tell me that they were not charging Matt with anything extra and that they had no proof he was the one who broke into my apartment.

Also, they have no leads on other suspects. They suggested it was more than likely random. But the phone calls persist. As do the raised hairs on the back of my neck whenever I step out of Jonah's building.

"Nothing wrong with having fun if your eyes are open," Margot encourages. Something about the way she says that makes me feel worse.

"Yes. And if the shit hits the fan, we're here for you. No matter what," Rina adds softly, her eyes sympathetic like she can tell I'm already there.

We finish brunch and step out into the bright summer sunshine, dropping our shades onto our noses to protect our eyes from the blinding rays. That's when I spot him, pulled up across the street in a goddamn Aston Martin convertible. The top is down, and Jonah's blond hair practically glows against the sun. He's wearing wayfarers and a white T-shirt and the way he leans against the open window driver's side door might be the sexiest thing I've ever seen.

"Oh dear God, Halle, if you don't have fun with that man, I will." Margot drools. "In fact, I think I'd take whatever he's offering." *I pretty much have.* "I can't tell which is sexier, the man or the car."

I smack her arm and hear her laugh lightly, but I can't pull my eyes away from the man staring in my direction. "The man," I answer automatically.

"Yes," Rina and Aria say in unison. "Definitely the man," Aria finishes.

"Are you coming, Carolina, or are you going to stand there staring at me?" he calls out. Aria, Rina, and Margot all let out simultaneous simpers. "Morning, ladies. Hope brunch went well."

"Stop flirting with my friends."

His lips spread into a full smile, complete with perfect white teeth and everything. "Then get your beautiful arse over here already."

"Keep your shirt on, I'll be right there," I yell at him across the street and I can hear him chuckle from here. I hug my ladies goodbye and then I run across the street, dodging an oncoming car until I'm on the sidewalk, standing in front of the passenger door. "Did you not think I was capable of getting back to your place on my own?"

Jonah grins up at me. "Get in, baby. I have something I want to do with you."

"Are you kidnapping me for naughty, naked fun?"

"Unfortunately, not. But you'll enjoy what I have in mind. Possibly." He tilts his head and quirks an eyebrow. "Or you'll kill me afterward." I hesitate. "Come on," he cajoles. "Where's your sense of adventure?"

In my feet. Or maybe in my apartment along with the rest of the mess that is my life.

I open the car door and slide onto the buttery soft dark gray leather. This car is nice. Like holy wow nice, and if I had any illusions about Jonah's money before, this car destroys them. "Did you steal this car?"

He smirks at me, leaning over and kissing the spot just below my ear. He smells like sunshine and fresh air and laundry and heaven. "I'm an Englishman by birth, Carolina," is all he says like that explains everything. Maybe it does. His lips press into mine, his tongue sweeping into my mouth, tangling with my own as he deepens the kiss. His hands rake through my hair. After I'm good and worked up and probably panting, he pulls back. "Are you ready?"

"Ready," I echo faintly.

Because I am. I'm ready for the fun. I'm ready for adventure. I'm ready for anything and everything this man has to throw at me.

Anything that will erase Matt and the nightmare that is my life and what is left of my home from my mind. Even temporarily. I'm not going to second-guess any of that. Escapism is real shit and I'm all about it today.

I'm not going to think beyond the moment. Because like I told my girls, I'm happy with this half-baked thing Jonah and I have. Life is short and oftentimes ugly and hard.

I'm learning that the hard way.

That might stop some. The smarter people out there. The ones who learn from their mistakes.

But like I said, my eyes are open. Fling, not a relationship. He's in love with his dead wife. Awesome. Fantastic. Let's do this. Yeah, that's not sarcastic at all. Those thoughts don't bring on a painful ache in my chest that I'd rather not think about. Not at all.

I get a quick kiss on the lips and fall silent as my inner thoughts take over. Then we're off, speeding south toward Plymouth through

Boston traffic, which is surprisingly light for a Sunday in August. We spend the drive listening to music, discussing our preferences, and watching the landscape pass as the warm summer wind whips through our hair. We talk a lot about medicine, which you'd think would be boring, but it's not.

I love telling stories of past cases and so does Jonah. His stories are super interesting, too.

And before I know it, our ride in this incredibly cool car is over and we're parking in a lot I would never imagine leaving a car like this in. Jonah doesn't even blink twice as he grabs a small duffel bag from the tiny trunk and then takes my hand, leading me toward some weird outdoor park thing.

But then I catch the sign and stop dead in my tracks.

"No. No fucking way. I mean it. Absolutely not, Jonah." He's grinning at me. The smug bastard is actually grinning at me. And if I weren't terrified of what I was seeing, I'd punch that smirk. Not hard, because he's adorable, even like this, but enough so that it would hurt a little. "No," I say one more time for emphasis, but I don't think my point is getting across.

Fly Zone. That's what this place is called. And from here, I can see all kinds of things like ropes courses suspended thirty feet off the ground, and tiny ass airplanes that look like they're bound to kill you before you hit cruising altitude, and bungee jumping.

"You can't live in fear of heights forever."

I can't even tear my petrified gaze away from the spectacle of terror in front of me. "See, that's where you're wrong. I can live my entire life on the ground. It's the way gravity and physics intends it to be."

"Just come check it out."

I shake my head back and forth, back and forth, but he clasps my hand and drags me along the dirt and grass until we've entered hell. "Two for bungee jumping," he tells the woman seated comfortably in a chair at ground level behind a counter.

"No. He's lying. It's just one."

"It's two. I can talk her into it. She's the bravest woman I know."
Bastard.

Chapter Twenty

Jonah

"I HATE YOU." Those are the first words out of her mouth after I pay for the tickets. She's scared. Not just scared, terrified out of her bloody mind. She's frozen in terror. Which makes me feel bad. I didn't think she'd be this freaked out. I figured she'd be nervous and talk a mile a minute, since that's what she does when she's nervous, but this near silence is unsettling.

I hate you was the last thing she said to me. Now we're in the restroom. I convinced the lady to let me take her into the single's bathroom to calm her down and help her change. Halle didn't argue, because Halle has gone near catatonic. I brought pink yoga pants and a yellow sports tank because you can't bungee jump in a dress, and that's all Halle wears unless she's at work or exercising.

She steps into the pants almost reflexively and I swallow down a hint of guilt. "We'll go home," I say, because I don't know what else to do. "Baby," I whisper cautiously, like she's some kind of feral animal, praying she'll blink or respond. "I'm sorry. This was a mistake. I'll take you home."

She shakes her head. That's it. Holy hell, I don't know what to do.

I finish helping her dress and then I lock the bag up in one of the lockers they have to rent. I take her hand, leading her over to the ladder we have to climb to reach the platform. She's still silent, almost robotic.

"Love," I try again, squeezing her. "Let's go, all right? I'll have you back home in no time. We can do anything you want. Go see a film, go for a walk, catch the end of the Red Sox game in a pub."

A man comes over to us, all big smiles and exuberance. He helps Halle step into her harness. She lets him. I'm too helpless and stunned by this change of demeanor to do much other than watch.

I put on my own harness and once we're both secure, I try again. "Let's go, Halle. We don't have to do this."

Another head shake and then she starts to climb. Silently.

I follow after her, suddenly wary that she might leave me when all this is done. That she might genuinely hate me for bringing her here and talking her into this. That she might have finally hit her breaking point with me. And that thought . . . wow, it hits me square in the chest. It crushes me on some strange, elemental level.

I don't want Halle to be done with me.

We reach the top of the platform, the heat of the sun over-heating us as it blazes like a fireball over everything it touches. The ocean in the distance fills the air with its salty brine. Sweat slicks my forehead and back. The warm wind is fierce up here, whipping Halle's hair in all directions, making us slightly unsteady on the wide platform.

I reach out for Halle's waist, trying to steady her, but she takes a faster step forward, forcing my hand to drop.

I've really buggered up.

"Halle—"

She shakes her head, again, effectively silencing me.

Now I'm truly panicking, and it has nothing to do with the tremendous height we find ourselves at. I think it's close to one hundred feet off the ground. There is a line of people ahead of us, three waiting their turn. As one of them goes free falling off the block, all arms and legs spread out like a starfish, screaming bloody murder, Halle spins to me, her pale blue eyes wild, her cheeks flushed, her limbs visibly trembling.

I take a step forward, desperate to pull her into me. To comfort her. To beg her to speak to me and promise me that I didn't damage us beyond repair. *I don't want to lose you, Halle.*

"I can't believe I'm here."

I practically sag in relief when she speaks.

"Jonah, I can't believe I'm up here." She looks to her left, down at the drop and her color fades, her pallor going completely ashen. "How did I let you do this? How did I let this happen? I can't jump off this. I'll die, right? I mean, people die bungee jumping, and here I am. I hate heights. Like seriously hate them. I might look all brave on the outside and put on a good show, but I'm a total scaredy-cat. And you can't jump with me, Jonah." She shakes her head. "I need to jump with you and you can't and I—" She swallows. "I'm scared." Her hands grip the thin cotton of my sweat-dampened T-shirt. "I'm scared of so much in my life right now. It's overwhelming me. Matt and the calls and my apartment and the possibility of some crazy person stalking me and testifying and you. I'm crazy about you and . . . and I need you to jump with me."

She finds my eyes and pierces me with an intensity I have no name for. It sucks all the available oxygen from my lungs. I'm dying just from looking at her right now.

She's not talking about the actual jump. At least, that's not how this feels. She just admitted she's crazy about me. And I'm . . . I blink, cupping her beautiful face and searching her eyes. They don't look like they're in touch with reality.

What am I?

"Oh my God," Halle cries out, interrupting my thoughts, which are plummeting faster than the woman who just jumped. "Look at her."

Halle begins to sag, her knees giving out. I reach out instinctively, wrapping her up in my arms. I can feel her heart pounding through her clothes and the rush of the wind.

"I've got you. I'm so sorry, Halle. So desperately sorry."

I hold her against me, kissing her face, her head, apologizing for so many, many things. What have I done? I'm constantly cocking things up. This woman trusts me, and I did this to her. Halle needs a man who can take care of her. Someone to love her without limits.

Not someone to push her past her breaking point.

Madeline is dead because of me. Because I brushed off her symptoms. Fatigue. Lower back pain. Bloating. Weight loss. Heartburn. Painful intercourse. Menstrual irregularities. All separately vague and slightly unimpressive unless you put them together.

But I told her it was nothing.

Me, a doctor. She told me her symptoms and I chalked them up to a million different things. Horses, not zebras, as Halle put it. She asked if she should get checked out and I suggested waiting a bit to see if they improved on their own.

There is no excuse for that. No rewinding the clock. I made a mistake and it cost me my wife. It cost Madeline her life.

She was diagnosed with stage three ovarian cancer. Ovarian cancer in a woman in her mid-twenties with no family history or a genetic link. My wife is dead and it's all my fault because I brushed off her symptoms. And if all of that wasn't fucked-up enough, I wasn't there when she had a stroke and slipped into a coma. I was away at a motherfucking conference where I was a bloody speaker. She was gone, and I never got to say goodbye.

Never got to tell her how sorry I am.

How much I love her one last time.

So Halle, this incredible, gorgeous, crazy woman who fills me with warmth and sunshine, deserves a better man. A man who is not me. I don't deserve anything—certainly not her. I gave my heart, my soul, my life away years ago. Madeline still holds them. And there is no possible way I could ever love someone else when I'm still in love with my wife. Right?

Halle shakes her head against me, like she's answering my unspoken question, telling my wrangled mind it's wrong.

"Next," the man running the show calls out.

Halle freezes in my arms.

"Let's climb down."

"No," she pushes out, drawing back and meeting my eyes. "We're here. I think it's time I face my fears. I'm tired of always letting the bitch win. I'm so tired of being weak and scared to live my life. Of tolerating the status quo because risk is a daunting prospect."

She sucks in a deep breath, her composure slowly returning. Her head swivels over her shoulder and then back to me, her teeth worrying her bottom lip to the point I'm shocked she's not drawing blood.

"I want to do this. Only, will you go first?"

I lean in and kiss her. I kiss her in a way I don't think I've ever kissed a woman before. Not even Madeline. It's carnal. Sloppy. All teeth smashing and tongues fighting and breaths mingling.

"I'll go first, Carolina," I breathe against her, my heart feeling like it's trying to leap out of my chest and jump into hers. And I shouldn't do that to her. So, I let her go and walk over to the man. I allow him to hook me to the thick cable that will prevent me from tumbling to my death.

Then I jump.

Just. Like. That.

I jump, because I suddenly feel claustrophobic on the top of the open platform a hundred feet in the air. My stomach launches into my throat. A thrill courses through my chest as adrenaline pumps mercilessly in my veins. My eyes are open, wide, and I watch as the trees, vacant fields and even the ocean in the distance blur at the speed of my descent.

But instead of exhilaration, I feel despair.

Instead of full, I feel empty.

I swing back and forth like a pendulum on the bungee until I land on a thick, blue, cushion-like mat. There is a woman here to greet me and I answer her questions reflexively when she asks if I enjoyed it. Once I step out of the harness and climb down from the mat, I march off toward the trees, needing an extra moment and distance before I'm able to turn back and watch Halle.

She's standing on the precipice of the jump platform, her copper hair glowing like red fire in the sun. My heart lurches in my chest at the sight of her. I'm in trouble. I know I need to pull back before this gets out of hand, but at that thought, my chest constricts like a vice.

Too late for that, my brain chastises.

Halle doesn't say anything before she jumps. She closes her eyes, and I see her chest rise as she heaves in a deep breath. Then she leaps like a diver, the picture of pure uncomplicated grace. She screams, but it's the sort of scream that comes out in a thrill of excitement, and I find myself smiling at my brave girl. She whips back once, and when she flies forward once more, she locks eyes with me, her magnificent smile spreading from ear to ear.

When she's on the ground and out of her harness, she flies over to me, catapulting herself up into my arms with an elated squeal. I catch her, holding her against me. She's breathing fast, but her smile is unstoppable.

"Oh my God, Jonah. Like holy shit, wow. That was incredible. The best thing ever. Thank you," she whispers now. "Thank you so much for bringing me here. I feel like if I can get through that, I can get through anything. I was so afraid, and I did it anyway. Thank you."

Her lips crash into mine and I kiss her back with equal ardor, desperate to hold onto this, onto her, for as long as I can before I have to stop.

If I can get through that, I can get through anything.

You're my biggest fear. Losing you. Keeping you. Both in equal measures.

"You're a goddess," I tell her instead. "I'm in awe of you."

"That was one of the best experiences of my life!"

"So, you're okay? We're okay?" I add, needing to hear it.

She tilts her head to the side, and at this angle, our eyes are lined up. "Yes. Everything is fantastic. This is exactly what I needed."

I release her, letting her body slide down mine until she is standing, and our hands are intertwined. I wonder if she has any recollection of what she said to me up on that platform or if it was all panic-induced. We walk away from the field to retrieve our bag and change our clothes, and then we make our way to the parking lot. For the first time all afternoon, my mind is silent.

"You know, when you first pulled up in that car, I thought you were James Bond."

I smile at that, leaning over to kiss the side of her face. I can't stop putting my lips all over this woman. "Doctor by day. MI-6 by night. What should your Bond girl name be then?"

"Pussy Galore is already taken."

A slow easy smile peels across my face. "So is Honey Rider, and your tits are far nicer than hers were."

That truth earns me another kiss. "Maybe Beaver Bandit, though I never loved the term beaver when referring to my beautiful lady area."

Now I laugh as I tuck her into my chest so I can hold her closer before I open the door for her and help her slide in. "I think you should stick to medicine instead of naming Bond girls."

AN HOUR LATER, I have Halle back home, sitting on the counter in my kitchen, her legs wrapped around my waist, her arms draped over my shoulders, her head thrown back in ecstasy. She's stunning. So absolutely beautiful when she gets close to the edge the way she is now. My cock pounds into her, her pussy squeezing me like a vice.

I wonder if I'll ever get enough of this feeling.

My forehead drops to hers as I piston in and out, in and out. It's so good that I close my eyes briefly. When I reopen them, she's right there, staring directly at me.

Our eyes lock, and in this most intimate of connections, something happens. Something so unexpected it makes me gasp and groan, the pleasure of her body bringing me to a new height. The last of the ice surrounding my heart cracks. More like melts in this heat. I'm open. I'm raw. I'm fucking exposed and I can't tell if I like the sensation of it or not.

Because Halle may tell me she's crazy about me. She may say that she wants me to jump with her. But Halle does not want a relationship. She does not want serious. She does not want love.

At least not from me.

That's what she said that night in the bar in the dark. *But when*

181

I'm ready to move on or you're ready to move on, that's it. No looking back. No regrets. I need honesty and openness and no bullshit. Because as I said, I'm going to want more eventually, and if you're not the guy for that, then fine. I'm cool with that.

Those were her exact words. And now that I'm staring into her eyes as I bury myself inside of her, I don't know what to do. So, I close my eyes and kiss her and ignore this feeling. This uneasiness. Halle comes on a loud cry, her voice hoarse from the bungee jumping and now her orgasm. I pull out of her, dispose of the condom and hold her against me.

"I think my friends were jealous," she says after a silent beat, her tone light and playful. I meet her eyes, frowning. "I think they were wishing they had been dared to hit on you instead of me."

"Wouldn't have mattered," I admit flatly. It's true. I kiss her again, holding her warm, naked body closer, because suddenly, any space between us feels like too much space. "Your friends are pretty, Halle, and I'm sure they're wonderful, but they don't hold a candle to you. I would have spotted you across the bar and wanted you. Not them." I look into her gorgeous blue eyes. "You're all I seem to want."

I watch her, studying her reaction. I don't get much of one. Nor experience the freedom I had hoped for by admitting that to her. Instead, my admission feels impetuous and foreboding. It feels like it's begging to destroy the perfection we have going.

After all, flings are meant to end. Flings are not meant to be serious.

And flings should never, ever turn into love.

Chapter Twenty-One

Halle

I THINK I might be in love. It's two-thirty in the morning on Wednesday night. Well, I guess it's technically Thursday morning, but who keeps track of that shit? Jonah is fast asleep, breathing softly next to me, his long eyelashes fluttering like he's in the middle of a dream. His arm is draped casually over my stomach, but this is not how we fell asleep.

No. I fell asleep on my side of the bed and he fell asleep on his, but at some point, he made his way over to me and wrapped me up in his arms. He's done this every night since I moved in nearly three weeks ago. We deliberately fall asleep separately, like this will somehow help us maintain our emotional boundaries, and then by morning, he's surrounding me like a cocoon.

Like he can't be close enough. Like any distance between us is too much distance.

Mostly, I don't think about it. Force myself not to.

But for the last couple of days, it's been nagging at me and tonight I stayed awake to see if I was the one who couldn't get close enough to him.

But no. It's all him.

When I realized that, I smiled. Not victoriously, though. It was the type of joyful smile that spreads traitorously across your face when you're falling hard for someone and they do something that makes you feel like you're not alone in the falling. It's the sort of smile that accompanies a swarm of butterflies in your stomach, some fizzy tightening in your chest and an elated thrill flowing through your veins.

And that's why I'm still awake. Why I can't fall back to sleep. Because Jonah is not falling for me the way I'm falling for him. That point seriously hit home when he was on the phone with his sister-in-law Erica. I've never been around when they've talked. At least not in the same room. He always manages to escape my general vicinity when she calls.

But tonight was different.

He spoke to her for over half an hour while I feigned reading a book. I've been dating, screwing, living with—whatever you want to call it at this point—Jonah for three weeks now. I've known him for well over a month—technically five weeks since our first hookup, but who's keeping track?

And he did not mention my name to Erica.

Not even in passing.

Not even as part of a "what have you been up to lately" answer. What does that tell me? It tells me I'm not important. It tells me I am absolutely no more than a passing fling he'll quickly be done with.

It tells me I'm fucking stupid.

Because I feel lost in the way he looks at me, like I'm a spark and he's air and together we ignite. I feel high when he holds me against him, kisses me and tells me the most perfect things in the history of modern language. I feel giddy when he holds my hand every time we go anywhere together. I feel buoyant when he takes me to dinner or to the movies or on walks. I feel coveted when we talk for hours upon hours and tell each other everything.

But worse than all that, I feel complete. I feel complete in his arms while he sleeps. I feel complete when I wake up in the morning and sip coffee with him over breakfast. I feel fucking complete when we laugh together over a home-cooked dinner and a glass of wine. I feel motherfucking complete when he sighs my name in his sleep the way he just did now.

My eyes close, and a tear escapes. *What are you doing, Halle?*

It's a good question. One I don't really have the answer to. Because I know this is only going to end one way. I know I'm setting myself up for the fall of my life. I know there is a very real chance I will not recover this time. But I can't make myself walk away. I can't stop myself from falling.

I. Can't. Stop. Myself.

As if all this wasn't bad enough, Matt called the other day, begging me to come over so we could talk in person. I haven't done that yet. I'm terrified to see him. Especially knowing I'm set to testify next week. Nothing with him is adding up. The calls haven't stopped. And I was right about them only happening when I'm out, either alone or with Jonah or even with the girls. It doesn't matter.

But I'm starting to believe that Matt isn't the one calling me. That he is most definitely not the one who broke into my apartment and trashed it. That he's not the one raising the hairs on the back of my neck every time I step outdoors.

But if not him, then who?

My apartment is cleaned up—thanks to Jonah. My insurance came through with a big check to cover all the damaged items. I could go home. I could leave Jonah's place, change my number, and ignore the feeling of being watched. I could get on with my life.

All this madness will eventually stop. It has to, right?

I'll move out and get on with my life without Jonah. And God, does that hurt. I clamp my lips together as a sob threatens to escape. Jonah shifts, like he can sense my inner turmoil, pulling me in closer and absently kissing the side of my head. I whimper before I can stop it. Mercifully, he doesn't wake up.

That is until my phone buzzes on the nightstand.

My heart instantly jacks up, because no one calls at this hour unless someone is dead or dying, right? Jonah groans, pulling away and slapping at his nightstand like it's his phone making this traitorous sound. I fly over and pick up my phone, gasping out when I see Aria's name.

"Aria?" I whisper-shout as I glance over at Jonah, who is blinking at me in the darkness, concern etched on his handsome features. He reaches out for me, taking my free hand and squeezing it.

"I'm sorry," she half-sobs, her voice thick with tears. "No one is dead, and I realize I probably scared the shit out of you, but I need someone to talk to and I can't wait and I'm sorry," she spits out at the speed of light. I blow out a breath and turn back to Jonah. I hope he can't see the remnants of my own tears.

"It's fine. Give me a second." I pull the phone away from my ear. "Go back to sleep," I tell Jonah, squeezing his hand back. "It's just Aria. Everything is fine."

"You sure? I can get up." I shake my head at him and he tugs on my hand, bringing me in for a kiss. "I'm here if you or your friend need me. Just wake me up." He kisses me again, humming against my lips. "Mmmm. Hurry back, I'm missing you already."

He releases me, rolls over onto his side and for a long second, I just stare at his back, before I remember a crying Aria on the phone in the middle of the night.

I creep out of the bedroom, closing the door behind me as gently as possible. It's dark as hell out here and I stumble into a bookcase, stubbing my toe in the process. "Shit," I hiss, hopping up and down a few times as I shake off the sting.

I make my way down the hall, all the way across the apartment to the far bedroom. This apartment has three bedrooms. *Three.* It doesn't take a Nobel Laureate to divine he and Madeline had plans to start a family.

What am I doing here?

"Aria?"

"Yeah. I'm so sorry, Halle."

I sit down on a plush white fabric chair in the corner of the bedroom, staring out the window at the buildings across the street.

"It's fine. Believe it or not, I was already awake. What's going on?"

"Drew broke up with me tonight."

My hand flies up to my mouth as my eyes bulge. "What?" I cry, utterly stupefied. "Why?"

She sniffles a few times before clearing her throat. "We've been fighting a lot lately. About my career. His career. The amount of time we're together. Or not. And tonight, he told me he was done. That it was getting to be too hard and I wasn't giving him enough. He left. Just like that. He packed his things and was gone. Like it was all so simple for him."

"Oh, Aria." I have no idea what to say. I sink back into the chair, my heart aching for my friend. She and Drew were together for a year and a half. They were living together, and he is, *was*, crazy about her. They always came across as the perfect couple. The one everyone was jealous of. "I'm coming over," I tell her.

"No." She sniffles some more. "It's the middle of the night, Halle. I just . . . God, I feel so angry and hurt. What the fuck, right? I mean, what the absolute fuck? Who does that? Who gives up on someone so easily? Someone you claim to love? I just don't get it. It's like the things that brought us together tore us apart, and instead of being supportive of my career, of my life, he resented it. Honestly, I think that dinner with you and Jonah a couple weeks back was the final nail in our coffin."

"What?" I gasp, completely taken aback.

"He kept commenting on the way you and Jonah are with each other. How in sync you seem to be already and how Jonah already cares so much about you. Love. He used the word love to describe you two and maybe it got him thinking about how he and I weren't really like that so much anymore."

I blink, flying out of the chair and moving over to the window, because for some reason, I can no longer sit.

I snort derisively. "Well, Drew is a moron then. Not only for leaving you, because women do not get better than you in this world, but for reading Jonah and me so wrongly. He doesn't love me, Aria. He doesn't even care enough about me to mention my existence to his sister-in-law. I'm living with him but I'm nothing more than the fling he asked me to be. The fling I *agreed* to be. I can't even blame him for it. I was completely on board. Said yes to the whole package."

Aria sighs, long and heavy, like she's exhausted and broken and men suck. "We're all fools then, aren't we? Do you remember when I told you about that guy in high school? Wes? My first love?"

"Yeah?"

"I couldn't help thinking about him tonight. Drew broke up with me and it was like I was comparing the two the way I always have. Tonight it was which one hurt me more. I haven't seen Wes in ten years, the bastard broke my heart, and yet, I always compare every guy to him. Still wondering about him. We're stupid when it comes to love."

I nod at that, but I can't find it in me to verbally agree. Mostly because I'm starting to take on some of Aria's heartbreak for my own.

"I should leave, right?" I ask. "End this now while I can still walk away with my heart intact?"

Aria lets out an incredulous scoff. "Is it intact?"

I don't reply, because it's not. It's chipping and cracking, like an ancient vase.

"Art is like love, Halle. Rarely black and white and always open for interpretation. Everyone will have an opinion. One person's beautiful is another's ugly. I guess there is a symmetry to that," she muses, before her tone turns serious once more. "Do you love him?"

I swallow hard, pressing the fingertips of my free hand to the pane of glass and sucking in a shaky breath. "Yes," I admit.

My insides quake at the implications of that admission. Those chips and cracks becoming more pronounced.

"Have you told him? Asked if he's still all about the fling?"

I shake my head even though she can't see it. I've been too afraid to mention anything. All that bullshit about openness and honesty is just that, bullshit. Or at least it is on my side of things. I am a deluxe-sized hypocrite. I need to brave up though. I need to face this or I'll really be ruined when it ends.

"If you feel as if you need to end it, then that's what you should do. But you need to talk to him first, Halle. Don't walk away from something without knowing the whole situation."

"I work with him, Aria. He's my goddamn boss. What happens to my job, my life, if I open up and tell him all this, only for him to reject me? Dead wife that he still loves, remember?"

She puffs out some air. "If you don't want to go home, you can come here. I have plenty of space and we can lament and mourn our failed love lives over ice cream and champagne. Sounds fantastic, right?"

I laugh lightly at that. It sorta does sound fantastic, in a masochistic way. "I might take you up on that." My smile slips. "Are you okay? Do you want me to come over tonight? I can, you know. No hour is too late or too early. We can talk more about it. Have a serious bitch fest about Drew."

"No." She half snickers. "I'm going to go paint some shit. Who knows, maybe all this heartbreak will turn into something brilliant and I'll sell it for millions of dollars."

"I have no doubt you will. I'll call you tomorrow, but if you change your mind about me coming . . ." I leave the sentence hanging.

"I'll let you know. I love you. Thank you for listening and distracting me with your crazy love life. And for not telling me that I'm better off without him. No one likes to hear that after they've invested so much in someone."

I chuckle, shaking my head. "Always happy to be of service. And I love you, too."

I move to disconnect the call, but the sound of my name stops me. "You need to talk to Jonah. Drew wasn't the only one to see what you two refuse to acknowledge."

She disconnects the call and I'm left alone in the dark. I have no idea how long I stand here, thinking, contemplating, hating on everything, but dawn groggily makes its way toward the sky when I feel strong, warm arms wrap themselves around my waist. Jonah's morning scruff brushes my cheek as he drops his chin to my shoulder.

"You never came back to bed."

"Drew broke up with Aria."

Jonah blows out a heavy breath. "I'm sorry to hear that. I rather liked them together. She all right?"

"She's strong and independent. Heartbroken. She'll be fine, though it may take a bit to get there."

"And how about you, baby? You're standing here, staring out the window like the world is weighing on you. You didn't even hear me call your name."

I open my mouth to speak and then close it. I don't know what I want to say to him. I work with him, *for* him, and that complicates this. I love my new job. I don't want to leave it, and I don't want it to become strained or awkward because I was stupid enough to screw and fall for the boss.

I'm the girl who is always getting hurt.

The one left behind.

The one cheated on.

The one who perpetually picks the wrong guy to fall for.

Yeah. That's me. And guess what? I did it again.

"Just thinking." Because I have a lot to figure out before I talk to him.

Only this time, I'm absolutely, positively positive I've never loved a man the way I love Jonah Hughes. And I'm absolutely, positively positive he does not feel the same way about me.

Chapter Twenty-Two

Jonah

MONDAY MORNINGS ARE for lying in bed, eating pussy for breakfast, followed by long, hot showers filled with up-against-the-tile sex. Monday mornings are for huge doses of coffee, percolated in a machine you forgot you owned, scarfing down homemade granola bars, while watching the crazy, sexy redhead you invited to stay in your home get dressed in boring scrubs.

"If you don't hurry up, I'm going to spank your arse again, Whitcomb."

She moves slower. The goddamn temptress, the destructor of my resolve, is moving slower. I did spank her the other night. In my defense, she asked me to.

Who was I to say no?

I spanked her until my hand print was pink on her porcelain ass. It was fantastic and so far beyond anything I've ever dreamed of doing with a woman before. I think she liked it. She might have loved it, if her wet pussy was any indication.

This woman. This adorable, beguiling woman. She has me going places I never imagined I'd go.

I don't know if it's Madeline's death, and the harrowing realization that comes with losing someone you love, but with Halle, I'm free. I can be my most unbridled self. The one I had systematically shut off. First after Madeline was diagnosed and then to a much greater extent after she died.

But Halle accepts it. Hell, I think she likes it. Likes *me*.

"I'm going as fast as I can," she snaps in feigned annoyance.

Liar. She's a bloody liar.

Because she's pulling on her white lace panties with aching deliberateness. She's attaching her matching bra behind her back as if it's the challenge of her life. Then the scrubs go on and her hair goes up and once she's finally, mercifully, dressed, I kiss her because it's probably going to be the last chance I get until tonight. Tonight.

Just the thought of being with Halle again tonight fills me with charged anticipation.

I like having her here. I like her cooking in my kitchen and covering my bathroom counter with her products. I like her clothes in my washing machine and her body sleeping next to mine.

It's a problem. It had me up half the night after our day of bungee jumping in the sun. I don't know what's happening between us. Her staying here doesn't feel casual. It doesn't feel like a fling. It feels real and it feels serious and that decimates my insides with guilt. Both for Halle and Madeline. I don't think the word conflicted quite sums me up.

I just don't know how to make it stop.

I was so close to telling Erica about her yesterday. I've been reluctant to do so. Not because of Halle, personally, but because of our situation. How do you tell your dead wife's younger sister that you have a woman living in your home? That you're engaged in a quasi-relationship with someone you don't believe is interested in anything more than sex?

It's impossible.

But it also feels like a lie by not telling her. So, I asked her to meet me this morning at the clinic. I plan on taking her out for a quick coffee and telling her. Face-to-face. The way it should be done.

But it still leaves me feeling hollow.

It's like I'm two different people stuck in some strange alternate version of my life, and I have no idea how to marry the two together. How to fuse them into one. It's moments like this I really wish Madeline were alive. I'd give anything to have my friend to talk to. That was always the bond that held us together, our friendship. Our friendship that turned into love. She'd likely have smacked me upside the head and told me to stop being so dramatic.

Just thinking about that makes me grin and hurt at the same time.

"For tonight," I start, grasping her hand tighter as I guide her around some slow pedestrians. "I was thinking we'd go out for dinner. Somewhere nice."

I want to talk to her about us. About what we actually are versus the rubbish we continue to try and tell each other we are. I'm ready, I think, to try for more. If there were ever anyone I would be ready with, it's Halle.

"Oh," she remarks, surprised as she glances up at me. "I . . . um."

I glance down at her. It's something in her tone.

"That sounds nice, but I was thinking maybe I should go back and stay in my apartment. Or even stay with Aria for a bit since she's going through her breakup."

I'm so taken aback that I stop dead in my tracks on the sidewalk in the midst of morning rush hour. Halle doesn't realize until the hand holding mine is tugged back and she stops, spinning around to face me. She pulls her sunglasses up, perching them on top of her head as she takes me in.

"Is that what you want? To move out?"

She blinks at me, desperate to unearth something in my tone, but she won't. It's completely impassive. If she's going to rip out my insides and end this, I'd rather her not be so aware of it.

She shrugs. I hate that shrug.

"Well, I . . . It's been three weeks of living with you, Jonah. Any longer and things are going to start—" Her eyes meet mine. "Living with you doesn't feel casual anymore and isn't that what we're trying to keep here? Casual?" I can't tell if she's genuinely asking or if her question is rhetorical.

"That's partly what I wanted to speak to you about tonight over dinner."

She nods. That's it. I have no idea what that nod means.

"Okay. We can talk about it then. We should talk about it. But I'm thinking it's not such a big deal if I go back home. The police said it wasn't Matt who broke into my place. I'm sure it was random, like they said, and you had an alarm installed."

I shake my head again. I didn't tell her this, but after her apartment was broken into and she told me she thought she was being followed, I rang an old mate of mine from university. He runs security for Hollywood stars and he gave me a number of a PI he's worked with.

He's been following Halle's piece of shit ex around for two weeks now and either her ex is quite clever, very crafty, or Halle was wrong about Matt calling and stalking, because my PI says the guy isn't doing anything. Not purchasing burner phones and not tailing her.

He says Matt spends a lot of time inside his apartment. I have some pictures to prove that. But still, someone broke into her apartment. Someone has been calling her and breathing heavily into the phone and she feels like she's being followed. Something is not right.

We start to walk again, my arm over her shoulder as I tuck her into my side. I need her closer than just holding her hand. It suddenly feels like she's slipping away.

"I like having you stay with me. It means I can see you, talk to you, touch you, kiss you and fuck you whenever I want."

Her gaze drops back to the sidewalk. Bugger, I'm doing this all wrong. "I think I need to go home."

That tone holds a litany of unspoken things in it. Her tone also

194

suggests she's afraid of getting hurt. But hurting Halle is the last thing I ever want to do.

Doesn't she know that?

Here's the problem with Halle. She's perfect for me. In every single way imaginable. She's smart. Feisty. She tests my limits emotionally while letting me test hers physically. I'm half in love with her and that's simply because I refuse to fall into absolutes. Why, you might ask?

Because I still love another woman. And I can't shake that. Madeline was my life. My wife. And I'm trying. I am. But it's not easy. Some moments it feels like the guilt and grief are going to swallow me whole. And I don't know where Halle fits into that.

It's why we need to talk.

It has to be all, or it has to be nothing. I have to commit to her completely or I have to let her go and walk away like the noble man I'm struggling to be.

"How about after you testify?"

And shit, I just put a deadline on this. She testifies against her ex next week. But if I don't give her something, she could leave as early as tonight, and I know if she does that before we have a chance to talk, I'll lose her completely. Or maybe that's her intention.

"I'll think about it. Can we go to work now? You're wasting my time with all this talking."

"You don't have patients scheduled for another hour."

She throws me a sideways glance as we enter the building. "Stop checking my schedule. It's creepy."

But she's blushing. And she's biting her lip to hide her smile. And goddamn, this woman makes me desperate in a way I've never known.

"Come with me," I growl. I don't release her hand the way I usually do when we enter the building. Generally, when we get to work, she walks off without so much as a goodbye or a backward glance.

Today is going to be different.

"We can't do this here, Jonah."

Except we are. She knows it. I know it, and she's not exactly fighting me. She's keeping pace and not pulling her hand away, so I'm going to take her words of protest as half-hearted. I open the door to my office, flip on the switch, close the door behind us, and lock it.

I spin around and find Halle against the opposite wall, her chest already heaving with her exaggerated breaths. Her blue eyes dark and heavy-lidded. Her cheeks stained pink. "God, you're so beautiful."

Halle's hands glide down to the drawstring on her scrub pants. They linger there for a beat before she begins to untie them. Slowly. So. Fucking. Slowly. They glide down the long silkiness of her legs and she steps out of them. Then she repeats the process with those white lace panties I was admiring not even an hour ago.

"Do you want me, Jonah?"

I shake my head and blow out a breath. "No. I don't want you." She stares me down but doesn't move, her beautiful pussy on display for me, but I keep my eyes on hers as I admit, "I *need* you, Halle. Desperately. Tragically. In every possible way I shouldn't."

There. How's that for honesty?

She pushes off the wall and moves toward me, but she doesn't touch me when she reaches me. Her eyes stay glued on mine and I can smell how turned on she is. I lick my lips, hungry to taste her, even in the air.

She smiles like she knows something I don't. Like I haven't fooled her for a second. Like she just won, and I just lost. Her hands run up my chest, slide over my shoulders until they find the hair at the back of my neck.

"Then take me, Jonah. I'm yours."

The way she says that means so much more than this. It means everything, and I can't help but lean in and kiss her, needing to absorb that.

I need her to be mine.

"I'm never going to be done with you," I realize.

She blinks up at me, like she's going to say something, but her mouth remains shut and her eyes gloss over. But it's there. In her silence is a plea. *Don't make promises you can't keep.*

I lift her and she snakes those gorgeous, mile-long legs around me and grinds her wet heat against me. Pressing her into the wall, I cup her ass with my hand and use the other to undo the tie on my own scrubs. They fall to the floor, and then I free my cock.

"This is going to be quick and hard. We don't have a lot of time for much else."

She moans, dropping her head back against the wall as our eyes lock. "I don't need much else. I'm already halfway there."

Shit. I push into her, no condom between us. It's just her and me in a heaven I never knew existed. A pleasure unlike any other. I find her mouth and capture her lips, her moans, as I thrust in and out of her. I open my eyes and watch the way her face is twisted up in concentration as she chases her climax. The way her cheeks turn from pink to red. The way a hint of sweat glistens on her brow. The way her eyes open and she pins me, knocking the breath from my body and making me push into her harder, deeper.

I can't get close enough to her. There is no limit. No end.

I'm done for.

I love her. I fucking love her. But this isn't just love. This is what being *in* love feels like. This crazy, all-consuming rush. This powerful swell surging up from within me. This clenching of my chest and tightening in my stomach and smile across my face. This need for her to be mine.

It's not possession. It's not claiming. It's more than that. It's knowing she's my everything. Anything less with her is unacceptable. It's self-satisfaction, a domination of the senses, a feeling of whole instead of broken and empty.

I want her to lose herself to me. I want her to fall in love with me just as hard and unforgiving as I have with her. I don't want her with anyone other than me ever again.

I fuck her harder, my hips pistoning with short, wild thrusts. She feels so good. So fucking good, I'm losing my mind.

"I'm so close," she pants, her head against the wall, eyes heavy. I reach down between us, finding her slick clit and thrumming in time with my thrusts.

That does it for her.

My eyes lock, watching my girl rise to her crest, knowing she's coming when her face falls into my neck and she shudders, biting my shoulder and moaning my name like it's a benediction. I follow her over the edge. I come so hard I see stars. I push my seed into her body, knowing beyond a shadow of a doubt it will not be the last time I do that.

Knowing that this is our start and not our end.

I open my mouth to tell her just that when there's a knock on my door. Halle's head snaps up, her eyes wide, a delightful synergy of amusement, dread, and embarrassment swimming in her blue depths.

I pull out, wincing through the urge to moan as I do, and set her on her feet. "Yes?" I call out as I reach over and grab some tissues from my desk. I hand them to her, then I tug up my boxers and scrub pants, tying the drawstring with clumsy fingers.

She scurries over to her discarded clothes, hastily shimmying up her panties and scrubs. "Doctor Hughes?" Laura, one of the nurses, cautiously asks. I have no idea how loud Halle and I were. Did we rattle windows in patients' rooms? Did everyone on this floor hear us come? Does my office reek of sex?

I risk a glance over at Halle sitting in the chair across from my desk. She's flushed to the nines with sex-tousled hair, but at least she's dressed. I point to her head and she blanches, ripping the elastic from her hair. It spills all around her shoulders.

Wow, that's a sight that could never get old.

I run my hands through my own hair, take a cursory look around and then open the door. "Yes?" I say again with a smile as I greet Laura. She looks normal. Not the least bit suspicious. I step back so it doesn't seem as if I just fucked my . . . girlfriend? . . . in my office. Halle is staring down at her phone to hide her flush.

"Sorry," Laura hesitates when she spots Halle. "I didn't realize you were in a meeting. There's an Erica Meadows at registration. She says she has an appointment to see you."

Erica. Shit. I completely forgot I'd asked her to meet me here this morning. And that high I was just enjoying rolls around in my stomach like arsenic. "Please let her know I'll be right there."

Laura nods and then quickly scurries away. I stand with my back to Halle, my hand on the open door as I take stock of everything.

Am I betraying my wife's memory by loving another woman?

I'm not. It's been two years. But it feels like I am. It feels like I'm turning my back on Madeline and all that she meant, *means*, to me. I need to tell Erica about Halle. It's time.

Halle is too important to pretend with.

And once I do that, I'm going to tell Halle how I feel about her.

"You can go," Halle murmurs, like she hates the words as much as the sentiment. "I understand."

I think I just died, because I hate her tone more than she hates the sentiment. I hate how dejected and sad and lonely it is. I did that to her. I made her feel like that and it makes me as sick as this entire situation does.

I shake my head because she can't possibly understand if I don't understand.

"You still love Madeline. I know this, Jonah. It's nothing new. You shouldn't feel bad about that. We had fun. I mean, that's all this was, right?"

Was? But I'm in love with you.

Yet, I can't make myself say it. Fun. That's all this was to her. All *I* was to her. She told me time and time again and I didn't listen. Not really anyway.

My chest tightens at that thought.

"Halle, it's not like that."

It is like that though, isn't it?

Because I haven't told her that it's not.

I turn around and stare at her for a moment, but she won't meet my eyes. She's ending this. I can see it all over her face.

I walk over to her. I don't give a shit that the door to my office is still open as I drop to my knees and cup her face in my hands.

"That's not how it is," I repeat. "Not at all. I need to talk to you tonight. Please. Just not here. Not at work. Not with Erica waiting on me."

"Sure," she says, her eyes searching me for something I'm not bothering to hide for once. Only, I'm not sure she finds it as she says, "We'll talk later."

Then she gets up, pushing past me and leaving my office. Everything inside of me hurts. I have a horrible feeling I might have lost her for good.

Chapter Twenty-Three

Jonah

ERICA. She looks so much like Madeline that my heart leaps in my chest before it clenches so tight I can hardly breathe. Dark hair. Bright chocolate eyes. Round cheeks that are permanently stained pink.

Beautiful.

Erica is so beautiful.

Madeline was so beautiful.

And I hate life as much as I love it. That practically stops me dead. I haven't loved the thought of life for two years. Until Halle.

"I saw this gif once," she begins without any preamble the moment I sit beside her. "Maddy sent it to me after she was first diagnosed, and we were still filled with absurd hope. It was one of those characters from *The Simpsons* and it said something along the lines of, 'Not sure if it's a flare or . . . The flu. Or bad tacos. Or allergies. Or an actual injury. Or too much coffee or not enough coffee.'" I smile, thinking about Maddy and her dry sense of humor.

"The list went on and I remember laughing my ass off before I balled my eyes out."

I swallow hard past the lump forming in the back of my throat, shifting beside her on the bench by the front door.

"She's beautiful, Jonah. The redhead, I mean."

I stare at her, wondering how she knew.

"I've been sitting here for a while," she says, reading my obvious confusion. "I watched the two of you walk in together. You love her." It's not a question, and again, I wonder at Erica. "It was written all over your face. All over the way you looked at her. You two were simply walking into the building, holding hands, and you looked at her the way you used to look at Maddy."

Fuck. That's just . . . shit. I can't . . . "I don't know what to say."

"You do though, right? You love her?"

I close my eyes and blow out a breath. Ignoring the pain, I say, "I think so. Yes." I couldn't seem to do the same with Halle. Tonight. I'll tell her tonight. And together we'll figure this thing out. I don't care if she doesn't want to jump into another relationship. I have no idea what I'm ready for, either. I just know I need her in my life. That I just plain need her, and I don't care how that happens. "Does that upset you?" I open my eyes, pivot my head and find Erica watching me warily.

"I remember the day you met Maddy. God." Erica laughs, shaking her head lightly. "She called me and said she'd met the most gorgeous man ever." Another laugh. "She said you were the perfect friend. Smart. Funny. Sexy. Caring." She shifts to face me now, her brown eyes killing everything inside me. "I asked her why you were her friend and not something more. She said you were too perfect to be more. That eventually your perfection would wear off and she'd be left with this asshole of a man."

I blow out the breath I didn't realize I was holding.

"Two years later, when you finally grew some balls and kissed her, she told me she'd been in love with you all that time. Since day one. I asked her if you were as perfect as she'd anticipated, and she said no."

I cover my face with my hands.

"She said you were better."

A strangled sound passes my chest, escaping my lips. I miss my wife. I love another woman. Life fucking sucks.

"You're not doing anything wrong by loving this new woman, Jonah. And you're still as perfect as ever. It's the right thing. Maddy is gone. She's dead and life . . . fuck, dude, life goes *on*," she emphasizes. "That's exactly what it's supposed to do."

My hands fall to my lap and I face my sister-in-law. "Is it? My love for Madeline has not dwindled. It's just . . . I don't know, changed, maybe. Shifted somehow to make room for another."

Erica shrugs. "It's been two years. How long do you want to be a brooding spinster?"

I laugh despite myself.

"Madeline would not be mad. She'd be *happy*. But more importantly, she'd be so fucking angry if she knew you'd given up on life and love because she was dead. That bitch was life personified. You held that in your hands, so you of all people should know this as a truth."

"I—" I swallow hard past the lump in my throat. I haven't cried over Madeline in a long time, but right now, I'm fighting the urge. "I didn't think I could be happy without her."

"It gets easier. You're already better with this new woman than you've been since Madeline died. Like ripping off a Band-Aid to use your terminology."

I stare at the little sister of my best friend. Of my wife. I watch as she watches people. She's young, but she doesn't always act it. Her and Madeline were so close. As close as Madeline and I were.

"You know, the redhead is the reason I asked you to meet me here this morning."

"No kidding." She snorts, leaning back and folding her arms. She turns to look at me, her eyes bouncing around my face until they land on mine. Then she smiles a smile I can't help but return. "Thank you for wanting to tell me about her. For doing it face-to-face and not telling me over the phone." She turns away from me. "I miss Maddy, you know?"

"More than words."

"So . . .," Erica trails off and glances in the direction of where Halle and I came in this morning. I follow her lead, but quickly turn back to her. "If she, the redhead—"

"Halle."

She nods. "Halle. I mean, if she, you know, helps you through this, you should go with it."

What do you say to the younger sister of the woman you loved? No, it was just a fling. Or, she's just having fun and isn't serious about me. Or, I feel as if this woman has become the answer to my prayers and the only sense I can make of her is that Madeline sent her to me directly? "Erica." I sigh. "I'm not sure—"

"Like I said, I saw the way you two were looking at each other. It was obviously there for both of you. We all need someone to make the unbearable bearable. It doesn't mean you don't love Maddy and it doesn't mean you're dishonoring her memory. I know you. Not as well as Maddy did, but I do know you. So, cut the shit, read between the lines, and then take me out to dinner tonight so I can meet her."

"Dinner?" I laugh. I laugh so loud. *Oh, Madeline, if only you could see Erica now.* "I can take you to dinner, Erica. Tonight, if you want."

"I don't want to lose you, Jonah. I need you in my life. I realize that might be weird at this point. You have someone new and Maddy is gone—"

I lean over and hug her, interrupting her rant. "I'm not going anywhere. You're forever my sister, Erica. New girl or not." I wrap her up in my arms and hold in my fucking tears. Because even though she may think she needs me, I need her. I needed her to tell me it was okay to be with Halle. More than she'll ever know. I needed to see her eyes that are identical to Madeline's and I needed this hug. *Ah, Maddy. We need you back.*

She pulls away, wiping her eyes that are barely more than glistening. "Tonight, okay? And you better bring your girlfriend."

I shake my head, smiling indulgently. "I have to make her my girlfriend first. We're not quite there yet."

Erica snorts out a sardonic laugh, rolling her eyes. "Men. Jesus, you guys. You might wanna get on that, dude."

And then she's gone. Like she was never here to begin with, and for some reason, even though they're so very different, it feels like I'm watching Maddy walk away from me. I hurt all over again. Will this pain ever go away?

No, I realize. It won't. And I think I'm okay with that. I think this pain will keep Madeline with me where she belongs.

I stand up, but instead of going back into the clinic, I head toward the front door. I need some fresh air, a few minutes to get my head together after that conversation, and I can't do it here. I'm serious about this thing with Halle. I'm utterly crazy about her, and that has me smiling in a way I haven't allowed myself to. I pull my phone out of my back pocket, glancing down at it quickly and thinking about texting her, but just as I start to move again, my right shoulder is slammed into with enough force to knock me back a few steps.

My phone slips from my fingers, clattering to the floor, and as I bend down to pick it up, the person who bumped into me hands it to me. "Sorry about that, doctor."

I right myself and find a pair of deep, dark brown eyes attached to a somewhat familiar face, though I can't place it immediately.

"That's all right." I offer a smile, resisting the urge to rub my smarting shoulder. The bloke hit me hard.

He stares me down, something wrong and unnerving in his penetrating stare. Then a smile curls slowly up the corner of his lips. "Heading out?"

"Um. Yeah. For a bit." I can feel my eyebrows furrowing together. He has to be a patient, because I am positive I know him from somewhere, yet something about him is setting my teeth on edge.

That smile grows. "Well then, I'm glad I ran into you. I would have hated missing you completely."

"Right."

"Bye, Doctor Hughes." And then he walks off, heading toward the patient area. I watch him for a few seconds, still bewildered by that encounter until I remember the phone in my hand. Pushing through the glass door, I glance east and when I find the street void of oncoming traffic, I jaywalk at a sprint until I reach the cafe across the street.

The door chimes as I enter, and I purchase a coffee I have no intention of drinking. So I'm not bothered, I find a secluded seat all the way in the back. I drop down, set my phone and my coffee on the table. *Be a fucking man.*

Me: **Erica wants to have dinner with us tonight if that's all right with you. I was hoping to talk to you about us before that. And just so there is no confusion or wayward thoughts prior to that conversation, there is an us. I want there to be an us. Text me after your last patient and we'll meet up.**

I breathe in. I breathe out. I hit send. I smile to myself. Life is too damn short. I'm in love with Halle. And I'm okay with that.

That weight mooring me to bottom of the ocean . . . gone.

I stand up, toss my coffee in the trash, tuck my phone into my pocket and head back across the street. I have patients to see before I tell Halle everything.

Chapter Twenty-Four

Halle

"HALLE, they added a walk-in onto your schedule." I'm staring at my computer screen without actually seeing anything.

I need to tell Jonah I'm done.

That things are getting out of control. That my feelings are too strong for this to be casual. I should have done it this morning. Or any time in between my middle of the night phone call with Aria and now.

But he looks at me like I'm the very air he breathes. Fucks me like he loves me. And I'm a total chicken.

Then Madeline's sister shows up like the proverbial slap to the face I needed.

He. Loves. Madeline.

Right. Thanks. Because I was seriously close to forgetting that small, not-so-insignificant detail about our mock relationship. Fuck. I hate men.

"That's fine. I don't mind," I reply without glancing up.

I feel like I can't look anyone in the eye. My not-so-secret fling with the boss is about to end and everyone will know. Everyone will talk about it. And once again, I'll be the punchline at my place of work.

I wonder if I'll have to leave this job, too. It can be done. It's not like I have a panel of patients yet. I'm new here and have been getting mostly sick visits and physicals that couldn't be scheduled with patients' primary providers.

"I'll be right there."

"He's in room eight. Came in complaining of chest pain but refused an EKG."

Now I look up and stare at Laura, the freaking nurse who practically walked in on me and Jonah having sex, with raised eyebrows. "He *refused* an EKG when he has *chest pain?*"

She nods and shrugs with an incredulous yet resigned expression. "I can't force him."

"I know. But for real? What is wrong with people?"

Another shrug. "He's young. Like late twenties, so maybe he doesn't think it's anything serious. Could be GERD."

"Yes, but still." I shake my head in disbelief. "Why bother coming in if you're not going to get the proper tests to rule out something potentially serious."

Laura gives me another shrug before she saunters off. I check the chart. He's a new patient. A guy by the name of Edward E. Cummings. Edward E. Cummings? His parents must have a sense of humor or be as big a fan of the poet as I am since he's my absolute favorite.

I stand up, log off my computer, and then head down the hall to room eight. I have to pass Jonah's office on the way and I can't help but look in there as I do. The door is open, but he's not in there.

It's a relief, I tell myself. I'm not ready to face him. Not here anyway.

I wonder if he's still with Erica. My phone vibrates in the pocket of my scrubs, but I don't check it now. It's probably just Aria texting me back anyway. I open the door to the exam room and practically fall over my feet when I see the patient waiting for me.

Matt.

My ex-boyfriend is sitting on the exam table, fully clothed with a glint I can't decipher to his eyes.

"I should have known," passes my lips before I can stop it. "Chest pain?"

"Of course." He smiles at me, but it's weak. And he looks . . . well, he looks like shit. Like he hasn't slept more than five minutes since I left him nearly three months ago. "The woman I love more than anything in the world left me."

I stare at him.

He grins. I don't. "I thought for sure you'd figure me out with the name."

"Clearly, I'm not that bright."

"Come in, Halle. Sit. We need to talk."

For a moment, I debate if I should. I mean, there are so many unknowns with this man. But I need to know once and for all if he's the one who's been calling me. If he's the one who broke into my apartment. I feel like if I can look him in the eye while he answers me, I might be able to tell if he's lying or not.

But still, I hesitate, before he adds, "Come on, sweetheart. Just for a few minutes? We have so much to talk about."

I shut the door behind me and sit down on the rolling stool, placing myself as far away from him as the small room will allow.

I smell his cologne. I take in his dark brown eyes and the purple shadows beneath them. I categorize the length of his beard and hair and state of his slightly disheveled clothes. He looks the same, but different. Those differences are everything. Those differences say he hasn't been taking the best care of himself the way he typically would—even for a hacker—and it simultaneously twists my gut with regret and fills me with jitters.

The scary kind of jitters.

The kind that make you hyperaware and on edge.

Matt sighs, like he wasn't sure I was going to sit and then his face drops into his hands. "How could you do this to me, Halle? Two years together. We were going to get married and then you turn me over to the Feds?"

"What?"

He lets out a humorless chuckle. "Don't play coy."

"Matt," I say his name and wait for him to look up. It takes him a beat. But when he finally does, hell, this man looks beaten down. So very broken and defeated. "I didn't turn you in to the Feds. I didn't even know what you were up to until after you were arrested, and they came into my workplace and hauled me downtown."

He stares at me, blinks twice before his eyebrows pinch together and he rubs a hand across his unkempt jaw. "You broke up with me. You ended it."

I nod, shifting in my stool to face him better. "It wasn't working anymore." I shrug. "I told you all of this that night. You were always on your computer and we were never together. Whenever we were, we hardly talked. Hardly spoke. Never snuggled or laughed. Never had sex. It was like all the light had faded from us."

He shakes his head. "We could have worked on it. I would have tried harder. You never talked to me about any of that. I had no idea you weren't happy."

I scoot closer to him, wanting, needing him to understand me. "It wouldn't have mattered. I'm sorry, Matt. I honestly, truly am. I never meant to hurt you. I just needed . . .," I pause, thinking about how I want to phrase this. "Something else. A change of life. Because you're right, I wasn't happy. Some of that was on you. Some of that was on me. In any event, we just weren't meant to be."

"Like you are with your doctor?" he bites out, his cheeks coloring with heat and agitation.

"How do you know about him?"

Matt grins and it's the most sadistic grin I've ever seen on him. My heart explodes out of my chest. My breaths come out in short bursts.

"I've had you followed. Or haven't you noticed?"

Shit. I knew I wasn't crazy.

I go to scoot back, but he reacts quickly, slamming his foot down on the leg of the stool and holding me in place. I try to get up, but his hand is on my arm, clenching it so tight I can feel the blood draining from my hand.

"Sit down. We're not done talking."

"Oh no," I sneer. "We're absolutely done talking. Get out of here, Matt, before I call the police or the FBI or whoever is set to put your criminal ass in prison."

"I said sit." His tone mixed with the murderous gleam in his eyes steals my breath. I can't move. I can't think. All I can do is shake my head because there is no way I'm going to sit down. There is no way I'm going to let him do this to me.

"Let go," I say, but my voice isn't as strong as I'd like. It quivers on the word *go* and I hate that. I hate that feeling of being powerless. Of being controlled.

He yanks on my arm, forcing me back down on the stool. I go to scream, but Matt pulls out a gun. It's a small, black gun, but a gun still the same. The kind little old ladies stuff in their handbags on the way to Bingo night. And even though it's small, it could kill me. It could kill a lot of people.

Matt sets it down on the exam table next to his thigh, his free hand lovingly resting on the textured grip handle.

Crapola.

"I saw your boyfriend, Jonah Hughes, earlier. I wouldn't have pegged you as a gold-digging slut, but obviously I was wrong."

I stare at him, stunned and sick with worry. *Jonah. He knows about Jonah.*

"It seems we're done with being nice, so where is it?"

I swallow down the bile threatening to come up. I can't keep track of what he's saying. All I hear is blood pounding in my ears. Jonah. The other people in the clinic. Matt with a gun.

"Where is what?" I whisper, my voice thick with panic.

"The flash drive. I know you have it. I slipped it into your purse. But that was before you walked out on me. Those stupid assholes I hired never found it when they flipped your apartment. The guy following you hasn't seen it either. It has to still be in your purse."

Holy shit. So that's what they were after. Something I didn't even know I had. Wow, that's just . . .

"What have you done?" I cry, desperate to stand. Desperate to get away.

I can't.

His goddamn grip is unrelenting. Bruising. I peek over to the gun, resting comfortably beside him. I won't be able to grab it before he picks it up and shoots me with it. I honestly have no idea how I'm going to get away from him without him hurting me or someone else.

"I got doxed. One of the assholes I was working with to get credit card numbers flipped. It's the only thing I can come up with. It all happened right after you left me. Ironic, right?" He leers at me with poison in his wild eyes. "I was convinced you helped him. That you were fucking him. The timing was just too perfect."

He squeezes my arm even tighter and I whimper before I can stop it.

"You're hurting me, Matt. Let go."

"But I actually believe you when you say you didn't turn me in," he continues, completely ignoring my plea.

I try to tug my arm away again, but he yanks me closer, the metal feet of the stool clattering into the exam table, smashing my knees into the unforgiving plastic.

"I put everything onto a flash drive. All the evidence I have on the other people in the ring. All my accounts. Everything. And I gave it all to *you*," he emphasizes. "Because I knew they'd be after me for what I had, both the Feds and the other assholes. I figured you were the safest one to hold it. I wasn't wrong about that. You're as sweet and innocent-looking as they come."

"Matt," I interrupt without much of an idea what I want to follow his name up with.

I lick my arid lips, my hand practically numb, the skin burning with pinpoint prickles. I get to my feet and he doesn't stop me, but he doesn't let me go. The stool slides back, and suddenly I find myself eye to eye with him. He looks deranged, like he's completely lost touch with reality and right from wrong and fucks to give.

"You're hurting me," I try again. "Let me go. I'll give you the flash drive. And then you can go."

"I'm not going to prison, Halle." He shakes my arm like it's a warning. A threat. "It's not fucking happening. I won't survive it. I'm looking at fifteen years minimum. You will give me that flash drive. But there is no goddamn way you're not coming with me. I know you. The second I'm out of sight, you'll call the police. So, here's how this is playing out. First thing, you're handing me that flash drive. Then, you're leaving here with me. We're going to *your* apartment to pack a bag. After that, we're going to Logan and hopping a flight out of here."

I have no idea what to do right now.

Like none.

Do I go along with this? Do I put up a fight and risk him shooting me? Do I insult him? Stroke his ego? I'm at a loss.

"Where are we going?" There is no way he can get a gun on a plane. Logan airport might be my best option to get away. That place is crawling with cops.

"I have a private plane waiting. We'll go someplace romantic. Someplace we can start again."

"Matt—"

"This is not up for discussion. You're mine, Halle. I knew it the moment I saw you in that bar. Seeing you again at that party only proved that. I have plenty of money stashed away for us to live on. You'll be happy. *We'll* be happy." He stares beseechingly at me. "It's the only way. I can't let you go. It's not possible. I know you understand that. If you don't do this, I will kill your lover before I kill myself. If I go to prison, I'm as good as dead. My life is over."

I'm going to black out. I can feel it. Everything is starting to dip and sway. He's going to kill Jonah. Oh my God. What do I do? I can't breathe.

"You want him to live? You don't want my death on your conscience, you do whatever the fuck I tell you to do."

I believe him. The Matt I knew once upon a time is gone. In his place is this crazy, sorry excuse for a man.

A gun.

The man drew a gun at me and is threatening to kill Jonah before he kills himself. He's so far from touching reality that there is no bargaining with him. No plea I can make that he'll heed. He won't go to prison. He'd rather die. That's what this is. He'd rather die.

And he'd take Jonah with him.

"Okay, Matt. Let's go pack me a bag." *And maybe by the time we do that, I'll have some sort of a plan.*

He smiles, like the wind was just pushed back into his sails. Like this is all going to work out the way he's planning. Shit. Mother-fucking shit. How do I do this? How do I get away from a desperate man with very little left to lose?

I need to get him out of the health center before he hurts someone.

I stand up and he tugs me into him, releasing my arm. I practically moan out in pleasure at the sensation of blood returning to my hand. That pleasure doesn't last long. Before I know what's happening, his mouth is on mine. He tastes sour, like stale coffee and desperation. I try to pull away, but there is no give to be had. He shoves his tongue into my mouth, cinching the back of my hair in his fist by the roots.

"Don't forget who you belong to," he growls against me. "Don't forget you're mine and not his."

"Never." I smile, bile climbing its way up the back of my throat. I quickly swallow it down. "I want to go now. I'm anxious to leave with you."

"Your boyfriend is lucky," he hisses under his breath as he gets off the exam table. He's nearly the same height as me. I angle to face him, needing to see his eyes as he talks about Jonah. "I saw him first. My plan was to come for you and then find him after. Show him that you belong to me and not him. That you could never belong to him. But he left before I found you and ruined that."

I hold onto the relieved breath desperate to escape my lungs. The thought of him hurting anyone makes me sick. The thought of him hurting Jonah fills me with a fear I have no name for.

"He doesn't matter. We do. Let's go."

A sparkle of light touches his eyes, lightening them to a notch below insane. Matt tucks his freaking horror-film gun back into the pocket of his pants, takes my hand and leads me to the door.

"Don't try anything. You tip anyone off and it won't end well for them."

My eyes track to the ground without lowering my head. I need to be able to watch him without making eye contact with anyone. I'm terrified out of my mind, but the thought of him shooting someone . . . I can't even imagine it.

We stop in my office, my eyes searching desperately for anything I can grab without him noticing. Nothing. I have absolutely nothing in this office that is helpful. Not even a syringe I can stab him with.

I lift my purse and slide it onto my shoulder. He smiles at me with a warmth I knew from him in a previous life. It makes me hate him more for putting me in this position.

Matt reaches into my purse, muddles through it until he retrieves his beloved flash drive. I hate that I've had this the whole time. I can't even question how that happened, because my purse is filled with lip gloss that is easily five years old, stale gum, and more crap than anyone needs.

He knew that about me.

He banked on it and won.

Matt tucks it into his pocket with a satisfied grin and nods his head at me as if to say he's ready.

I wordlessly turn off the light and close the door to my office, a sick knot of dread coating my stomach. Sweat slicks the back of my neck. My heart races so loud I'm shocked no one can hear it. I'm shaking. It's a minor miracle that I'm able to stand and walk in a straight line.

We make it down the hall. We make it through the door. We make it down the stairs and to the lobby before we're stopped.

And everything turns to chaos.

Chapter Twenty-Five

Halle

IT STARTS OUT SLOW. Like a bass drum in the background. Like a bradycardic heartbeat. Bump-bump. Bump-bump. It's like those dreams where you're watching yourself from outside your body, or a sequence in a movie where everything is moving in slow motion.

Matt is holding onto my arm, his fingers wrapped firmly around my bicep. We're heading to the front door, side by side. Matt is talking about the plane he has waiting for us at Logan. How we have to go someplace far and very foreign. That I can no longer be Halle Whitcomb, but that's okay because he has a fake passport for me with a different name on it.

I'm nodding and doing everything in my power to keep him calm and nonviolent while systematically going through every possible escape scenario in his plan.

Then Jonah walks in the front door.

He spots me and his entire face lights up. Like the finale of a fireworks display on New Year's Eve. Or a little boy on Christmas morning as he finds all the presents under the tree. Like I'm just what he's been searching for his whole life and seeing me here, in this unexpected way and place, made his whole day.

That look lasts a total of three seconds.

I know, because I count.

One. Two. Three.

Bump-bump, bump-bump, bump-bump.

That's when the smile spreading across his gorgeous face falls. Possibly because I do not return his look of elation and adoration. Or possibly because he notices the man on my right holding onto me like I'm a flight risk.

Or clumsy because I've already tripped over my sneakered feet twice, but I'm going to blame that on the panic.

"Halle?" That's Jonah, and this time, it takes less than a second for his confused expression to turn to a delightful cocktail of fury, deadly intent, and fear. "What's going on?"

Matt pauses, freezing mid-step at the sound of my name. Strangely enough, he hadn't noticed Jonah, who is now practically in front of us. I wish he weren't standing so close. I wish he would step back and away from me, but he's only getting closer, as if he's about to separate Matt from me by force.

"I'm leaving," I tell Jonah sternly. "I don't want to see you again." *Please leave, Jonah. Please walk away before you get hurt.*

Jonah stares at me for a beat. Then at Matt. Then he shakes his head like nothing is adding up and one plus one no longer equals two, and the world is spinning on an entirely different axis.

But the thing about Jonah, he's a smart guy.

A very smart guy.

And I believe the record has already stated that I have a terrible poker face.

"Has he hurt you?" he asks me, his eyes scanning mine before they drop to my body and end on Matt's hand around my arm.

Matt laughs mirthlessly, raising his chin in defiance—a vain attempt to even out his sightline with Jonah's, though Jonah still has a good half a foot on him.

"No. I haven't hurt her." His grip on my arm tightens as he jerks me to his side. "She's the one who hurt me, doctor, by jumping into your bed when ours wasn't even cold. But it doesn't matter because Halle chose me and not you. She wants *me*." He thrusts a thumb into his chest. "Not you." A smarmy grin curls up the corners of Matt's lips. "As she said, she doesn't want to see you again. So back the fuck up unless you want to be the one who gets hurt."

That's when Matt's free hand lowers to his side. The side carrying the gun.

I can't look away from them. If I do, even for a split second, this could all go very wrong.

I have no idea if we've drawn a crowd or not. If someone has called the police by now. I'm hoping so. I'm hoping there are dozens of people around and that someone is savvy enough to realize there is a real threat.

Jonah glares at Matt, his flinty gaze turning to impenetrable stone. His fists ball up at his sides, his knuckles turning white. His cheeks grow rosy as his rage slowly boils up to a crescendo, ready to explode like a volcano. I'm hoping Matt is smart and thinking clearly enough to realize that if he shoots someone, his escape plan is for naught.

That he still might have a way out of this that does not involve murder and suicide.

But something tells me Matt hasn't been thinking clearly for a while. Something tells me he's hanging on by a very loose, thin strand of reality.

My eyes bounce back and forth between the two men, my vision blurring along the edges as I try to focus through the panic-laced adrenaline coursing through my bloodstream.

I can't breathe, or maybe it's that I'm breathing too much because I feel like I'm hyperventilating.

"Release her now, and if you're lucky, I'll let you live long enough to make it to prison."

I shake my head, begging, pleading, dying. *Please don't do this, Jonah.*

Matt's trembling uncontrollably, and I can't determine if it's from anger or fear.

"He won't go to prison," I say, wondering if Jonah understands my meaning, knowing there is no way he could. "Just go, Jonah. Leave us alone."

Jonah, the stubborn, protective, wonderful bastard shakes his head. "I can't do that."

"Leave," I plead, my voice shrill. I don't know what else to do. Tears breach the divide, streaming futilely down my cheeks. "Please," I sob. "Please let us leave. You have to let us go."

"He'll call the police, Halle." I shake my head. I shake it over and over again. I need to tell Matt that Jonah won't do that, but I'm losing my ability to speak. "It's too late now."

"No," I wail, my body crumpling.

Three things happen at once. Matt goes for his gun, sliding it out of his pocket in one smooth motion, gripping it like it's high noon at the O.K. Corral. Jonah seizes my other arm, attempting to pry me away from Matt.

Instead of allowing that, I step in front of Jonah, desperate to shield him from whatever Matt has planned. Matt won't shoot me. *I think.*

And all that slow-motion suddenly speeds up to live action.

Matt lifts his gun, sweat rolling down his flushed face, his expression sick with menacing conviction. I don't know this Matt. The man I lived with, loved at one point in time, would never threaten people. Would never hurt anyone. Then again, I would never have imagined he'd be stealing from them, either.

I have to get to the gun.

I lunge for it just as an arm wraps around my stomach, wrenching me back. "No!" I scream out so loud my voice cracks on the end, my arms flailing wildly, extending helplessly toward the gun.

Jonah wrenches me back, lifting me into the air and pushing me aside as if I weigh nothing. I fall, hard and fast, my ass slamming on the ground as my body skids back a few feet from the momentum.

Jonah wastes no time. He lunges for Matt, tackling him and taking him to the ground. The air whooshes out of Matt's lungs, momentarily dazing him, as he's slammed down on his back.

But the gun. The gun that always goes skittering away in movies stays firmly planted in Matt's hand. He moves to strike, recovering faster than I would have expected. I gasp, crawling to my knees, forced to watch in stunned horror. I'm terrified any wrong move I make will end in Jonah being shot.

Killed. Oh, God. I can't take this. I'm going to be sick.

The two grapple, moving this way and that. Striking back and forth like deadly snakes, rhythmically dancing. It's as hypnotizing as it is terrifying.

Matt cracks the butt of the gun into the side of Jonah's face. My hands fly up, covering my mouth and the resulting sob that's pressing through my raw lips.

Yet somehow, Jonah shakes it off, managing to capture the hand holding the gun. Matt's eyes are narrowed slits of determination, as he fights back, desperately trying to shake Jonah off and regain control of the gun.

Jonah's fist collides with Matt's face, knocking his head back against the uncompromising tile floor. He growls out, spitting blood on the floor.

But before Jonah can do anything else, Matt swings with his other arm, nailing Jonah across the chest and knocking him back. It's enough to secure the upper hand.

Matt twists around and pins Jonah to the floor. He raises his hand, twisting the gun into position to fire it. I hear sound all around me, but I can't look away. Jonah reaches for the gun, but he's going to be too late.

He's going to be too late!

I scream, collapsing to the floor. Matt presses in on the trigger and my eyes close, but nothing happens. There's no bang. No thunderous crack. My eyes fly back open to find Matt studying his gun only to realize that he had the safety engaged.

Thank God.

The breath I was holding flees my lungs. Matt moves to disengage the safety, but Jonah takes advantage of his momentary distraction. He grabs the arm with the gun and twists it hard, wrenching it back at an awkward angle until Matt howls out in pain.

Jonah thrusts up with his elbow, cracking Matt's nose with a sickening crunch.

Matt's done.

He has to know this is the end of the line.

Crouching down on all fours, I crawl slowly toward them. If only I can grab that goddamn gun, I can stop this. But before I can even get close, Matt thrusts, swinging his arm wildly, doing everything he can to free himself and the gun.

A deafening *crack* fills the air.

I scream again as Jonah's body lurches, a groan of pain slipping past his lips. His face turns ashen, his eyes wide.

Oh my God, Matt shot Jonah.

A thin line of red slowly discolors the ripped material on the back of Jonah's pale blue scrub top, saturating the fabric, but I can't determine how badly he's hurt.

Jonah rises, the wound barely registering as his elbow slams down on Matt's stomach before his forearm swings back. He nails Matt directly across the throat, snuffing out the air from his lungs.

Matt falls back, grasping his throat as he thrashes, choking for air that seems to elude him. The hand with the gun goes slack before he brings it up to his throat, like that will make his plight for air easier.

The gun clatters to the floor. I scramble for it, but Jonah is already there, beating me to it.

"Jonah?" I blink, frantic to catch his eyes. He doesn't reply, but the wound can't be that bad if he's able to move like this. Right?

Lifting the gun off the ground, he reengages the safety and hands it to me, far out of range for a struggling Matt to reach. I've never held a gun before and I hope I never have to again. Jonah's hair is disheveled, face red and angry, clothing wrinkled and ripped, body bleeding.

Despite all that, he drops back to his knees, hovering over Matt's prostrate form. "Breathe, Matt." His cadence is slow and encouraging. "You're panicking. Try taking a slower breath."

Matt does, greedily sucking air in past his angry trachea.

"That's it now."

I stare at Jonah, awed. Matt just tried to kill him. Tried to shoot him and kidnap me, yet, he's helping him, calming him down and ensuring he breathes. I reach out and touch Jonah.

I have to. I have to feel that he's okay.

That he's still here with me. Jonah rolls his head over his shoulder, meets my eyes, and gives me the smallest of perceptible smiles. It's one that says he's okay. It's one that says we're alive, and holy shit, that really just fucking happened.

I mean, hell.

"Halle," Matt rasps, his eyes shifting every which way for me. But I can't face him. I don't have it in me to look into his eyes. To speak to him.

He tried to take me out of the country by force. He threatened me with a gun. He freaking attacked, shot at, my . . . well, Jonah. The man I love.

So, all that guilt I had before about him going to prison and becoming someone's bitch? Yeah, I think it's safe to say I'm over it. He deserves to rot there. He deserves for his life to be over.

In fact, I'm angry.

So goddamn angry.

Angry with myself for ever being with the man, for loving him once upon a time. But if I'm angry with myself, I'm furious with him. How did he let this happen? How did he become this man? Where did he lose sight of right versus wrong?

The police arrive seconds later, knocking Jonah away from Matt and slapping handcuffs on Matt's wrists before I can blink twice. Matt stares at me, his expression saturated with devastation, his eyes brimming with tears. I have nothing left to say to him, so I watch him go, my thoughts empty and chaotic all at once.

I turn to Jonah, and I find him already there, watching me with something indiscernible in his gaze. And for the first time, in all this madness, I take in the very real possibility that he's done with me. That he wants absolutely nothing to do with me ever again.

I mean, my ex just tried to kill him.

And that happened in his health center. And he said we needed to talk tonight. And he loves another woman.

I stare at him, and I know how this is going to end for us. My heart is shredding to teeny, tiny bits of pulp. My insides are ugly, raw, and overused.

You knew this would happen.

I did. I absolutely did, and I have no one to blame but myself. I don't regret it. None of it.

Still, I wish it had lasted longer.

Jonah Hughes is inside me. Under my skin and etched into every cell I'm comprised of. I can tell myself this is rebound love. That it's a natural reaction to a man like Jonah after everything I've been through, but it's bullshit. Even I can't digest that lie.

I have no idea how I'll get over him.

It's not a thought I've had before. With the others, I knew it would suck for a while, but then I'd be okay. Right now, looking into his green eyes, I wonder if I'll ever be okay again. If everything that just transpired has irrevocably changed me.

He shifts on the ground, his fierce expression softening as more of my tears fall. I don't even know if they're for him or from the ebbing adrenaline.

"You okay?" he asks and all I can do is shake my head, because no. I'm not okay. Nothing about what happened is okay.

I want to laugh at just how preposterous his question is. How crazy it is to be attacked like that. To have this entire situation become part of my, part of his, story, but I can't find the humor in any of this.

"Baby," he breathes, rising up slowly on his knees like he's going to lunge for me. Like he's going to grab hold of me and dissolve every single one of my doubts.

But he never makes it.

The police are there, surrounding him and surrounding me. The gun. Jesus, I'm still holding Matt's gun. And people. God, there are so many people standing around us, yelling out questions. Asking if we're all right and what happened amongst a crap ton of *oh my Gods*.

It's like the world started again, only it's nowhere I want to be. I feel like I need to run and hide under my covers until I fully grasp everything I have no understanding of. And if I wasn't in such an odd emotional state at the moment, I might cringe at the fact that this happened in my new place of employment.

I swear, I'll never find another job as a nurse practitioner in this city again.

Someone lifts me to my feet. I blink. I come back to reality. I come back to the now. I divert my attention away from Jonah. It's just too much to keep it there.

The police are spit-firing a zillion questions my way before someone tells me that I need to go with them downtown. Been there, done that, own the fucking T-shirt, I want to tell them, but I stay silent and allow them to escort me out to a waiting cruiser.

I spot Jonah being treated in an ambulance, a paramedic tending to his back. I'm assuming it's just a flesh wound and the words *lucky break* come to mind.

Our eyes lock for a flicker of a second, and when he doesn't smile or call out to me, or even look as broken as I am, my head dips into the back of the waiting car. Time to face the firing squad.

Chapter Twenty-Six

Halle

THE ENTIRE PROCESS TAKES HOURS. First, I'm questioned by the police. And let me tell you, if you've never been to a police headquarters, you're missing out. It's everything you'd ever expect it to be. Exactly like it is in *Law & Order*. Old. Smelly—like bleach, coffee, and body odor. Loud and cramped. At least the room they put me in was cramped.

I was initially questioned by the police. I recounted every detail. Twice. I answered all of their questions, even the ones that sounded more like an accusation than a question. Even the downright insulting ones. I answered them all calmly. I didn't even bother with my attorney. I've done nothing wrong and I will not cower. I'm done with that.

Then I wait. And wait. And fucking wait. This is after they took my purse and phone from me. I don't even have the luxury of googling today's events, so I can see my name splashed across the headlines. Or recount everything a dozen times over to my friends who are no doubt trying to call me. It's the first time in my life that

I'm glad my parents are dead. I couldn't have handled them witnessing the disaster my life has become. That fills me with a whole new level of despair.

Finally, the FBI detective who interviewed me after Matt was initially arrested waltzes in. I'm assuming he's who I was waiting for, but I can't be sure because no one tells you anything here. It's worse than being a patient in the hospital. I never liked this guy, this Agent Fellows. He's young, arrogant, and generally speaks to me like I'm an idiot. I get it in an odd way. I felt like an idiot the last time I spoke with him. But not today. Today, I'm not an idiot. I'm just mad.

So, when he begins with, "I hear you were attempting to leave the country with an accused felon," I lose the last shred of my patience.

He's standing, all tall and proud like he's got power over me. He doesn't, so I stand as well. Since I'm not accused of anything and I'm here on my own goodwill, I'm not cuffed, and he can't do much about it.

"You wanna know something funny, Agent Fellows?" He stares at me, clearly not about to answer my rhetorical question so I power on. "That accused felon you just mentioned? Yeah, he was able to get himself a gun. He was able to set up a private jet at Logan Airport. He was able to obtain a fake passport, not only for himself, but one for me. He explained the multiple offshore accounts that could fund him for the remainder of his life. He had a flash drive with everything you're looking for and probably a shit ton more. And you," I point at him, "knew nothing about this. Not a goddamn thing."

He crosses his arms over his chest, pointing to the chair I just vacated. "Please sit down, Miss Whitcomb."

"I'd rather stand. I won't be staying much longer."

"I was informed you were the person in possession of the flash drive."

"Yep. That was me. But you can't blame a woman for the mystery that is her purse. And as I already explained to the police, I didn't know it was there. Had I known, I would have given it to you. Or them, since they're nicer to me."

His eyes narrow. It's the only indication that I'm getting to him at all, and that sort of makes me want to laugh. He's an FBI agent and I'm me. I assumed these men were unflappable.

"You do understand that your involvement in all of this does not paint the best light on you. You were in possession of crucial evidence. You were helping Mister Lyons leave the health center. He was planning on fleeing the country with you."

I hold up my arm. The one Matt had a field day with. He peeks at it and then back to me. "I assume since you're an FBI agent, you've been threatened with a gun before. You might have even been bruised at the hands of another man. I can assure you that today was a first for me on both accounts. I wasn't given a choice about leaving the health center with Matt. The man had a gun and threatened to kill my boss before killing himself. The flash drive I already explained. So, you can stop this now, Agent Fellows. I'm seriously done for the day."

"No, Miss Whitcomb, you're not."

I shake my head. Because he's wrong. I'm absolutely positively done for the day. I lean forward, bracing myself with my palms flat on the old ass-stained, wooden table between us, and level him with my eyes. "Do not come in here trying to play bad cop with me when you haven't even done your job properly. If I treated my patients with the same level of diligence as you treat your criminals, I'd be killing people left and right." He opens his mouth, but I'm not done so I interrupt before he has the chance. "I'm in no mood for your attitude. I was threatened with a gun. My arm hurts like hell and is bruised to sin from the way he gripped me. My boss was attacked, *shot*, and nearly killed. I've been sitting here for hours. You took my phone and purse, so I can't even leave. I'm tired and hungry and want to go home, so unless you have anything of value to add, that's what I'm going to do."

Agent Fellows stares me down. I don't think he was expecting this from me. The first time we met, I was a demure little doll, scared out of my wits. I thought I was going to be charged with something like accessory. I thought my life was over because I was previously engaged to the wrong man. But today I'm so very different. The attack this morning rests on the FBI as far as I'm concerned, which means it's on Agent Fellows. He's lucky Jonah is okay, otherwise he'd find out just what sort of woman I can really be. My mama may have raised me with good-girl manners, but my daddy raised me never to take shit from anyone.

"Sit down, Miss Whitcomb."

I shake my head.

"I'm not finished interviewing you."

"I've already given my statement to the police. You know everything that transpired, and I answered your questions about the flash drive and my 'leaving' with Matt." I punctuate my ire with air quotes. "I can't imagine there is more to add." I head for the door and when I reach it, I roll my head over my shoulder to face him. He'd be cute in another life. Dark hair and eyes, similar to Matt, but his face is more chiseled than Matt's. More movie FBI. "I'm going home, Agent Fellows. If you need anything further from me, you can speak to my attorney. Have a nice day."

I knock on the door, because I'd bet serious money it's locked from the outside. The door opens a few seconds later and I exit, walking with my head held high even though I really want to bury it in the sand. I'm so sick with this, but I won't let them see that. How am I supposed to go to work tomorrow? That is, if I still have a job. I sigh at that before I can stop it.

Fucking Matt. Why did he have to be the worst of all the men in my life? The one to ruin it when I don't even care about him anymore. It seems so ironic and so unfair. I retrieve my belongings from a woman sitting behind a desk. She has me sign something and then I have my belongings back. That's when I see it. I have about fifty missed calls, but what stops my heart is a text message from Jonah. Only it didn't come in after the attack. It came in this morning right *before* I went in to see Matt.

Erica wants to have dinner with us tonight if that's all right with you. I was hoping to talk to you about us before that. And just so there is no confusion or wayward

228

thoughts prior to that conversation, there is an us. I want there to be an us. Text me after your last patient and we'll meet up.

He wants there to be an us. I smile so big before I can stop myself. This was before Matt came after him with a gun. I sigh again, tucking my phone back into my purse, unsure what I should do with myself now. Do I go to Jonah's apartment? My apartment? Back to work? Christ. That last one makes me want to hurl.

No one stops me as I make my way through the desks filled with officers doing their work. They don't care about me. I'm the least of their problems. I reach the front of the building but stop in my tracks when my name is called.

I twist around to find Jonah standing over by a bank of wooden benches against the far wall. He's a mess. A beautiful mess, but a mess all the same. His blond hair is tousled, he's still wearing the same wrinkled, ripped-up scrub top he was before, and he has a cut on his upper lip I didn't notice before. Before I can take a full inventory of him, he swallows up the dividing space between us and wraps me in his arms.

His face drops to my shoulder, breathing me in. "I was so fucking scared." The tension in his body eases as he squeezes me tighter. "I can't lose you, Carolina. I thought . . ." He trails off on a deep breath before he pulls back and cups my face in both his hands, staring into my eyes like the world starts and stops in them. "I thought he was going to take you or hurt you. Or both. I thought that was going to be it, especially when I saw the gun. All I thought was 'I can't lose her. I can't let him hurt her.'" He sucks in a rush of air and wipes away my tears that I didn't even realize were falling. "I love you, Halle. I'm *in* love with you. I was pretty damn sure of it this morning, but after what happened, I'm absolutely positive now."

I blink at him, stunned stupid for about two seconds before I regain my faculties, my eyebrows knitting together. There is no way I heard that correctly. "You love me?"

He smiles warmly, and God, that smile. It lights up everything. It makes this rank police station in downtown Boston disappear. It's all him. He's the only thing I care about. Funny how quickly that happens. One minute he's my hookup, my fling, my undeniable chemistry. The next . . . the next he's my future.

"I do. Totally. Completely. Madly." He tilts his head. "In a very healthy, non-aggressive way."

One side of my lips quirk up at that.

"I didn't see it coming until it hit me over the head like a sledge-hammer. You're irresistible. Impossible not to love. You brought me back to life, Halle. The whole me. The me I never thought I'd see again." His forehead drops to mine, our noses brushing, our eyes locked. "I know we haven't known each other long. A couple months really, but I don't care. None of that matters when I'm with you."

"But—" I shake my head, unable to finish my thought.

"But what about Madeline?" he supplies for me.

I nod, swallowing hard, my eyes burning with tears.

He blows out a breath, the sweet warmth flittering across my lips. "I will always love Madeline, Halle. She will always be a piece of my soul. But she's gone, and I can't change that. I never expected to meet anyone. I certainly never expected to fall in love again. But I did. That doesn't mean I'm dishonoring her memory. If the roles were reversed, I'd like to think she would have found someone who makes her as happy as you make me. I realize I might not be explaining it well—"

I press my fingers to his lips and shake my head against his. "You're explaining it perfectly. And that's all I needed to hear. I love you, Jonah. In a way I'm positive I've never loved before."

"Thank God." He laughs, closing the small gap between us and crushing his lips to mine. Jonah kisses me the way a man in love kisses his woman. With reckless abandon and zero fucks to give for whoever is watching us. Despite the auspicious circumstances that led us here today, I think this might be the best moment of my life.

But then I realize something vital and pull back. "I'm so sorry about what happened with Matt. Sorry doesn't even begin to cover it. He nearly killed you and it's my fault. I tried to save everyone, and I couldn't."

He gives me a knowing grin, his nose brushing back and forth against mine. "You did save everyone, Carolina. You nearly got him out of the health center. You were ready to sacrifice yourself for everyone, including me. You're the bravest woman I know. So fucking strong." I open my mouth to object, but he kisses me, cutting me off before he continues, "You're strong enough and smart enough to know when to accept help and when to do it all yourself."

I can accept that. I may even like it. Because I want him to always be the one. The one by my side. The one helping me when I need it. The one bolstering my strength. Because that's how I feel when I'm around him. Like I can slay dragons. Even if he got the kill shot today and not me.

"I think it's finally over," I say, and he nods against me.

"I think so, too. So, can I take you home now? To my home?"

"Yes." Because there is nowhere else on earth I'd rather be.

WE STEP OUTSIDE into the hot Boston sunshine and the press immediately surrounds us. They're everywhere, shouting out questions to both Jonah and me. It's something I hadn't really taken into consideration. And now that I think on it, I have no idea where Matt is. If he's inside the building we just vacated. That thought makes me shiver.

Jonah wraps his arms around me, tucking me into his side as he pushes us through the relentless masses to a waiting Uber I'm suddenly so thankful he ordered. The cab of the car is cool and quiet, the only sound is Top 40 pop coming from the speaker. It's annoying and distracting and I'm so grateful for it, because my mind is going a million miles an hour. I need a shower. I need a drink. I need something to eat and I need to sleep for the next two days straight.

Jonah takes my hand, squeezing it three times. "That was fun," he deadpans, and I burst out laughing.

"I love you," I say, because I do. I don't even care anymore. And you know what? It feels good to say it. Natural even. Like it's something I'm going to be telling him for the next sixty years.

His head swivels in my direction, his smile managing to relax me.

"We're supposed to meet Erica for dinner, but I think it's best if we postpone that one, don't you?"

I nod. Even though I feel a little bad about that. I'm sure she'll understand. I mean, how often has the excuse "my ex-boyfriend attacked my new boyfriend with a gun" been used? Probably not much.

"How many stitches did you get?"

"Eight. It wasn't deep. I'll let you play naughty nurse with me later."

Wow. He really is the perfect man for me.

"I'm sorry," I tell him because it needs to be said. I think I might have said it once already, but who cares?

"Never apologize to me for what happened. I don't blame you. I only care that you're here with me."

"Can I tell Erica I'm sorry then?"

"No. She'll understand."

"I went on a blind date once," I say, turning to meet his eyes, wondering why I'm telling him this but not allowing that to stop me. "Toward the end of dinner, he took a call and when he came back, he told me his little sister had just been kidnapped so we couldn't have dessert. He left. Didn't even pay the bill."

Jonah's lips are twitching, amusement dancing in his eyes as we speed through the city toward his building. "I see. Did they ever find her?"

I shrug. "No idea. He never mentioned a little sister when we were discussing our families."

Jonah laughs, leaning in to kiss me. "Well, I think a shower and a rest are in order. And once we've done that, I'll take you out."

"Are we talking mob-boss style or ninja?" He stares at me with a bemused expression. "Never mind. I think it's the day. We can just blame it on that."

He shakes his head at me and I wonder if he knows what he's

gotten into with me. Our car pulls up in front of the building and I step out, but before I can make it inside to that waiting shower and supremely comfortable bed, Jonah stops me with a tug of my hand. He pulls me into his chest and snakes his arms around me, and just holds me in the middle of the sidewalk on Arlington Street.

"There are so many things I love about you, Halle Whitcomb," he whispers in my ear after a few silent moments. "But I think one of my absolute favorite things is your ability to adapt. To roll with the punches and always make me smile, even when I'm reluctant to do so. My life will never be boring as long as I have you."

"And my life will always be full as long as I have you."

Epilogue

Jonah

A YEAR *and a half later*

I'M in love with a woman whose least favorite holiday is Christmas. Her parents were killed in a car accident on that day, so who can blame her? Honestly, since Madeline died, Christmas hasn't been my favorite, either. Last year, Halle and I went to a movie and then ate dinner in Chinatown. I didn't push it last year because we were both recovering from being attacked by her ex and him finally being sentenced to twenty-five years in prison. Figured it wasn't really the best timing.

That flash drive Matt had stashed in Halle's purse was loaded with information. Lists of other hackers Matt had worked with. Communication streams from the dark web. Numbered offshore bank accounts. The list went on and on. A lot of people were brought down because of that one small drive. Since then, no strange numbers have called Halle. She no longer feels as if she's being watched. It's done. Matt's gone. And we've spent the last year and a half together.

So yeah. Christmas.

I get the strong impression that once upon a time, Christmas was Halle's favorite holiday. I can imagine her running down the stairs, wearing pink slippers with some cuddly animal on the front, matching pajamas and giggling in excited awe when she spots all the presents under the tree. Every time I picture her like that, it makes me smile. So, this year, I've decided to try and change her negative mindset on this miserable holiday.

This year, the timing is perfect.

Her one rule for tonight was that we walk everywhere we go, no driving. I complied and took her to the Top of the Hub. We ate in the restaurant with a view of the city.

They did a whole Christmas Eve dinner thing and it was perfect. She's perfect.

Now we're walking back home, hand in hand, looking at the beautifully decorated storefronts. The more time I spend in this city that is ever-changing around me, the more I love it. We walk past the health center we both still work at, but neither of us pay it much attention. It's closed now anyway. At first, after the attack, she was reluctant to return. Not because she was scared, or because the building made her anxious, but because she was embarrassed.

But Matt had already ruined a job for her and I was not about to let him ruin another. The staff was good about it. They were more concerned for her than anything. Especially Oliver Fritz, who has somehow managed to become a close mate. That's something I never expected. We spend a good deal of time with Halle's friends. Probably because I didn't have many of those before she came into my life. I had work. I had Madeline and Erica. But that was it, really. And we all know how my life was after Madeline.

Erica has become like a little sister to Halle. The two of them spend loads of time together. Even Madeline's mother has taken to Halle. Which is something I never expected in my wildest dreams. It makes me feel like Madeline is still with me. Like I haven't lost her completely, and that she's okay with what's become of my life. Maybe even happy about it.

Halle never actually went back to her apartment. She gave it up and brought whatever furniture and belongings she wanted over to my place. Everything else was either trashed or sold. It wasn't even something we discussed. It just happened naturally. I don't think either of us wanted to live apart after living together those weeks.

"I love this city," she says, echoing my thoughts from just moments ago, a flash of cold winter air whisking past us, forcing her to slide farther into my side. "It feels the way Christmas is supposed to feel. Cold. Sparkly. Snowy." She angles up to meet my eyes. "It's beautiful."

She's beautiful.

Her long red hair is up tonight, a rarity for her when not at work. She's wearing a red cocktail dress that drives me wild with what it shows and what it doesn't.

She drives me wild.

"Are we going home so you can finally see what's under my dress?"

I want to see what's under her dress. She's had the undergarments in question tucked away in a box that I wasn't allowed to breach. The crazy lady even duct-taped the sides so I couldn't sneak a peek without getting caught. And now my cock is growing hard, to the point that I'm starting to rethink my plans for the next few hours.

"Not yet, Carolina. I thought we'd stop in for a drink first. It's Christmas Eve. Seems the thing to do."

She smirks at me. "Oh, so that bottle of wine we shared at dinner was just a warmup?" I nod, and she laughs, shaking her head lightly. "You don't have to get me drunk to get lucky tonight, Doctor. I can tell you with absolute certainty, I'm a sure thing. I may even let you use those handcuffs on me."

Fuck. Did she have to mention the handcuffs? How am I supposed to take her out for a drink now when all I can think about is cuffing her to our bed and spanking her perfect ass, before I fuck her blind.

"Later. We're definitely using those later. One drink and then home."

She sighs, but doesn't say anything else until we come upon the bar we first met in. The outside is decorated with lights and wreaths, the windows covered in condensation obscuring the view in.

She pauses when she catches where we're going and then she pivots to face me. "Here?" I nod, and she grins at me like she likes that I took her here. "You're a romantic bastard sometimes. I mean, if bringing the woman you're living with to the place you met before your one-night stand can be considered romantic."

"It's the place we met. The place that forever changed my life."

"Yep. Definitely romantic. Okay, let's go have a drink before you take me home. Not a shot though, I'm not feeling *that* nostalgic."

"Deal."

"And in case I forget, thank you. You've made me so happy."

She makes me so happy.

I kiss her and then open the door for her. She prattles on about something or another as she enters, but I don't hear her above the racing of my heart and the blood pounding my ears. She takes exactly four steps in when she freezes. Her hands fly up to her mouth and stifle the "oh my god" that stutters out.

She's doing that laugh-cry thing she does when she's happy and overly excited. She takes two more steps in and Aria rushes over, hugging her affectionately, followed by Oliver, Rina, and Margot, as well as some other friends. She's looking up into Oliver's eyes, laughing and smiling as she does.

I love her laugh and smile.

"It's a surprise Christmas party for the girl who hates Christmas," he explains to her, glancing at me quickly and winking. Halle spins around, taking in everyone around her. I've rented out the entire pub just for this. Just for her. My mother and sister are here. Erica and her mother. Halle's aunts and uncles all the way from South Carolina. Everyone we know and love is here.

"You're here? You're all here on Christmas Eve for me?" She points to her chest, shaking her head back and forth.

"Jonah set it all up," Aria explains.

Halle spins around to find me, still hanging back while she takes in her moment.

Her eyes lock with mine, beautiful pale blue and glassy. "You did all this?" she asks, staring at me in awed wonder. "For me?" She still doesn't understand how loved she is.

I love her so much.

That's my cue. I close the distance between us. She smiles brightly, her eyes glowing, overflowing with love and elation. She watches as I drop down to one knee and then her expression transforms to one of utter disbelief. Her eyes widen and her mouth pops open. Fresh tears well up in her gorgeous crystalline depths. "Oh my God," she whispers.

"Halle Jane Whitcomb, I knew the moment I saw you that nothing was ever going to be the same for me again. You were the perfect antidote to my dark life. The one I never even knew I wanted. I've brought all of your family and friends here tonight, so you would not only know how much you're loved, but so you would see it, feel it. And if you say yes, I promise to spend every day for the rest of our lives ensuring you know, see, and feel how much I love you. Will you do me the tremendous honor of being mine forever?"

I pull out the red velvet box housing the ring and open it. She gasps, covering her mouth with her hand as she quietly sobs. "Yes," she manages through her tears. "Yes, of course I'll marry you." Standing, I slide the round-cut diamond in the platinum band onto her finger and then tug her hand, slamming her into my chest and kissing the hell out of her in front of all our family and friends. She tastes like chocolate and wine and tears.

I love her taste.

The room erupts into a chorus of laughter, cheers, and whistles. We smile against each other; our noses kiss and our eyes lock.

"I love you," I whisper.

"I love you, too," she whispers back. "Forever."

I nod. "Forever."

"Thank you for turning all my sad memories into happy ones."

I lean down and kiss her. I kiss her the way I'm going to kiss her forever. "I may have turned your sad memories to happy ones, but you must know, I now only have happy moments because of you."

Epilogue 2

Aria

"I CAN'T GO ON," Margot moans. "Just leave me here. Save yourselves. This will only end one way." I'd say my friend here is being dramatic, but considering her head is now pressed against the side of the wood bar, eyes closed and hand lingering next to the now empty shot glass she just finished off, I know she's not. Because she's right. This will only end one way.

With her facedown in the toilet.

"I told you not to take that last shot," Rina chastises with a disapproving scowl on her face. She puffs out a breath, her hand going to her lean hips.

Margot manages to flip Rina off, but that's all she's got left in her.

I sigh, silently cursing our other friend, Halle, for leaving early and leaving us with a drunk Margot to clean up. I turn to Rina.

Time to get serious.

I raise my hands, curling one into a fist and positioning it above my other hand that is open, palm facing up. "You ready?"

Rina nods. Brushing her long dirty-blonde hair over her shoulders so it doesn't detract from her focus, she rolls her neck, cracking it once. Then she pivots to face me head-on. Getting her game face on, she mimics my position. She nods her head again, this one a signal that we should start.

"Rock, paper, scissors, shoot," we say in unison before throwing out our best offering. I go with paper and she hits me with rock.

"Ha." I grin, giving her a hip bump. "Have fun with drunk Joe over here."

"Hey," Margot objects to my pet name for her, but she doesn't really have the energy to do much else. "I resent that."

"You also resemble it, babe. Keep this up and it's intervention time."

Margot doesn't respond.

"Best two out of three?" Rina begs with wide big puppy dog eyes. That shit never works on me, so I don't know why she bothers.

"Nice try, dollface. But I had this distinct honor last time, and it took me two weeks to get the smell of vomit out of my car. Plus, I didn't drive tonight so…," I trail off with a shrug.

"Fine," she concedes her loss with grace. "But we really need to put a cap on Margot's shots. I mean, if the girl can't handle her liquor—"

"I swear, this is the last time," Margot slurs out, attempting to raise her head off the wood of the bar and not getting all that far.

"You always say that, sweetie." I squeeze her shoulder. "But for real, next time, we're putting you on a limit. Think of your liver."

"Seriously," Rina agrees. "You're a nurse. You know better."

Margot offers up a weak shrug, her brown hair is, well, it's everywhere. Probably stuck to the beer encrusted bar top. Even the people sitting next to her have shifted to give her a wider berth.

"Didn't you outgrow this madness in college?" I ask.

Margot is finally able to raise her head, her eyes opening into tiny bloodshot slits. She shakes her head and then winces. "I went to an all-girls Christian college. It was worse than my all-girls Christian high school. No men. No alcohol. I might as well have been in a convent. I think I've still kissed more girls than I have boys. I

241

know I've had sex with more and I am most definitely not a lesbian."

Rina and I exchange looks of horror. "How did we miss this?" I ask.

"No idea," she replies. "How many men have you had sex with?" Rina asks, turning back to Margot.

"Five. And they were all awful. Especially the guy last night." Ah. So now the shots make sense. "Tiny dicks that couldn't last more than a couple of minutes. The women were actually better. Sort of made me wish I batted for the vagina squad."

"That's quite possibly the saddest thing I've ever heard."

"Ditto." We both stare down at our poor friend, Margot. In truth, we've only known her about a year and we've never talked much about college, so that's probably how we missed it, but still. I feel like that's something we should have known right off the bat. "Have you at least had an orgasm?" She nods, but her expression is grim. And then it hits me. "Holy shit. You've never had one by a member of the opposite sex."

She shakes her head this time and I think I might pass out. That's how distressing this news is.

"Next time we go out, you're staying sober and we're getting you a guy. Someone hot. Someone who knows how to work his fingers, and mouth, and dick." That's Rina, and she's clearly taking this situation as seriously as I am. "We did it for Halle and we can do it for you too."

But Margot just shakes her head at us again. "I'm done with one-night stands."

Okay. I guess I can understand that. I don't ride that train myself. Then again, I was in a relationship up until six months ago for over a year and a half. It's how I met these two lovely ladies and Halle who ditched early to go home to her hot man. And sex was not why we broke up.

"Fine then. We'll find you a hot doc." Rina looks to me for encouragement.

"Yes. Definitely." And then something occurs to me. "You can have Drew." I get raised eyebrows for that. Apparently, offering up your ex-boyfriend to your friend is a no-no. "Okay, maybe not Drew. But someone hot. Someone sexy."

"Sounds good," she mumbles. "Discussing my miserable excuse for a sex life has been awesome and all, but can someone take me home now. The room is starting to spin."

Shit. Margot is a puker. "Um, yeah. Maybe you should get her out of here?"

Just as the words leave my mouth, Margot lurches, her shoulders jerking forward. Both Rina and I spring into action, hauling our petite friend off the stool and dragging her outside without so much as a good night or a see ya later.

At least she's getting it out now instead of in Rina's car.

Which basically means I get stuck with the tab, but I don't really mind. Money isn't an issue for me and it was a fun night, despite Margot's propensity for drunken oblivion. Signaling the bartender, I ask to settle up before I make my way home.

I'm so exhausted all I can think about is my bed.

I sat, holed up in my house all day painting. It was productive but after a day of that, I needed to unwind some. Or a lot in this case because I wasn't loving what I was creating.

My phone chimes in with a text and once I notice it's from Drew, my ex, I ignore it. I don't even pay attention to what he sent me. The last text was about how much he missed me. So not helpful for the whole getting over him thing. The previous text was about a cool-ass case he had in the emergency room that actually made my stomach turn. Before that, it was about a dream he had about me. It's been going on over the last few months, and lately they're coming in with more frequency than they used to.

And really, he's the one who ended it, so I don't exactly feel the need to text him back. I've been hoping he'd get the message that I don't want to talk to him, but it doesn't seem as though he is.

Whatever his game is with me, I don't like it.

My feet carry me east for more blocks than I care to think about before I bang a right onto Dartmouth, hopping up the steps to the brownstone I own.

Unlocking my door, I toss my keys onto the entryway table, lock everything back up tight and then head immediately upstairs. My teeth brushed, I strip down into my panties and then climb into bed with a loud, grateful groan.

My eyes close and they stay that way until a blaringly loud noise startles me awake.

I jolt upright, but I cannot figure out what that sound was. I'm foggy, disoriented, and for the briefest of moments, I have no idea where I am. My eyes zip around the interminable darkness, my muddled senses taking in the scent of snow when I spot the barely open window. I'm home, in my bed, and I left the window open. In January. Again. Ugh!

The sound that woke me starts again, loud and unforgiving.

My head whips over, locating my ringing phone lighting up my nightstand. Heavy, uncoordinated limbs slow me down as I scramble across the bed to answer it. Glancing at my alarm clock, I notice it's 12:43. No one ever calls you at this hour with good news, and my mind immediately flickers to my parents as a mild dose of panic crawls up my spine.

My thoughts are almost confirmed before I pick up the phone as I catch the Boston area code attached to a number I do not recognize. I swipe my finger across the phone. "Hello?" I answer hesitantly, praying that maybe it's just a wrong number.

The gravelly sound of someone clearing their throat fills my ear. "Is this Miss Aria Davenport?" a very male voice says with the studious air of professionalism.

"Yes," I answer reflexively, but my heart is exploding in my chest as I lean back against the fabric of my headboard, drawing my knees up to my chest like they'll somehow protect me from the bad news I know is yet to come.

He clears his throat again. "Aria," he starts, using my first name. "My name is Doctor Tim James." He pauses, and my mind is swimming, trying to place a name I'm nearly positive I've never heard before. And then I realize what he led with, *Doctor*. "I'm a doctor at Massachusetts General Hospital in Boston." Drew works at MGH. So do Rina and Margot. "I'm sorry to call you, but you're listed as Joshua Brown's emergency contact and healthcare proxy."

"What?" I practically shriek, my hand flying up to my mouth. "Josh?" Disbelief and a fresh wave of terror fills me. "Is he..." I can't even finish that thought or sentence. I just can't.

"Mr. Brown is alive."

Relief floods through me but just as quickly recedes, because I'm still getting this call, which means something is terribly wrong.

"He was brought into the emergency department, suffering from several injuries including a fractured fibula, three fractured ribs, as well as other internal injuries that we're going to need to surgically explore. He also has a severe contusion to the right side of his head—"

"What the hell are you saying?" I snap, interrupting his medical rant. None of this means anything to me. This man might as well be speaking Russian for all the sense he's making. "Is he okay?"

"He suffered a head trauma that resulted in pressure and swelling on his brain as well as the other injuries I mentioned."

"Oh God, no. Josh." My chin drops to my chest as my hand slides up to cover my eyes. Tears leak out despite my best attempts at reining them in.

"The surgical team is about to wheel him to the OR now to repair the internal injuries he sustained. His broken leg will not require surgery, just setting."

I shake my head. I can't handle this. I. Cannot. Handle. This. "What happened?"

"I'm sorry, I don't know the specifics. I just needed to make you aware. But if you're able, you should come. He may need someone here to make medical decisions for him."

"Uh. Okay." I shake my head, wiping furiously at my eyes. "I'll be there soon."

Then he hangs up. That's it. But I don't really have the mental capacity at the moment to think too deeply on that. Flipping on the lights, I squint against the brightness before riffling through my drawers for something to wear. I dig out a black long sleeve thermal and a pair of jeans, put my hair up in a messy bun, grab my phone, and I'm out my door in less than ten minutes.

Without my coat.

Shit.

But it's too late to go back as the Uber is pulling right up and I'm in too much of a hurry to get to the hospital or care all that much about freezing. Coats can wait. Josh cannot.

Once I get inside the enticingly warm car, I call Tyler, Josh's boyfriend. I spoke to Josh two days ago, and he was most definitely still with Tyler. I want details and I want them now. The phone rings three times before his groggy, sleep-filled voice fills my ear.

"What the hell, Aria?"

"Tyler," I clip out. "Have you talked to Josh?"

Silence. I'm greeted with freaking silence and I'm about to lose my mind.

"No. Not since last night." He's confused. "We had a late dinner and a drink and then we called it a night. I have an eight a.m. client I'm supposed to meet…" He trails off as silence once again ensues and I can't find my voice to fill it. "What's going on?"

"A doctor from MGH called me." I swallow hard, staring sightlessly out the windshield of the car. "Tyler, Josh was in an accident or something. I don't know the details, but he's really messed up. They're taking him into surgery."

"What?! Surgery? No. That's impossible."

"I don't know anything, Tyler. I'm sitting in the back of an Uber on my way to MGH, but you need to get your ass over to the hospital now."

"Shit." He's silent, but I hear rustling in the background, so I assume he's getting out of bed. "I'm on my way. Fuck," he growls, anxiety leaching from his voice. "I'm on my way. I'll call you when I get there." He's frantic. Good thing he lives down the street from the hospital.

"Take a breath, Tyler. I don't want to get a call about you next."

He takes that breath, but then he starts to gulp, and I wonder if he's holding back tears. "I feel so…I can't stand this."

"I know. Just get to him and I'll be there as soon as I can."

"Right. Talk soon, honey."

"Talk soon."

Slipping my phone into my purse, I lean back in the seat. The driver is silent, and I'm not even afforded the luxury of awful background music to distract me from my thoughts. One question continues to torture me.

What happened?

Because Josh is a strong guy. A big guy. But he's also a gay guy. A gay guy who has been in more fights because of his sexuality than I can count. And since the doctor didn't mention a car accident, I'm going with worst-case scenarios here. Josh was attacked.

THE END

DOWNLOAD your copy of The Edge of Forever continue to meet the gorgeous doctor who flips Aria's world upside down. Plus you get plenty more of Halle and Jonah in this story!

Want a look at Jonah and Halle's extended HEA? You can get it HERE.

Also by J. Saman

End of Book Note

For those of you who've read me before, you know this is the part where I babble on about the book a bit. I wrote this book for the ILLICIT box set and I have to admit, it felt different for me. The story, at least. It's not my norm. I can't even put my finger on what it was, but I labored over this one.

I really fell for Halle and Jonah as a couple. I think that's what drove me forward when I struggled. I wanted Jonah to find love again. I wanted Halle to believe that true love was possible. It wasn't an easy journey for either. Or for me.

I think the reality is, we all have baggage. No one enters a relationship (any sort of relationship) without bringing their past experiences (both good and bad) into the mix. And the older we get, the greater the baggage. Maybe that's why I love writing so much, everyone has a story.

As you may or may not know, this book is what drove me, as part of ILLICIT to becoming a *USA Today* bestseller. That has forever been one of my goals as a writer so thank you to everyone who helped support me along the way.

The next in the series (yes, they're all standalone) is The Edge of Forever. It's Aria's story and actually, I wrote it way before I wrote this book. But this story felt like the better jumping off point. Subscribe to my Newsletter- as mentioned above, you get a free book and my latest updates as well as promotions, freebies, etc. Find me on Facebook, Goodreads, Pinterest, Instagram and/or Twitter. I love talking with you. Oh, and PLEASE leave me a review!! I'm an indie and I need all the help I can get with those.

XO ~ J. Saman

Love to Hate Her

BLURB:

A rare moment of weakness. A burning desire impossible to deny. Forbidden words I should never have spoken...

Seven years ago, I confessed my darkest secret to my brother's girlfriend.

When she broke up with him and walked out of our lives, she took my secret with her.

But, with my band set to go on tour around the world, I have a problem. I need a nanny for my autistic daughter. And unfortunately, Viola Starr, my brother's ex, is the perfect fit.

Now, there is no escaping her. Or our past.

Especially when my brother seems determined to win her back.

Five months and she'll be out of my life again.

Five months of ignoring lingering, heated glances.

The fire she draws out of me. The way she loves my daughter.

Five months... And my world is about to come crashing down around me.

Prologue
Viola

The air is hazy, thick with the cloying scent of weed as I meander my way through the throngs of people laughing, smoking, and generally having a great time. I don't belong here. At least that's how it feels. Especially since I have a sneaking suspicion what I'm about to discover.

"Hey, Vi," Henry, the bassist for the band, calls out to me with shock etched across his face as he grabs my arm and tugs me in for a bear hug. His tone is an infuriating concoction of surprise, delight, and panic. "What brings you out here?"

I'm tempted to laugh at that question, though it's far from funny. As such, it forces a frown instead of a smile. It really should be obvious. But maybe it's not anymore, and that only solidifies my resolve that I'm doing the right thing tonight.

Even if it sucks.

"I'm looking for Gus," I reply smoothly without even a hint of emotion, and his grin drops a notch.

Knowing that my boyfriend of four years is cheating on me should resemble something along the lines of being repeatedly stabbed in the back. Or heart. It should feel like death is imminent as the truth skewers my faith in men, my sense of self-worth, and my overall confidence into tiny bite-sized pieces of flesh. I should be a sniveling, slobbering mess of heartbreak. I should be nuclear-level pissed while simultaneously seeking and plotting a dramatic scene and meaningless revenge.

That's how it always goes for girls like me versus guys like Gus. And maybe I am just a touch of all those things. But right now, I just want to get this over with and go home.

"He's umm…," Henry's voice trails off as he makes a show of scanning the room as if he's genuinely trying to locate Gus amongst the revelry. My bet? He knows exactly where Gus is and is attempting to buy him and his current lady of the minute some time.

"It's cool," I say, plastering on a bright smile that I do not feel. "I'll find him."

Because when you've been friends with someone your entire life, in a relationship with them for the last four years, you don't expect them to betray you. You expect loyalty and honesty and respect. *You expect fucking respect, Gus!* Gus cheating and lying about it is none of those things.

"I can find him!" Henry jumps in quickly. "I'd probably have a better shot of locating him in here than you will. Ya know, cuz I'm taller so I can see around the crowds better. Do you want a drink or something? Why don't you go make yourself a drink while I look for him?"

I shake my head and step back when he moves to grasp my shoulder.

Henry pivots to face me fully, a half-empty bottle of Cuervo in his hand, his eyes red-rimmed and glassy. He crumples, his shoulders sagging forward.

"It's not what you think, Vi. It's not. It's just…" He waves his free hand around the room as if this should explain everything. Sex, drugs, and rock 'n' roll. This room is the horror show definition of that cliché.

I don't begrudge Gus or his bandmates success. I'm sublimely thrilled for them that their first album is taking off the way it is. It's been their dream—*our dream*—for as long as I've known them, and that's forever.

Which is why I should have ended it when Gus left for L.A., and I left for college.

I knew the temptations that were headed his way. I knew women would be throwing themselves at him and that I was going to be thousands of miles away living a different life.

Does it excuse Gus's actions? Hell no. Have I cheated on Gus once while in college? Absolutely not, and it isn't like I haven't had my own opportunities to do so.

But do I understand how this happened? Yeah. I do. I just held on too long.

"It was coming anyway," I tell Henry. "But it's nice to know he won't be lonely."

Yeah. That's sarcasm. And I can't help it, so I might as well allow the bitterness to make an entrance and take over the sadness that's been sitting in my stomach like a bad burger you can't digest. Especially as Gus has been adamantly denying his trysts, and Henry pretty much just confirmed them.

Henry's like a fish out of water, and I lean in and give him a hug. I always liked Henry.

"He's going to be so broken up about this, Vi. He loves you like crazy. Talks about you all the time."

I pull back, tilting my head and shrugging a shoulder. "That doesn't matter so much, though, does it? I'm at school, and he's out here with…" Now it's my turn to gaze about the room, my hand panning out to the side, reiterating my point. "Good luck with everything, Henry. I wish you all the success in the world. You guys deserve every good thing that's headed your way."

Henry scowls like I just ran over his dog as he shakes his head no at me. "You can't end it with him. You're a part of this. We wouldn't be here without you. We wouldn't be anything without you. You're like…," he scrunches up his nose as he thinks, "our fifth member. Our cheerleader."

"Maybe once," I concede, swallowing down the pain-laced nostalgia his words dredge up. The backs of my eyes burn, but I refuse to let any more tears fall over this. I cried myself out on the flight here, and now I'm done. "You guys don't need me anymore. You have plenty of other cheerleaders."

He opens his mouth to argue more before just as quickly closing it.

"Stay safe, okay? And be smart," I add.

"You too, babe. I'm gonna miss you."

This is the moment it hits me.

I'm not just saying goodbye to my relationship with Gus, but to my friendships with these guys. To late-night band practices and weekends spent down by the lake just hanging out. I'm saying goodbye to my entire childhood, knowing that we're all headed in different directions, and there is no middle ground with this. My throat constricts as I try to swallow, my insides twisting into knots.

Bolstering myself back up, I hold my head high.

I need to find Gus, and then I need to get out of here.

Wild Minds, the band that Gus is the second guitarist and backup singer for, opened for Cyber's Law tonight. *The* Cyber's Law. One of the hottest bands in the world. They're also on the same label that just signed Wild Minds. This show is a big deal. This contract an even bigger one.

This is their start.

They had given themselves two years to make it big. They needed less than one.

Heading toward the back of the room, I skirt around half-naked women dancing and people blowing lines of coke. It's dark in here. Most of the overhead lights are out, but the few that are on mix with the film of smoke, casting enough of a glow to see by way of shadows.

I bang into a table, apologizing to someone whose beer I spill when I catch movement out of the corner of my eye. Jasper, Gus's fraternal twin brother and the lead singer of the band, is tucked into an alcove, a redhead plastered against him as she sucks on his neck.

Where Gus is handsome, charming, and completely endearing, Jasper is the opposite.

He is sinfully gorgeous, no doubt about that, but he's distant, broody, artistic, and eternally happy to pass the limelight to an overeager Gus. Jasper was actually my first crush. Even my first kiss when we were fourteen. But that's where it ended. Since that day, and without explanation, I've hardly existed to him.

Sensing someone's watching, he pulls away from the girl on his neck, and our eyes meet in the miasma. His penetrating stare holds me annoyingly captive for a moment before he does a slow perusal of me. Unlike Henry, Jasper is not surprised to see me. In fact, his expression hardly registers any emotion at all. But the fire burning in his eyes tells a different story, and for reasons beyond my comprehension, I cannot tear myself away.

He tilts his head, a smirk curling up the corner of his lips, and I realize I've been standing here, staring at him with voyeuristic-quality engrossment for far too long.

But I don't know how to break this spell.

The smoldering blaze in his eyes is likely related to what the girl who was attached to his neck was doing to him. Yet somehow, it doesn't feel like that.

No, his focus is entirely on me.

And he's making sure I know it.

A rush of heat swirls across my skin, crawling up my face. I shake my head ever so slightly, stumbling back a step.

Noticing my inner turmoil, Jasper rights his body, forcing the girl away. She says something to him that he doesn't acknowledge or respond to. He runs a hand through his messy reddish-brown hair as he shifts, ready to come and speak to me when my field of vision is obscured.

Gus. I'd know him in my sleep.

My gaze drops, catching and sticking on his unzipped fly.

"You're here," he exclaims reverently, the thrill in his voice at seeing me unmistakable. I peek up and latch onto the fresh hickey on his neck. A hickey? Seriously? I didn't even know people still gave those. When I find his lazy gray eyes, I want to cry. Especially with the purple welt giving me the finger.

"I'm here."

He wraps me up in his arms, and I smell the woman who gave him that hickey. Her perfume possessively clings to his shirt, and I draw back, crinkling my nose in disgust.

"What's wrong, babe?" His thumb strokes my cheek. "Long flight?"

I step back, out of his grasp.

"Your fly is unzipped, and you have a hickey on your neck."

He blanches, his eyes dropping down to his groin while immediately zipping his family jewels back up. "I just took a leak."

I nod, but mostly because I'm not sure how much fight I have left in me. It *was* a long flight. And a long eight months before that. But still, it's one thing to know your boyfriend is cheating on you; it's another to see it in the flesh, literally.

"And the hickey?"

"Not what it looks like, Vi. I swear."

I reach up and cup his dark-blond stubbled jawline. My chest clenches. "Don't lie, Gus. It just ruins everything. I don't want to hate you, and I think if you lie to me now, I might."

He shakes his head violently against my hand, his expression pleading. "You're here, Vi. You're finally here. Nothing else matters."

"But it does. It all matters. The distance. The way our lives are diverging. I love you, Gus, but it's not like it used to be with us. None of it is." I swallow, my throat so tight it's hard to push the words out. "Let's end this now before it turns into bitterness and resentment."

"I could never resent you."

I inwardly sigh. He really doesn't get it. "But your penis might. You're fucking any woman who looks at you. Where does that leave me?"

"You seriously flew out here to end it?" He's incredulous. And hurt. And I hate a hurt Gus. Even if we're not the stuff of happily ever afters, I do love this man. I'm just not so sure how in love with him I am anymore. He broke my heart. He broke my trust. And absence hasn't made my heart grow fonder. It's made it grow harder.

But I still don't want him hurting. He's my... *friend*?

Shit and hell, he's my friend.

And God, I'm going to miss him.

So I hug him. I wrap my arms around his neck because I need to. I ignore the scent of that faceless girl because I need to feel him close to me, even if for the last time. That lump is back in my throat, and my eyes are once again burning with those tears I refuse to let fall. Gus squeezes me, gripping me as if his life depends on it, and it's breaking me apart.

"Would you rather I ended it on the phone?" His face meets my neck, and my eyes fling open wide, only to find Jasper watching us from over Gus's shoulder. A curious observer, and my insides hurt all over again. His expression is a mask of apathy lined loosely with disdain. The way it's always been with me. All that earlier heat a thing of the past. I don't care either way.

"I don't want you to do it at all," Gus's voice is thick with regret as he holds me. "I love you, Vi. I love you so goddamn much. I just…"

"I know. I really do." I squeeze him back, feeling like I'm losing the only good part of my childhood in saying goodbye. "We're just in different spaces now, with different lives, and that's the way it's supposed to be."

He shakes his head against me, holding me so close and so tight, it's hard to breathe. He smells like that girl. But he smells like him underneath, and I cling to that last part because the scent of some unknown meaningless girl hurts too much. It rips me apart, knowing he did that to me.

To us.

I close my eyes for a moment and push that away. It's useless at this point, and I don't want to leave here more upset than I already am.

"Don't end it," he pleads, cupping my face and holding me the way he always has. "I can't lose you."

I lean up on my tiptoes and kiss his cheek. Tall bastard. "And I can't come in third. I handled second well enough, but not third."

"Third?"

"Music first. Other women second. Me third. I need to end this Gus, or I'll hate you, and I'll hate myself."

"No," he forces out, but it's half-hearted. We're nineteen, and just too young. There isn't enough of the right type of love between us to fight harder for something we both know will never work. He doesn't want to be the bad guy. The cheating guy who pushes his long-time sweetheart-best-friend away. "You're breaking my heart." A tear leaks from my eye as I battle to stifle my sob. "I'm in love with you, and you're ending it." I blink back more tears, watching as he accepts what's happening. "I'm going to regret this," he states matter-of-factly. "Letting you go is going to be the regret of my life. Years from now, I'm going to hate myself for not making you stay."

But you're not fighting for me now.

260

"And that's why I have to go." I lean in and kiss him goodbye and then run like hell.

I make it outside, the heavy door slamming behind me. Warm, stale air brushes across my tacky skin, doing nothing to comfort or bring me clarity. I'm a mess of a woman as useless tears cling to my lashes.

"You're leaving already?" Jasper's voice catches me off guard, and I start. Why did he bother following me? "You just got here."

"Yes," I reply, twisting around to face the green eyes that have been fucking with my head since I caught them ten minutes ago. "You can't be surprised."

"He loves you. He's just lost in this life, ya know?" I shake my head at him. Jasper takes a long step in my direction, wanting to get closer and yet hesitant to. "So that's it? You just walk away from him?"

"Am I supposed to ignore the fact that he's been *cheating* on me?"

"No. I suppose not. And I can't make excuses for it either."

"What do you want, Jasper? You can't honestly tell me you're disappointed to be rid of me."

"I see we're at the zero-fucks-left-to-give portion of the evening."

I shrug. That just about sums it up.

His eyes, filled with anger, indecision, and frustration, bounce all around, the street, the lights of the neighboring storefronts, the crowd still dispersing from the show, everywhere but at me. I can't stand this any longer, so I turn away and start to walk out into the Los Angeles night, away from the arena where Wild Minds–the band and the boys I've loved my whole life–just performed.

"It's yours," Jasper calls out, and I'm so confused by his hasty words that I freeze, turning back to him. His expression is completely exposed. Utterly vulnerable. And he's staring straight at me. Directly into my eyes in a way he hasn't dared since we were fourteen. My heart picks up a few extra beats, my breath held firmly in my chest. God, this man is so intense, I feel him in my fingernails.

"What is?" I finally ask when he doesn't follow that up.

"The album," he answers slowly, reluctantly, like it pains him to confess this, his darkest secret. "Every song on it is yours. All of them, I wrote about you."

I stand here, lost in space as I grasp just what he's saying. What it means, as random lyrics from random songs on their album flitter through my head. Song after song filled with the most achingly beautiful poetry.

"Jasper?" I whisper, my hand over my chest because I'm positive my heart never beat like this before.

But he is already at the door, having confessed his sins without waiting for absolution.

"Why did you tell me?" I yell after him, praying he'll stop. Needing him to explain this to me. *Why did you tell me, Jasper? Why did you pick this moment to ruin me?*

His hand rests on the frame of the now open door, his head bowed, his back to me. "Because I didn't think I'd ever get another chance, knowing I'll probably never see you again." He blows out a harsh breath. "But it doesn't change anything, Vi. Absolutely nothing. So you can move on without us and pretend like I never said a word."

And then the door slams shut behind him.

Jesus.

It takes me forever to move. To force myself to try and do just that. To try and forget his words and ignore the havoc they just created.

Knowing it's futile. Knowing those words will reside in me forever.

Want to know what happens next with Viola and Jasper? Get your copy of LOVE TO HATE HER now and get lost in the tempting world of forbidden love and rock stars!

Just One Kiss

London

"Dad, just stop. It can't be helped," I groan, leaning back in the seat of my two-door Boxster, heading up I-91 North through Vermont on the way to my parents' winter home through what appears to be the beginnings of a storm. "The Weather Channel mentioned some snow. Like three-to-six inches max. I'm sure it's going to be fine."

"When was the last time you checked that?"

I have to think about this for a second. It's been a long couple of days. "I don't know. Friday?"

"It's Monday, London," he not so kindly points out, his tone growing shrill and agitated. "Monday. Weather changes in this part of the country on a daily basis. We're supposed to get eighteen-to-twenty-four inches at a *minimum*, and it's expected to come down fast and hard with the added bonus of some ice mixing in. Hence why your mother and I have both been calling you non-stop for the last two days. The last two days that you've been ignoring us."

I bluster out a frustrated breath. "I was on deadline."

"I know. You told us that on Friday. At the exact same time we told you that you can work from anywhere."

I roll my eyes like the petulant child he's making me feel like. "Stop it with that. I can't write in a house full of people screaming and watching old movies and shouting at me about decorating the tree or which color of tinsel works best."

"Or making out like two horny teenagers," I hear my sister grouse in the background, the ick in her voice unmistakable and loud, since my father always has to have me on speakerphone. Why? Who the fuck knows! That's just how he rolls.

"Your mother and I have not been making out like two horny teenagers."

"Liar," she coughs. "They're worse than me and Maverick." Maverick is my eldest sister, Charleston's—or Charlie as we call her—fiancé. That's obviously not his real name, but since my sister's favorite movie is *Meet The Parents* (Not *Top Gun*, as you would think) everyone calls him Maverick since she's his Iceman. I don't question the logic behind it, since technically it was Goose to his Maverick and Goose dies, but it's really not worth the effort.

"You wanna talk about horny people going at it all the time, go pop in on Savannah and Royce. They've been like bunnies in heat since she got pregnant." That's my mother chiming in, and I can't help but growl into the phone.

"How do you think they got pregnant in the first place?" Charlie cackles.

"You know what?" I interject, my nose scrunched up. "Maybe I'll turn back around. You're right, the weather is getting bad."

Being the only single in a house full of over-love and over-sharing can get to be a bit much.

Especially this time of year.

My mother laughs, knowing I'm kidding. As much as I know my family is crazy, I love them to pieces and then a bunch more. And it's Christmas. The universal time to be with family, crazy or otherwise.

At least that's how we do it.

No matter what's going on in our lives, we stop and get together as a family. It's tradition. Evidently I'm a little late to the party.

"If you had tried to write from here, you'd already be *here*, safe and sound," my father cuts in, hating my mother's over-sharing as much as I do. "But instead you're driving into an area with blizzard warnings in a car that does not have front-wheel drive, let alone all-wheel drive. You could have stopped at the house and picked up one of the SUVs, London. I swear, sometimes you just love screwing with my sanity and blood pressure." He sighs and I fall silent. "Where are you?" he asks, his tone softening. "Maybe you *should* just turn back or find a place to stay that's safe. As much as I need you here to help me balance out your sisters and your mother, I'm worried about you driving in this."

I glance over at my navigation screen and then quickly back to the road. The snow is falling so thickly, I can hardly see the road ahead of me that is so terribly plowed, it's ridiculous. This is ski country after all, is it not? Isn't plowing snow what these people live for up here?

"It looks like I'm close to I-89." I think. It's nearly impossible to tell, even on the navigation screen because every few seconds, it cycles like it's lost. Not all that reassuring.

My dad starts cursing into the phone. "In this weather, that will take you a minimum of two to three hours. Find a motel, London. I don't like you driving in this."

"Dad, the day after tomorrow is Christmas Eve. The day after that Christmas. I just want to get there and be with all of you for the holiday. Who knows how long this storm could go on for?"

"That's why we told you to come up three days ago!"

"Blood pressure," I remind him. "And now is not the time for the I-told-you-so speech."

"London, for the sake *of* my blood pressure and your mother's, please. I'll send Fletcher down to fetch you with an all-wheel drive truck, but I hate you driving in that Porsche."

I look to my left and right out my foggy windows, but there is nothing but evergreens and snow. No towns. No signs. Not even a roadside gas station.

I puff out a resigned sigh. "Okay, I'll find something," I tell him, hoping this weather abates a bit so I can just push on and make it up to the house.

"Call or text when you're somewhere safe. We love you."

"Love you too, Dad." I disconnect the call, wiping with my hand against my windshield that is fogging up despite the defroster I have going and the heat I have blasting.

I left New York at eight this morning and the snow started once I hit the Connecticut/Massachusetts border. It's now noon, which means I've been driving in this mess forever, epically slowed down to practically a crawl since the roads are slick and visibility is shit. There are no other cars on the road, and this is what you'd call a major highway. No holiday traffic or ski warriors who are not deterred by the treacherous white stuff.

It makes no sense to me unless they were smart enough to leave early and beat the storm. Obviously, I need to check my weather app more often or (shudder) listen to my parents more than I do.

Instead, I am alone in a car that is not meant for this, going about twenty-five miles per hour and hoping—hell praying—that I don't miss the exit for I-89 that will lead me up toward Burlington and my parents' house on Lake Champlain, hovering a solid ten miles from the Canadian border.

This wouldn't have been so bad if I could have snaked my way up through New York and then over into Vermont, but no, the highway north of the city showed a massive accident this morning and my GPS rerouted me. My stomach growls loudly, choosing this moment to remind me that I haven't had anything to eat all day since I woke up late and had to run out the door, slurping down a to-go coffee from the deli on the corner by my apartment.

"Don't start," I snap at my empty belly. "I can't feed you. We have to make it through this shit first."

Turning up the music humming through my speakers, I lean forward, singing aloud to a song I know by heart. It helps to settle my slightly frazzled nerves and I push forward, scanning every snow-covered sign for the one I need. But as the miles stretch and the road grows more and more empty, my heart rate begins to spike with panic.

Did I miss it? Did I miss the exit?

Just as those thoughts hit me hard, my GPS starts in with 'recalculating route' in that annoying, nasal voice it has. I glance over to the map, but it's like my car is driving out into the middle of nowhere and not on a highway. The gray circle in the center of it just keeps spinning and spinning, and this is the moment that I go from a seven on the panic scale to twenty-eight.

"Balls," I curse. "You're supposed to run on a freaking satellite," I yell at the screen.

I slow down further, glancing out my window first and then the passenger one. But it's all the same, and I have no idea where I am. In a moment of desperation, I hit the button on my steering wheel to bring up my phone so I can call my father back, but now that's not even working. All the names and numbers are gray.

What the hell is going on?!

Picking up my phone from my center console, I unlock it with my face only to find that I have no service. As in none. Zero. Not even 3G.

"Dammit!" I scream at the top of my lungs, slamming my fist into the button to shut off the music that is happily chirping from my speakers. "Shut up!" I yell at it, running a frazzled hand through my hair and trying to rein myself in. Panicking like this will get me nowhere. I need to think. I need to calm the hell down.

Sucking in a deep, meant to be fortifying breath, I straighten my spine and steel my nerves and resolve.

I catch a sign that says something about a glass warehouse, a motel, a gas station, and *yes*. "That's what I'm talking about!"

But in my stupid enthusiasm, I press a little too hard on the gas pedal, and as if my car is chastising me the way my father would, the front tires start to slip and sway, skidding on the packed snow and ice that coats the road.

"No," I bellow, my voice skipping up a notch to a startled screech as the back tires start to get in on the action, overcompensating for the front. "Stop that. Don't do this. Please, I swear, I'll ease into whatever motel I find if you just stop doing that." My hands grip the steering wheel tighter, twisting it to the right and then the left frantically, trying to realign the suddenly out-of-control vehicle.

Oh my god, this cannot be happening.

My foot hits the brake and the wheel shimmies, the tires making a horrific grating noise. I press on the gas once more, but instead of correcting the problem as I anticipated, the car starts to spin, doing a full 360. I slam back on the brakes but to no avail.

We're not stopping.

We're not even slowing down.

If anything, the car is moving faster. Terrifyingly so. My heart is racing out of my chest, blood thrumming through my ears at a deafening decibel.

My hands are flying this way and that, but now the car is gaining speed, heading straight for… "Ahhhh!" I scream, my eyes wide and unblinking, my hands white-knuckling the wheel as I barrel toward a row of trees on the side of the highway without any way to stop.

My eyes close just at the moment of impact, my body tense and coiled as the front driver's side hits the tree with a sickening *crunch.*

The impact throws me, my head smashing into the window, and then my body lurches, slamming against the steering wheel. No airbags. I have no idea why they didn't deploy in a seventy-thousand-dollar car, but that's a serious problem as my head explodes with blinding pain.

Warm stickiness dribbles down my face as the car shifts and moves a little more before stopping completely, wedged against and under the tree.

I fall back into my seat, panting for my life and searching around the car. I sit here for a stunned, silent moment, mentally assessing everything. I have no idea if anything else is injured other than my forehead. I move my toes in my Uggs then my fingers.

"Jesus Christ. I can't believe I just crashed," I whisper.

Outside, I see nothing but white. Trees and an endless fucking sea of white.

I glance down at my lap and then over to the console, but I can't find my phone. A splatter of blood drips from my face onto my jeans.

Blood.

Oh my god. My stomach immediately rolls as my vision sways. I take a few deep breaths, forcing myself not to think about that. About the red, wet, sticky stuff that's now everywhere. I touch it with my fingers and that's just the wrong thing for me to do because it makes the dizziness worse. But holy bejesus, it really *is* everywhere. I scramble for my purse that fell into the well on the passenger side, searching for something, anything that will help wipe the blood off my face and body.

I have to get rid of it.

Dizziness consumes me as I move. A fresh wave of nausea hits me hard, cold sweat coating my skin like bad makeup. I close my eyes, fighting the black prickly dots around the edges of my vision before I reopen them, find my purse, and pull out my pack of tissues.

I wad up a ball in my hand and press the paper into the cut on my forehead. A whimper passes my lips at the sharp, shooting pain that accompanies that, but I soldier on, determined to find my phone and get the hell out of here.

My cell is on the other side of the passenger seat, but the second I pick it up, I know it's useless. I had no service before the crash and looking at the screen now, I see it's no different.

Fucking hell. What am I going to do now?

Want to meet the gorgeous man who comes to London's rescue? Keep reading JUST ONE KISS now and enjoy all the swoon-y, feel good holiday romance!

Made in the USA
Middletown, DE
07 July 2023

34713737R00163